GW01339231

EARLY RISING

by the same author
THE HAPPY PLANET
FOXON'S HOLE

JOAN CLARKE

Early Rising

Illustrated by
PAULINE MARTIN

JONATHAN CAPE
THIRTY BEDFORD SQUARE LONDON

FIRST PUBLISHED 1974
© 1974 BY JOAN CLARKE
© ILLUSTRATIONS 1974 BY JONATHAN CAPE

JONATHAN CAPE LTD, 30 BEDFORD SQUARE, LONDON WC1

ISBN 0 224 01001 8

SET IN 11 PT. BASKERVILLE 1 PT. LEADED

FILMSET AND PRINTED BY
BAS PRINTERS LIMITED, WALLOP, HAMPSHIRE

To L.M.K.H.

Chapter 1 · Midsummer Eve

About ninety years ago there were five children called Cecily, Erica, Christopher, Clare and Molly. They lived in a long, low house in a village called Woodhuckle. They had a big room of their own to play in when it was wet, and the run of the garden when it was fine. The five children were mostly happy and quite often good; all except Erica, who never seemed able to please anyone, though she tried the hardest of them all.

This is the story of Erica, from the time she first remembered anything at all to the time she was sixteen and refused her first offer of marriage. There is not much to say about Erica as a very small child, because she herself could only recall bits here and there about the earlier years. Almost her first memory was of the death of her mother, and that was when she was already six. All five children had been sent away to stay with their great-aunt at the seaside, and Erica never knew how she had learned that her mother was dead. She only saw herself sitting there on her bed crying, and Chris calling her a cry-baby – although he was only four. Great-Aunt Libbie's maid, who was putting her and Chris to bed at the time, said it was quite right for a child who had lost her dear mother to cry. Then Chris began to cry, too. He had not understood about dying, but when he heard the word "lost" he realized that his mother would never come back.

The only other memory Erica had of that time was of being put into new black clothes. She had been – or thought she remembered she had been – rather proud of the black ribbon tied round her hat. She seemed to see her small six-year-old self parading in front of a mirror and twisting round to see how the ends of the ribbon streamed down her back. Had she really been too young to understand her loss? Or had the loss been so unbearable that a kindly forgetfulness had wiped out everything but that one glimpse of childish vanity? She never knew.

She could not call to mind anything which showed how she had missed her mother after they had returned to Woodhuckle either; but perhaps that was because there had been Bessie to turn to. Bessie was clever and strong. Bessie always understood. Bessie seemed to Erica one of the wisest people she knew. Only years later did Erica work out that Bessie was only just thirteen herself when she came to look after the five motherless children. Bessie Hunt had been the brightest girl in Woodhuckle school. Her teacher said she was throwing herself away going as a nursemaid. She wanted her to stay on at school and become a teacher herself; but Bessie's mother said teachers did not learn anything that mattered. As soon as her daughter was twelve and could leave school she was to go out to service in a good house. There she would learn things which would be useful to her when she herself married. Perhaps Bessie's mother was wrong, but if so, it was the luckiest thing in the world for the five little Stocks. If they grew up as happy as any motherless children could, it was because they had Bessie to love them and be loved.

It was probably luckiest of all for Erica, who was the one who most needed help.

"I'm just the one in the middle," she said one day when she was nearly seven years old. "Cecily is the eldest, and Clare is the prettiest. Molly is the baby, and Chris is the only boy. I'm not anything. No one is interested in me. They just tell me to run away and not fidget."

"Don't talk nonsense," Bessie had said. She was mending socks at the time and sounded cross, but Erica knew it was only the darning she was cross with, so she did not mind.

"It's not nonsense," she said.

"Yes, it is," contradicted Bessie. "They wouldn't tell you to run away if you were a good girl like Cecily, or if you worked at your books like Chris. Besides, it's true that you fidget, you know that it is. Just look at you now! You'll break that tape-measure if you keep pulling it out like that."

Erica put the tape-measure back in Bessie's work-box, and then sat on her hands as the only possible way of keeping them still. They were up in the nursery at the time, Erica sitting in the window seat, and Bessie in the big rocking-chair. Clare and Molly were in the room but so busy with their dolls that it was as though they weren't there, and Erica could say what she really thought.

"I can't be good," she said sadly. "And it's not my fault if I'm not clever like Chris."

Bessie bit off her sewing thread. "You're clever enough," she said sharply. "Don't let anyone tell you different or they'll have me to deal with."

Erica jumped up. She hugged Bessie so hard that she crushed her white apron, tipped over her work-box and jerked the thread out of her needle.

"Now, then ... " began Bessie. But already Erica was out of the room and racing down the back stairs to the garden to play with Chris.

Bessie, of course, could not look after all five children all the time. The three older ones, Cecily and Erica and Chris, spent each morning with a governess called Miss Pringle. Erica's early memories of Miss Pringle were mostly unhappy ones, because when she was small she was not good at lessons at all. In fact, right up to the time she was seven she could hardly read. Cecily had learnt to read when she was five and Chris when he was only three, so no one understood why Erica couldn't. Miss Pringle could never decide whether Erica was stupid or naughty, but rather thought it was the second. Most people did find Erica naughty, and that worried her because of her father. He was the vicar of Woodhuckle, and she thought it must be embarrassing for him, when he stood up in Sunday school and spoke about being naughty, to know that his own little daughter was the naughtiest of all.

In the end Erica at least learnt to read, even though she did not become good. She always remembered the day when she first read a story by herself because it was also the day on which she tried to die in order to make people sorry for her. It was just before her seventh birthday. She had been out in the garden playing with Cecily until Alice, the housemaid, opened the back door and rang the dinner-bell to tell them to come in for lessons. In the boot-room Cecily changed from button-boots to indoor slippers. Erica couldn't because she had her slippers on already.

"I forgot," she said guiltily. "But they're not very dirty. It was only dew. Perhaps Miss Pringle won't notice."

"You always do forget," said Cecily. "Besides, they're wet. You ought to change them."

"They'll dry just as well on me," said Erica.

Miss Pringle was waiting for them in the dining-room which they used as a schoolroom. Chris was writing at the big mahogany table. He was still so small that he had to sit on the thickest book from his father's study to be able to reach, but already he could write and spell a great deal better than Erica. Miss Pringle threw up her hands when she saw Erica.

"My dear child! Where have you been?"

"In the garden with Cecily."

"Then why is Cecily still clean and neat? Just look at yourself."

There was a long mirror hanging between the windows. Erica and Cecily looked in it. Cecily's dress was white and stiff. Her fair hair was smooth. Each slipper was held in place by black elastic neatly criss-crossed over her white stockings. Erica's dress was wet and limp because she had carelessly run through the wet bushes. There was a big mud stain on the skirt where she had knelt to look at a robin's nest in the hedge. One slipper had lost its elastic. Her dark hair flopped in her eyes because she had lost her ribbon. It had caught on the gate when she thrust her head through the bars to watch the village children trooping to school and she had never even noticed.

"You are a disgrace," said Miss Pringle. "Go and find Bessie, and ask her to make you tidy."

Bessie was not best pleased, but she got out another dress and clean stockings.

"It's nothing but wash and mend for you! You might think as how it's other people who get the work when you're so careless. Now I'll have to sew elastic on the slipper, as if there wasn't enough already on my day off. It'll be tea-time before I get away."

Erica watched her as she got out her work-box.

"It's all Miss Pringle's fault," she said indignantly, "making you do all that work on your day off, just because she doesn't like me to look untidy!"

Bessie laughed, forgetting her anger. "Well, I like that! Whose fault was it you got untidy in the first place?"

Erica laughed, too, at that, and Bessie helped her with the stockings and the clean dress, and brushed her tangled hair.

When she got back to the dining-room, they were having a writing lesson. Erica picked up her pen reluctantly. Cecily was writing in a beautiful flowing hand, almost more beautiful than Miss Pringle's own. Chris didn't have to do copy-books, because for some reason boys didn't. He was learning Latin verbs for his father.

"Write, *I have been a very bad child*," Miss Pringle ordered, writing the words up on the blackboard for Erica to copy.

Erica dipped her pen in the ink and wrote *I have been a very dab chidl*. She looked at what she had written and was sure there was something which wasn't quite right. Perhaps *very* had two *r*'s? She tried to fit in a second one, but the ink ran and made a blot. She saw Cecily looking at her.

"It's all wrong, I know it is," she whispered in despair.

Miss Pringle came round the table and looked over Erica's shoulder.

"What a very silly little girl!" she said mildly. "I wonder if I shall ever teach you how to spell? Look, I will write it out for you at the top of the page. Now copy it out fifteen times, so that you learn it." Erica tried to obey, but her eyes were so full of tears she could not begin.

"Now, don't dawdle," said Miss Pringle.

Erica dug the pen so hard into the paper that the nib crossed.

"Oh dear, how clumsy you are," said Miss Pringle.

The morning ground on. Cecily and Chris did what they could to help. Cecily wrote sentences so quickly that Miss Pringle could hardly tick them fast enough. Chris became so stupid that she did not know what to make of him. He had to have every word spelt out for him. He lost his pencil. He lost his india-rubber. He was sure he saw a spider climbing up the table leg. Miss Pringle shrieked and Cecily giggled. Erica wrote doggedly on. Sometimes she wrote *bad* and sometimes she wrote *dab*. Sometimes she wrote *chidl* and sometimes *child* and sometimes *chlid*. What did it matter anyway? She was still writing when Alice came in with three glasses of milk and three buns on a tray.

"No bun for Erica," said Miss Pringle. "She does not deserve one."

"I don't want a bun," said Erica loftily. "I am not hungry."

She tried not to look at the buns as the others ate. Cecily soon finished hers, but Chris was slowly picking the currants out of his to save them for last. He always did that. One day at a party a kind lady had said, "Don't you like currants, little boy?" and eaten them all for him before he could speak, but even that had not taught him.

"Drink up your milk, Erica," said Miss Pringle.

Erica did not see why she should drink milk, which she did not much like, if she was not going to get a bun anyway.

"Put it on the floor. Perkins may drink it," whispered Chris. He put the glass on the floor himself. Perkins, the immense tabby, took no notice, but continued to sleep in his patch of sunlight by the window. Chris screwed up a scrap of paper and threw it at him. It missed. Then Erica tried, and hit him. Perkins twitched his ears, but went to sleep again. Then Chris tried again and then Erica.

"Erica! *What* are you doing? Come here at once!"

Erica jumped up guiltily, and in doing so kicked over the

glass of milk. Perkins woke up at last, jumped down from the window-sill with a thump, and began licking up the spilt milk. Chris laughed. Erica laughed. Even Cecily laughed.

"You are very impertinent children," said Miss Pringle. "I shall tell your father how naughty you have been; especially you, Erica."

"But ... " began Erica, and then stopped.

"Please, it was me who put the milk on the floor," said Chris. "Erica doesn't like milk."

"Erica should like milk. She is a very lucky girl to have it. There are thousands of poor children starving in our big cities who would be glad of that glass of milk, would they not, Cecily?"

"Not thousands," said Cecily, who was a very exact girl. "Even hundreds of children couldn't really share one glass."

So Cecily had to write out twenty times *I must not be impertinent*, and Erica and Chris had to stand each in a corner till Alice came to lay the table for dinner, and lessons were over. Miss Pringle was not really unkind, but she believed she had to be very strict or she would not be obeyed. She had never had anything to do with children before, and had never even thought of being a governess till her father died and she and her mother found themselves with almost nothing to live on. Miss Pringle had been an only child herself and knew nothing of big families. The natural liveliness of the young Stocks seemed to her to be downright disobedience, and she punished them accordingly. Yet underneath her strict manner she was really very fond of Cecily and Chris. She would like to have been fond of Erica, too, but she was a bit afraid of Erica's temper. Also, she thought she might be blamed because Erica was so bad at lessons. She could not imagine what she and her mother would live on if she lost her post.

The children had dinner alone. Their father was out, Miss Pringle always went home to her widowed mother, and Bessie was upstairs looking after Clare and Molly. Alice brought their meal in and set it on the table. There were bowls of soup, and bread hot from the oven to eat with it. To drink there was water. Chris seized the jug to pour himself a glass, but Alice stopped him.

"Finish your soup first," she told him. "Hot soup and cold water together is more than any stomach can take. Your poor Ma knew a boy who died just from drinking water with his soup."

Chris sighed and pushed the jug away. They had always been told that you died if you drank water and soup together. Alice said so, Sarah the cook said so, Bessie said so. Even before that, their mother had said so. The only one who didn't say so was their father, but then he didn't say it wasn't so either. In truth, he didn't like to let on that their mother had had a bee in her bonnet on the subject, but they didn't know that. They all believed that to drink hot soup and cold water killed you – or at any rate, nearly believed it.

The soup was a mulligatawny and Sarah had put more curry powder in than usual. Erica looked longingly at the jug of water. She looked so longingly that she did not pay enough attention to what she was doing. Her hand jerked and a trail of brown spots shot across the tablecloth. She looked at the spots anxiously.

"It's because I'm so thirsty," she said hopefully. "Being thirsty makes you clumsy."

"You don't need anything special to make you clumsy. You always are," said Cecily. She wasn't being unkind, only truthful, but it was too much for Erica. Every single thing had gone wrong for her that day from the moment she got up. Miss Pringle was going to tell her father she had been naughty, and her father would look sadly at her. Bessie was cross with her, which was almost worse than Daddy looking sad. She was too stupid to learn to spell and now she could not even drink soup without spilling it.

"I'm going to drink water with soup," she announced.

There was a shocked silence. Erica picked up the jug and poured herself out a glass while the others watched.

"Don't," begged Chris. "I don't want you to die."

"I'm so thirsty I'll die anyway if I don't," said Erica.

"Leave her alone, Chris," said Cecily. "She won't really drink it."

"Yes I will," said Erica at once. "Which first, soup or water?"

"First soup, then water, then more soup," said Chris after careful thought. He didn't want Erica to die, but if she was determined, he wanted the thing done slowly and properly so that he could watch. Erica took a spoonful of soup and then drank half her glass of water, but nothing happened. She waited a moment and then took another spoonful of soup but still nothing happened, though her heart was beating so hard it seemed to be trying to jump into her throat.

Chris was staring at her open-mouthed. It was nice that Erica was still alive, but he couldn't help thinking it would have been more exciting if *something* had happened.

"Alice! Alice!" he shrieked as Alice came back with the next course. "Erica drank water with soup and she didn't die at all. Why didn't she?"

Alice collected up the soup bowls and put down plates of cold meat and potatoes.

"It doesn't always show straight off," she said.

Erica was very silent for the rest of dinner. Cecily said Alice had only been joking, but Erica wasn't sure. She was beginning to feel a bit odd in her inside. After dinner she went and lay among the daisies on the back lawn, and thought about dying. Of course, if she were dead she would not have to see her father looking sad at her, and people would not keep on calling her stupid. They might even be sorry for her and wish they had been kinder to her when she was alive. This thought comforted her for a little, but then the tears began to flow again. What was the good of people being sorry for her if she was dead? She thought of herself lying still and cold, and the tears welled up faster and faster.

Suddenly she jumped to her feet. If this was to be her last day alive then at least she would enjoy it. She darted off to look once again at the robin's nest. While she was peeping in at it Chris came into the orchard. He came to see what she was looking at, and they both watched as the two robins fluttered fearlessly back and forth feeding the nestlings. Erica and Chris were so near, they were almost within touching distance.

"I do wish I could really hold a bird in my hand," sighed Erica. "I've always wanted to. Only just to know what it felt like, of course. I'd let it go straight away."

Chris looked at her. He could see that she had been crying, and he thought of a joke to cheer her up.

"I know how to catch a bird," he said.

"No, you don't!"

"I do too! You have to put salt on its tail. William Long told me." Erica believed him then, for she thought the gardener the wisest man in the world after her own father. There seemed nothing he did not know about plants and animals, and if he said you could catch a bird by putting salt on its tail then it must be so.

For the next quarter of an hour Erica forgot all about dying. Chris had begged a little paper bag of salt off Sarah. Erica ran about the lawn with the bag in one hand and a pinch of salt ready in the other. There were plenty of birds on the lawn but she never got near enough one to put salt on its tail. After a while she heard an odd sound behind the hedge. She stopped quite still to listen. Then she flung the bag away and rushed round to the far side. There she found Chris, Sarah and Alice and her own beloved William Long all in fits of silent laughter.

"Oh, Erica!" gasped Sarah. "Fancy your brother taking you in with that old story!"

"But . . . but Chris said . . . William said . . ."

Erica broke off because she had just seen how stupid she had been.

"But if I was near enough to put salt on a bird's tail, I'd be near enough to catch it anyway. I wouldn't need salt."

The others fairly howled. Erica was trembling with rage and shame, but they were laughing too much to notice.

"Wasn't it a good joke?" shrieked Chris. "Erica, wasn't it funny? I knew it would make you laugh."

It was too much. Erica rushed at him, hitting and kicking in her rage. Chris tried to run away, but Erica grabbed him and shook him as hard as she could shake.

"For shame, Erica!" said Sarah. "Your own little brother."

"I thought you'd like it," said Chris as well as he could through the shaking. "I wanted to cheer you up."

Erica was beyond hearing him. She went on shaking him and finally pushed him so hard that he fell. Alice and William seized hold of her and pulled her away. They held her arms so tightly that she could not escape.

"Let me go! Let me go!" she screamed.

They did not let her go and she felt she could not bear it. She *had* to get away. She bent her head to William's hand and bit for all she was worth.

Erica was in disgrace. Erica had been carried upstairs and dumped on her bed. Nice little girls, she was told, never bit. She was to stay in her bedroom till she came to her senses. Erica lay on the bed and sobbed. She sobbed and shrieked and sobbed again, but no one came to her. She remembered she might be going to die. Suppose she were to die all alone upstairs? Surely someone would come! But the kitchen, where Alice and Sarah were consoling Chris, was a long way off. There was no one else in the house. Everywhere there was only the deep silence of a country afternoon. Erica buried her face in the pillow and cried and cried till she cried herself to sleep.

She woke up hours later. The evening sun glowed on the windows of the house opposite. Outside the thrushes were singing. In the still evening air she could hear quite plainly the clanking of buckets in the yard. William Long was watering the horses before he went home. Erica had forgotten all about dying. She only knew she was hungry and bored. She looked around the room for something to play with, but there was only a book of Cecily's lying on the window sill. She was so bored that she actually tried to read it. Very slowly she spelt out the first sentence. *Fire! Fire! screamed a ragged little boy, running as fast as his bare legs could carry him.* Erica felt a slight stirring of interest. Where was the fire? Was the little boy running away from it or towards it? Had he gone for help or had he even lit it himself? She tried the next sentence, and then the next. She read many words wrong and left others right out, but she read on to the end of the story.

Her father came home late. He rather hoped the children were already in bed. He was very fond of them, but not at the end of a long day when he was tired and hungry. He made straight for his study, but Bessie stopped him in the passage and asked if she could speak to him. His heart sank for he knew that meant one of the children had been misbehaving.

He hoped it was not Erica. He did not know which was more exhausting, Erica defiant with rage, or Erica repentant and engulfed in tears. He went slowly upstairs and pushed open her door.

"Daddy! Daddy!" shouted a piercing voice. "I can read! It's perfectly easy! I can read *anything*!"

Mr Stock was so relieved to find her happy that he forgot about scolding her. He sat down beside the bed and made her read a page aloud. She read so well that he was really pleased with her. He kissed her kindly and would have gone away without saying more if Erica herself had not remembered.

"I've been very bad," she said sadly. "I don't believe William Long will ever love me again, or Chris either."

Chris heard this from his room opposite and protested loudly.

"Don't be so silly! I thought you'd think it funny about the salt. Truly I did!"

Erica thought about the birds on the lawn, and herself running after them. Perhaps she had looked rather funny? She smiled in a way that was rather more like crying, but her father looked so happy that she began to smile properly.

"Anyway, tomorrow is my birthday," she said more cheerfully. "We're to have strawberries and cream. That's *one* thing I'm lucky about. If your birthday is in June you get strawberries and cream for your birthday tea. Everybody likes strawberries and cream, so everybody likes coming to my party." Her father smiled down at her, and then glanced out of the window.

"Look!" he said. "They have lit the fires on Carne Hill. They are for your birthday."

Erica looked out of the window to watch the leaping flames on the hillside, and smiled to herself. She knew the bonfires were not really for her birthday. They were for St John's Eve. The village boys and girls went out to light them each year to keep the witches away. Bessie had told her. Erica snuggled down to sleep. She felt very old. Last year she had really believed the bonfires were for her. Even that afternoon she had believed you could catch a bird by putting salt on its tail. She could read too. And tomorrow she would be seven.

18

Chapter 2 · Keep the pot boiling

Being seven wasn't very different from being six after all. Erica did the same sort of things – climbed trees and paddled in the brook in summer, and, when autumn came, ate the windfall apples and went to look for blackberries in the lane. Outside in the road she could hear the school-boys as they went to and from school. "Obbley obbley onker! My first conker!" they chanted as someone else's chestnut was smashed to smithereens.

Altogether it wasn't a bad life for the five Stock children. If the house was a little quiet and desolate downstairs, upstairs in the nursery there was plenty of laughter. There were plenty of people, too, who went out of their way to be kind to the motherless children. Indeed, many of their troubles arose because people were rather too interested in them. Woodhuckle seemed very full of old ladies with nothing better to do than come and tell the vicar of his children's misdeeds. When their mother had been alive, no one had thought they ought to tell her if her children had been naughty, but everyone seemed to think the vicar needed to be told, or he would not notice. They may have been right, but, as Chris said, it seemed all the more of a pity to tell him about things which would only upset him. Chris was probably saying that because he had just been in trouble himself. There were two sisters, Miss Browne and Miss Emmeline Browne, who lived on the corner of Church Lane and saw everything that went on in the village. One day they called to tell the vicar that Chris had been reading other people's postcards from the postman's bag. Poor Mr Stock! He asked Alice to go and find Chris. Chris didn't deny that he quite often went on the rounds with the postman, and that, if there were any postcards, Mr Baines gave them to him to read.

"Mr Baines *likes* me to read them," he said earnestly. "He says I read them very well. He says his eyes aren't what they were, and he can't afford proper glasses or he'd read them himself. I thought that you'd be *pleased* that I read the postcards for him. You always *say* we should be kind and helpful, and I *was*."

The small five-year-old was so comically indignant that Mr Stock rather wanted to laugh, but he couldn't with the Miss Brownes sitting there looking shocked. He tried to explain to Chris how wrong it was to read secrets from letters which had been entrusted to the post.

"Oh, I wouldn't read *letters*," said Chris happily, thinking the difficulty was now cleared up. "Mr Baines wouldn't read those either. Postcards are different. People don't write *secrets* on postcards. It'd be silly!"

The vicar laughed outright at that, but the Miss Brownes still looked shocked and Chris's pocket-money had to be taken away from him for a whole month. He was most hurt.

All the children got into trouble from time to time because of what the neighbours said, but Erica was a particularly easy child to complain about because she liked doing things which elderly people thought wrong in a girl from the vicarage – such as tree-climbing, and wading in the brook, and generally rushing about. If there was nothing else to complain of, they could always say that she had not sat still in church.

"You'd think they'd have better things to do with their eyes in church than prying at other people's children," Bessie used to say. Bessie did not like the Miss Brownes, because they tried to tell her how to bring up the children. They said she fed them on all the wrong things, and let Clare play outside without her sun-bonnet, and left baby Molly sleeping where a cat might sit on her head and suffocate her.

"I wish a cat would sit on Miss Browne's head!" said Bessie bitterly. "When I want to know how to bring up children, I'll go to our Mam that's had six, and not to a couple of old maids that wouldn't know the top of a baby from its bottom!"

When winter came, Erica found another occupation that the Miss Brownes considered unladylike. They were sure she ought not to go sliding on the ice with the village boys. Every year, as soon as it was certain that the frost was going to hold, the school-children flung buckets of water over the steep path down which the cows went to drink in summer. The water froze and made a long slide all the way to the pond. One after another, children hurtled down the slide and shot out on to the ice. Then they scrambled back to the bank, and so round and up to join the queue waiting to come down. They called it "Keep the Pot Boiling". There must never be a gap with no one on the slide, for that meant the pot had gone off the boil. Faster and faster grew the fun, smaller and smaller grew the gap between one slider and the next. The little children and the more timid of the big girls stopped playing then, because in the end someone was bound to fall; and if that happened, the next person would trip over him, and then the next, till everyone was in a heap on the ice. The ones at the bottom could get badly hurt if they were unlucky.

Erica was terrified of falling but she went on sliding, however hard the pot boiled. She could never have enough of the cheering and the danger and the speed. "You're a game 'un," the big boys and girls would say, and that was enough to send her hurtling down the slide again.

Once she did fall – a really bad fall – flat on to her face; blood poured from her nose. The next boys were so close behind her that they could not stop, and they all fell on top of her. In the scrimmage Toddy Baines accidentally trod on her hand with his hob-nailed boot. She nearly fainted, but still did not cry. Billy-Bob, William Long's son, picked her up and carried her home. The repentant Toddy ran alongside.

"I didn't mean it, Erica! True's I stand here, I didn't," he cried. "You'll not want to keep the pot boiling no more now."

"But of course I will," said Erica. She wasn't showing off, either; she really meant it. The boys cheered, and for all her bloody nose and throbbing hand Erica was happy.

Unfortunately, Miss Emmeline Browne was just drawing the sitting-room curtains as Erica was carried past her house. The next day, after church, she and her sister stopped the vicar to give him good advice about his daughter. Erica had been allowed to stay at home because of her bruised face. She had been left with her father's big prayer-book so that she could follow the service even though she wasn't there; but she could not read half the words and was very bored. So she was delighted at first when her father came in to see her.

"Erica, my dear," said the vicar gravely, "perhaps you had better not go sliding on the ice with the school-children any more."

"Oh, Daddy, why not? I must. I said I would, and they'll think I'm a coward if I don't go just because I hurt myself."

"But there's no need to go with the big boys. Other little girls don't. Why not play on the slide when the big boys are in school? Cecily and Chris could go with you, and you could invite Letty Upthorpe and her brother Hector."

"Hector Upthorpe!" said Erica scornfully. "Why, he was the one who tripped me up and made me fall."

"What! ... Now, Erica, think carefully what you are saying. You know he did not do it on purpose."

"Yes, he did. He was cross because he's such a cry-baby the big boys won't let him play Keep the Pot Boiling. They said, 'Look, even young Erica doesn't snivel like you if she falls.' So then when I went past he pushed a stick between my feet to make me fall. He thought I'd cry, but I didn't. Well, not till there was no one to see me but Billy-Bob, at any rate."

Her father was horrified and asked why she hadn't told anyone what Hector had done. Erica said indignantly that she wasn't a sneak.

"Besides, the boys would have half killed Hector if they'd known."

"What, because he hurt you?"

"Well, perhaps," said Erica doubtfully. "But mostly for spoiling their game."

Her father couldn't help laughing, and when Erica asked if she could go sliding again, he said she could. He wasn't going to have people saying his daughter was a cry-baby like Hector Upthorpe! All the same, he sighed as he went upstairs to get ready for dinner. He sometimes felt too tired to cope with small children. He was already nearly sixty when his first wife died, and when he fell in love again some years later, people said he was much too old to think of remarrying and raising more children. He had laughed then and said it did not matter, because if he was old his new wife was young. It had been she who died, though, and he was the one who had been left to bring up their five small children.

The next day, Erica's head still ached and her hand throbbed. She was allowed to stay in the nursery instead of going down to lessons. Bessie had gone out with Clare and Molly, and the room was peacefully silent except for the crackling of the fire. The nursery was one of the most pleasant rooms in the house. It always seemed full of light, even on the darkest days; for there were windows in two of the walls – a side window looking out into the big yard where the stables were, and a back window over the smaller yard where the wash-house was. Against that window stood a chest with a padded top, so big that two children could lie full length on it. There was usually more to watch in the stable yard, but the small yard was the busier on Mondays because Monday was always wash-day. Erica curled herself up on the chest and rested her head on the window-sill, so that she could watch what was going on.

Mrs Poine was doing the washing; Erica could see her moving about inside the wash-house. Mrs Poine had four children, and a husband who left most of his wages at the inn. So she was glad to get any work she could. Her cottage was always full of other people's wet clothes hanging round the fire to air. Mr Stock was not in favour of that. He said that if any house had to be full of washing it should be the house the clothes belonged to, particularly when it had over a dozen rooms instead of Mrs Poine's two or three. So he paid for Mrs Poine to come to the vicarage and do the washing on Monday and the heavy ironing on Tuesday.

Monday and Tuesday were the happiest days of Mrs Poine's week, for Sarah saw that she got a hot meal; and if the vicar happened to meet her he always raised his hat with grave politeness and asked how the children were doing.

"Almost as though I was a yooman creature after all," said Mrs Poine, "and not speaking to me as though I had no more feelings than the soap in my hand, like some I could name." Sarah knew she meant her husband but said nothing and just nodded.

Mrs Poine always wore pattens to keep her old boots out of the wet. She clattered over the cobbles in the yard with almost as much noise as Greyo the big carriage horse. When Erica was still lying in bed, she had heard her clopping across the yard to light the fire in the wash-house copper. Now sheets and towels were seething in the bubbling water and eddies of steam billowed out of the wash-house windows. Erica waited hopefully for the moment when Mrs Poine took the bung out of the copper and all the hot soapy water came cascading out into the yard, burying the cobbles in a sea of grey suds. Then Mrs Poine came out, her thin shawl tied tightly about her to keep out the cold, and chased the water away with a stiff broom till all the cobbles gleamed clean and fresh in the frosty air. Erica was still watching with lazy pleasure when Bessie came in with a glass of milk.

"Oh come and look quick! Who's that with Mrs Poine?" asked Erica. A small girl of about five had come out of the wash-house to watch the water rush away, and she was dancing and hopping with excitement. Erica had never seen the child, and that in itself was interesting. Everybody always knew everybody else in Woodhuckle.

"That'll be Mrs Poine's little niece, Gwen," said Bessie. "Mr Poine's niece, I should say, for it's his brother's child, poor little scrappit."

"Why poor little scrappit?"

"Because her father was another Ben Poine, only worse. Drank away his wages so fast that there was nowhere for the family to go but the work-house." She saw Erica's eyes fixed on her in horror and broke off hastily. "Now don't you go spreading that about. It's not little Gwen's fault, but there are those who would hold it against her if it got around that she had been in the House."

"No, of course I wouldn't spread it!" said Erica, quite shocked. She was not very clear why it was so terrible to go to the work-house, worse almost than having a relative in prison.

"It was very good of Mrs Poine to have Gwen to live with them," Erica went on.

"Ah, it was that. 'Specially when you remember she's often not got enough to feed her own three. Catch me marrying a no-good like Ben Poine!" Bessie could afford to speak proudly. She was now keeping company with a very fine young man, a soldier in a scarlet coat, who was already a lance-corporal and looked to be made a sergeant before very many years.

Gwen Poine stayed on in the village, for her mother had died in the work-house infirmary and her father had emigrated to Canada. He said he would send for Gwen when he had made his fortune, but no one really believed he would do either. Gwen went to the school with her cousins, and people were beginning to forget she wasn't just another little Poine. Erica saw her in Sunday school and at church, but her next real meeting with her was at Hector Upthorpe's birthday party the following summer, when Erica was nearly eight.

The Upthorpes hadn't been living in Woodhuckle very long, but already it was difficult to remember the time before they came. Stock and Upthorpe children had got into the habit of doing many things together and always thought of each other as friends, though in fact they didn't always even like each other. It was partly that they lived so conveniently close. "Next door," they said, though actually there were four cottages between the vicarage and The Limes, where the Upthorpes lived. Also, they were very much of an age. Tom, the eldest and the one they all liked best, was twelve. Then came Letty, who was ten, the same age as Cecily. Hector, who was then eight, like Erica, came next; and last of all there was

Effie, who was five and came between Clare and Molly in age.

If it had been Tom's or even Letty's party, they would have been happy enough to go, but none of the Stocks liked Hector. However, there was to be cricket on the front lawn and tea outside, if it was warm enough. "What fun if Cecily bowls Hector out," said Chris hopefully. "She's getting very good."

"He'll only complain it wasn't fair, and we'll have to agree because it's his birthday," said Erica.

"Not if Tom's there," said Chris. "He wouldn't let Hector get away with it."

But Tom wasn't there. At least, he couldn't come and play cricket, because he'd fallen that morning and sprained his ankle. He had to stay indoors with his leg propped up on cushions. However, two school-friends of his, Johnny Rae and Jim Franklin, had come to keep him company; so they took charge of the cricket and made everybody stick to the rules. At first they had not wanted the girls to play, but Tom said Cecily and Erica were much better cricketers than Hector, so that was all right. In fact, Erica had the satisfaction of catching Johnny himself out.

It was a good game of cricket, and one or two passers-by stopped to watch. Hector got very angry when they did, and said people oughtn't to look into other people's gardens. After a while, the three Poine boys came down the lane with Gwen and stopped to stare too. They looked a pathetic lot with their ragged clothes and runny noses. They had been turned out of the cottage because their father was in a temper and said he didn't want them under his feet. They had had no dinner because he had come home from the inn the previous Saturday night without a penny of his wages left. The Poine children had nowhere particular to go and nothing particular to do; so they stopped and stared with vague pleasure at the brightly dressed children playing cricket in the garden. A few minutes passed before Hector noticed the four faces peering over the hedge.

"Go away!" he ordered.

They scrambled down quickly from the bank, but they stayed in the road and went on watching.

"Go away, I tell you!" said Hector.

"They don't have to unless they want," said Cecily severely. "They're not hurting you, and it's not your road anyway."

Hector hated to be told off. He went bright red with fury and rushed to the hedge.

"Go away, you beastly little brats!" he shouted. "You've no right to come staring at gentlemen's children. I'll tell my mother about you, and she won't give your mother any more washing to do. Be off!"

The threat was enough to send the boys away. They were no fighters, the Poine boys. Bread and scrape and boiled turnips are not a diet to fight on, and they might not get even those if their mother could find no work. They trailed off with their heads hanging. Only Gwen lingered. She was as pale and puny as her cousins, but there was a spark in Gwen which even semi-starvation could not quite put out. She stood where she was, silent but defiant.

"Go away, you work-house brat!" said Hector.

It was too much. Not even the unkindest village child had ever said that to her openly. Gwen picked up a stone and flung it as hard as she could. It missed by yards: she burst into tears and fled.

"Cry-baby!" jeered Hector.

Erica thought she would burst with fury. There didn't seem anything bad enough to do to Hector except kill him then and there, and she couldn't do that because guests weren't even allowed to be rude to the birthday boy. It was Cecily who stepped forward. Her grey eyes looked oddly dark in her pale face. Hector was standing in a lordly way with his back to the low hedge, and there was a smug smile on his face now.

"That'll show these village children how to behave," he said.

Without any warning Cecily stepped straight up to him and she pushed so hard that Hector vanished heels over head through the hedge. Though it was only a small hedge, it stood on the top of the bank and there was quite a way to roll down into the ditch outside. There was a dreadful moment's silence before a thump and a yell told them that Hector's fall was over. They rushed to the hedge and looked. Hector had already scrambled to his feet and stood in the bottom of the ditch howling.

Johnny and Jim burst out laughing.

"Now who's a cry-baby?" asked Cecily.

The bell for tea rang at that moment, which was perhaps fortunate, and they went back into the house. Erica found Jim Franklin walking beside her.

"I say, what a corker your sister is!" said Jim with simple enthusiasm. "Didn't she just give Upthorpe minor what he deserved! She looks good, too, not a bit like a tomboy."

"She is good," said Erica. "As good as good, always. I can't think what got into her ... well, I can, of course, because I wanted to as well, but I didn't dare. I'm afraid Mrs Upthorpe will be very angry with her, though."

"I shouldn't think she'll ever know what happened," said Jim comfortingly. "How could she?"

"Hector will tell her," said Erica bluntly.

Jim looked down his nose. "The boys in our school don't tell tales," he said loftily.

Erica said nothing. She did not like to contradict a boy so much older than herself, but privately she thought Jim must be rather a fool.

Hector didn't actually tell his mother; only, as soon as the last guest had gone he began to limp. Not quite on purpose, because he really had bruised his leg and it was beginning to get stiff. All the same, he needn't have limped quite so exactly where his mother was sure to see him. Mrs Upthorpe was rather a silly woman, though very kind. She spoiled all her children a bit, and Hector most of all. Once, when he was a small baby, he had nearly died of pneumonia, and she couldn't get it out of her head that he was still delicate, even though he was now as fat and strong as a little pony. When she heard what had happened before tea, she was quite distraught.

"My poor Hector! Those dreadful vicarage girls! You might have been killed! And you've been sitting all through tea in damp clothes! You'll get pneumonia again! Oh, whatever shall I do? You must go straight to bed, and I'll go and tell the vicar how his precious daughters behave. You must have a hot bottle in the bed. I'll order a hot carriage – I mean bottle – immediately and tell them to bring the carriage round to the front door."

28

She tugged at the bell-pull, but because the maid didn't come quickly enough, she rushed out to give the order herself. Hector tried to slip out after her, but Tom reached out a long arm and caught hold of him.

"Take that grin off your face!" he ordered furiously. "Just wait till my ankle's better. Won't I make you sorry for being a sneak!"

"I'm not a sneak," whimpered Hector. "I didn't say a thing. I couldn't help mother seeing I was limping, could I? It was Effie who told." Hector dragged himself free and ran away, thanking his stars that Tom couldn't come after him.

"Why, Hector," Letty called after him, "you're better! You're not limping any more! Isn't that nice!"

Hector's limp suddenly returned. He banged the door noisily behind him, but not in time to shut out the sound of Tom's laughter.

Chapter 3 · Being good isn't easy

When Mrs Upthorpe arrived at the vicarage and told the vicar that Cecily had brutally attacked her son, he simply could not believe her at first; he was sure Cecily could never have done such a thing. But to his horror, Cecily at once agreed that it was she who had pushed Hector into the ditch. Poor Mr Stock felt as though he himself had been knocked off his feet backwards. As soon as he could find his voice he ordered Cecily to apologize to Mrs Upthorpe. Cecily looked at him gravely.

"I cannot say I am sorry, Father. I am not sorry. Hector deserved to be punished."

So Cecily was sent up to her room and told to think over her faults. She was not to come down until she was ready to apologize, and she was to have no supper. Cecily made no attempt to argue. She kissed her father, she said good night politely to Mrs Upthorpe and then went sedately upstairs. After she was gone there was a silence in the room which was broken at last by the vicar.

"I thought Cecily at least knew how to behave," he said heavily. "If I cannot bring up Cecily, I certainly cannot bring up the others. I have failed."

He looked so unhappy that Mrs Upthorpe forgot her anger and tried to comfort him.

"Oh, my dear Mr Stock, it wasn't so bad after all. Children will be children, you know, especially when they get together. I shouldn't have left them out there in the garden so long without even Tom. They excite one another, and then someone's bound to do something silly. But it's only mischief when all's said and done."

"To push a child so hard that he has a dangerous fall, is more than mischief," said the vicar.

"Oh, well," said Mrs Upthorpe, a little embarrased. Now that she was calmer she began to feel she had been making a fuss about nothing. She knew her husband would say so when he came home. "Perhaps it wasn't such a bad fall. I mean, it was only a ditch after all ... and if there were nettles in it, there can't have been *very* much water, can there?"

But now that Mrs Upthorpe was no longer exaggerating, Mr Stock was ceasing to believe her. Why had she made such a fuss in the first place if there had been no danger? The more Mrs Upthorpe tried to say that the accident had been nothing, the more he was convinced it had been really dangerous.

"If only Cecily would apologize," he said wistfully as Mrs Upthorpe got up to go.

"Oh well, that's a thing I never would do myself when I was little," said Mrs Upthorpe playfully. "I just *couldn't* bring myself to do it, not even when my mother said she would beat me. I dare say you were the same when you were a boy."

"Oh no ... at least, I don't know. I can't remember."

"No. I don't suppose you do. Such a long time ago, wasn't it, vicar?" said Mrs Upthorpe with one of her inane laughs. "I always say you make my dear Henry look *quite* young, with your beautiful white hair – quite a picture! Though of course I shouldn't say it to your face!"

She was gone at last, and Mr Stock went slowly back to his study. He stopped for a moment by the mirror in the hall and looked at his reflection. Beautiful white hair indeed! How dare that idiotic woman be so impertinent? He turned away impatiently, but even when he couldn't see it, he knew the white hair was there. He had even been rather proud of it, had thought it was a fine head of hair for a man of his age. He groaned again. His age! Was he really an old man – too old to understand and bring up children?

Cecily was quite happy up in her bedroom. Indeed, her father knew it hadn't been much of a punishment to send her. She often spent hours there of her own accord, just looking out of the window or dreaming. It was true she was to have no supper, but she wouldn't really miss that after an enormous birthday tea. Anyway, Chris and Erica managed to smuggle some of their supper bread and jam upstairs and share it with her. Bessie saw them doing it and pretended not to see. She had already heard what Cecily had done from Hannah, Alice's sister, who was a housemaid at the Upthorpes. Hannah was not fond of Master Hector and the story had lost nothing in the telling. Bessie, who sometimes privately thought Cecily was a bit too good, was delighted with it and she told Erica and Chris not to worry.

"Your father will soon hear the rights of it all. Mr Upthorpe is coming after dinner this evening to see him. Our Hannah was in the sitting-room making up the fire when Tom told his father, and Mr Upthorpe laughed out loud. He knows what that Hector is like, even if his ma don't!"

All the same, Erica and Chris remained bothered. It was all very well for Cecily to say nobly that she knew that what she had done was right and didn't mind how she was punished, but that wasn't really the point.

"Father keeps saying that if you don't know how to behave, then he'll have to *do* something about it. What do you think he means?"

"I don't know," said Chris with a shrug. "What can he do except beat us? He might beat me, but I'm sure he wouldn't beat you girls."

"And I'm quite sure he wouldn't beat you either, Chris," said Erica. "He's not the beating sort."

They sat on the chest in the nursery and talked it over, still feeling worried. Clare and Molly were already fast asleep in the night nursery next door, and Bessie was down in the kitchen.

"I don't like Daddy saying he must *do* something to make us good," repeated Erica. "I don't want anything done to *make* us good. We're all right as we are."

"I tell you what," said Chris. "Let's both be very good. Then he'll know he doesn't have to do anything special about us."

"We couldn't be good for ever," objected Erica.

"Of course we couldn't. But for a long time we could. Three days, perhaps."

"A week," said Erica firmly.

The next morning, Erica came down to breakfast full of a new idea. Her father had already had his breakfast and gone off early to visit the bishop in Gloucester, so she was able to tell Chris straight away. She had been reading a book before breakfast about another family who wanted to be good, for some reason or other, and had invented a clever way to help themselves.

"Is it a Sunday school book?" asked Chris suspiciously.

"Yes, it is," admitted Erica. "But it's interesting all the same."

"Oh well, go on then," said Chris tolerantly.

"It's about these children who had an uncle," began Erica. She saw Chris frowning and said hastily, "Now don't stop and ask which children. It doesn't matter. Just any children and any uncle. And this uncle gave them a little box each, and if they did something naughty they had to put a black bead in the box, and if they did something especially good they put a white one in. And the uncle said he'd give a prize to the one who did best."

"I bet it was the most namby-pamby one who got it," said Chris.

"I haven't read that far yet, but truly they're not namby-pamby."

So Chris said he would try it. Erica cut the string of her one and only necklace. The beads were blue and white, not black and white, but it came to the same thing. Chris said it was wrong to cut it up, and so Erica ought to put a blue bead in her box straight away. Erica said he would have to put one in his box, too, because it was his knife. Chris was just going to argue, when he stopped.

"Bother! If I'm angry I'll have to give myself a blue bead, I suppose."

"You see," said Erica. "It's working already."

Erica had always been told in Sunday school that children who were good were happy. But after being good for three whole days on end she began to wonder if the Sunday school teacher had got it wrong. She had seldom felt so cross. Chris said the same. They were sitting gloomily on the chest in the nursery. The rain was beating against the window-panes. Cecily was crying over a book, and Clare was crying over a broken doll. The only really cheerful person was Molly, who was sitting in the dark corner behind Bessie's rocking-chair unwinding her sewing-reels.

"Let's count up the beads and tell each other what we got them for. It'll be something to do," said Erica at last.

So Chris fetched the old tooth-powder tin he had been keeping his beads in, and Erica brought out a tiny wooden box with "A present from Bournemouth" on it, which Bessie's mother had given her. They sat down at the table and began taking out beads in turn. Erica had given herself a white bead for giving Chris twopence out of her pocket-money.

"That's not worth a white bead," said Chris scornfully. He was feeling contrary because the rain had stopped him playing cricket with Tom and his other friends. "You didn't give me the twopence; you only lent it to me. You'll get it back next week."

"I bet I won't," said Erica. She, too, was feeling awkward, through being shut indoors all day. "You never save anything, so you won't be able to. Besides, you gave yourself a white bead for letting old Mrs Daviot kiss you, and Cecily and me have to let her kiss us every time we go to see her."

"It's different for girls. Anyway, you never gave yourself a blue bead for not getting your spelling right."

"But if I put in a blue bead for every spelling mistake I made, I'd have nothing but blue beads; and spelling mistakes aren't naughty, they're just stupid."

"Then I'm going to put a blue bead in your box for being stupid," said Chris, and did so.

"And I'm going to take that white one out of yours," said Erica, and did so.

"No, you're not to! And if you do, I'll give you a lot of blue ones for stealing."

What with Erica trying to get white beads out of Chris's tin, and Chris trying to put blue ones in her box, something was bound to happen. It was Erica's box which went first, when Chris knocked it with his elbow in the scrimmage. It clattered on the floor and the lid broke off at the hinge.

"I hate you!" said Erica, and turned Chris's tooth-powder tin upside down on his head. The beads bounced off him and down to the floor. Molly gave a shriek of delight and threw herself on them. Erica shrieked still louder and jumped down from her chair. After all, they were her very own beads, off her only necklace. She began trying to grab them in handfuls and pushing them anyhow into the box. Chris laughed unkindly and tried to kick the box away to tease her, but slipped on one of the scattered beads and landed crash on the floor. It was Erica's turn to laugh, and Chris got to his feet in a rage.

"This is a stupid game," he shouted. "I'm not playing it any more." He stormed out, banging the door behind him.

Erica sat quite still on the floor after he had gone; she didn't even bother to go on picking up beads. It felt queer to be quarrelling with Chris, for they hardly ever did. Chris might quarrel with Cecily, and Clare with Molly, and Erica with Clare, but she and Chris always just seemed to get on. Erica felt there must be something very wrong about this bead game. She decided she had better finish the book in which she had read of it. Perhaps she and Chris were playing it wrong. She fetched the book from the bookshelf and began to read at the table. It was growing dark by then, but there was still enough light to read.

Erica began to feel a little more cheerful. Clare and Molly were laughing together, and Cecily's canary sang softly in the corner. Nobody was cross and nobody was trying to be particularly good. Cecily, who had paid no attention to the quarrel except to put her fingers in her ears, was still crying over her book. She loved books which made her cry, so that was all in order. Clare and Molly were putting beads in their mouths and seeing who could spit them furthest, so they were all right, too. Erica went on reading. The children in the book hadn't quarrelled over the beads as she and Chris had done, but it turned out to be all a bit of a take-in. The uncle had given the prize not to the one with the most white beads but to the one with the most black beads. He said the children who gave themselves too many white beads must be conceited, and the children who gave themselves hardly any black beads weren't being honest.

"Well, really!" said Erica out loud.

No one paid any attention. Erica shut the book with a bang. She saw what the uncle meant, of course, but it did make the whole game seem even sillier.

Then Bessie came in with the oil lamp, to hang it on the hook from the ceiling. She was very cross to find herself slipping on beads and made Erica finish picking them all up. It took a long time because everything on the floor was in shadow now the lamp had been hung up. Bessie wouldn't let her set the lamp on the floor because, she said, it was too dangerous and would burn the whole house down if it got knocked over.

"I wish it would," muttered Erica. "Then it would burn all these stupid beads too. Chris ought to help me; he spilt half of them."

"It's not Chris's necklace," said Bessie. "And how did you come to break it anyway? Really, you ought to be ashamed of yourself. You break every pretty thing you're given. And you were quarrelling with your brother, too. I heard you. Now, you know what your father says – 'Let not the sun go down upon your wrath.' You'd better go and tell Chris you're sorry."

"I shan't," said Erica. "Besides, it's too late. The sun must have gone down ages ago. And it's silly that you have to forgive people earlier in spring than you do in summer."

"I can see you've got that black dog on your shoulder all right," said Bessie sharply.

Bessie picked up little Molly, who crowed with delight, and

Clare gave Bessie a big kiss. Bessie kissed her back and called her "Heart's darling". Erica pretended not to hear, but she hated it. Bessie and Chris were the two people she loved best in the world, and now Chris had quarrelled with her and Bessie was ignoring her. When Bessie had gone off into the night nursery with the two little girls, Erica found that tears were running down her cheeks. She quickly opened her book again and bent over it, pretending to read so that Cecily should not see.

The next morning was just as bad. Chris, who never did anything by halves, not even quarrelling, was still angry with her. They had to spend a quarter of an hour alone together in the schoolroom while Miss Pringle gave Cecily a piano lesson, and Chris did not talk to her. Erica tried to tell him about the book and the foolish way the bead game had been ended by the uncle, but Chris wouldn't let her. He said he didn't want to hear another word about the silly book. So after that they sat in silence until Miss Pringle and Cecily came back. Then the first lesson was English, and this morning they had to read verses of poetry turn and turn about. It was Cecily who had to begin.

> "Birds in their little nests agree,
> And 'tis a shameful sight
> When children of one family
> Fall out and chide and fight."

Erica kicked Chris under the table to tell him to listen. When Erica was reading her verse, Chris kicked her back. Altogether, Erica managed to kick Chris five times and Chris kicked her three times. They weren't hard kicks, because Miss Pringle mustn't notice, but they kicked as hard as they dared. Erica's last kick was a bit too sharp; Chris yelped, and Miss Pringle turned round to see what was happening.

"Erica! I cannot bear any more of your fidgeting. Go and sit in the punishment chair!"

Erica got up reluctantly. The punishment chair was a high-backed chair which stood in the window. It faced straight out into the front garden, but there was little to see from that window because of the big laurustinus bush growing just outside. Miss Pringle would tell someone to sit there for two minutes or three minutes or five minutes, according to how bad they had been. This didn't make much difference to Erica, for she couldn't sit still anyway. She just had to wriggle, or try to peep at the clock, or rub a tickling nose; and then Miss Pringle would tell her to start again. After a while Erica would give up trying. It was easier to sit there a whole morning wriggling than remain absolutely still for two long minutes.

This time Miss Pringle said five minutes; but Erica was so angry with Chris for not saying he'd been kicking too, that she was determined to keep still. She did not turn her head to look even when the garden gate squeaked. It was the butcher's boy with the meat for dinner in a covered basket on his arm. Georgie Jones was a particular friend of Erica and Chris. He made them whistles out of elderberry stems and he whittled peg tops for them to whip. When he saw Erica sitting in the window he waved cheerfully to her. Erica stared straight ahead as though he wasn't there. The butcher's boy disappeared round the side of the house. When he came back he did not wave. He gave her a long hard look and then strode off whistling down the path. He hoisted himself up into his cart and drove off. Erica could see him above the thorn hedge perched high on the driving-seat.

"The five minutes are up," said Miss Pringle.

Erica got slowly down from the punishment chair and went back to her place at the table.

"That was very good, dear," said Miss Pringle, glad to be able to praise Erica for something. "I think you deserve a star for that, because I know you find it difficult to sit still."

Erica watched while the star was drawn in her exercise book with a red crayon. Erica loved getting stars, and she loved being praised still more. She thanked Miss Pringle very much, and then without warning burst into tears.

"My dear Erica," said Miss Pringle, rather touched. "You really must learn not to take things to heart so."

"Please cross the star out," sobbed Erica. "I don't deserve it."

It had come to her all in a rush what Georgie Jones must have thought. He wouldn't know she was sitting still because she was in the punishment chair. He would think she had grown into a spoiled snob like Hector and considered herself above waving to a boy who was delivering the meat.

"Now stop that foolish noise at once, and tell me what you mean," said Miss Pringle more sharply.

"You shouldn't have given me the star," explained Erica, still sniffing. "It was wrong to give me a star for being rude to Georgie Jones. I should have waved back to him – I should! Even if I had to sit in your silly chair for hours and hours."

Miss Pringle was angry. Little girls should not tell their governess that her punishments are silly. Miss Pringle told Erica that she was being very ill-mannered, and that anyway she did not approve of her waving at butcher's boys. She thought she would have to tell Erica's father. At that, Erica exploded. She forgot all about being polite to older people and about doing what the governess said. She stamped her feet. She shouted.

"I'll wave to anyone I like! I don't mind if you do tell Daddy! It's you he'll be angry with, not me. He says we're not to be rude to anyone. You shan't make me be rude to people. You shan't!"

"Stop shouting at once," said Miss Pringle firmly. "At once!" But Erica went on stamping and shouting. Miss Pringle shook her, but it only made her worse.

"I don't think Erica *can* stop when she gets like that," said Cecily helpfully. "We just leave her alone."

"It is disgraceful!" said Miss Pringle, who was becoming fussed. "I never saw such behaviour in all my life. Like a wild animal! It is a good thing your step-sister is coming to look after you. You will be sorry if you behave in that way to her."

Erica stopped her noisy sobbing all at once and stared at Miss Pringle. So did the other two.

"What did you say, Miss Pringle?" asked Cecily.

Miss Pringle looked flustered. She realized she should not have said that, for Mr Stock had asked her not to speak to the children about it while he finally made up his mind. She frowned at Cecily.

"Girls should not ask questions. Continue your work now. Your father will explain anything he wishes you to know."

They obediently bent their heads over their work, and Miss Pringle sighed with relief at getting over an awkward moment. She thought they had not quite understood what she had said; but as soon as lessons were over, the children rushed upstairs to find Bessie. They pelted her with questions.

"That Miss Pringle! You'd think she was old enough to hold her tongue when she was asked to," was the first thing Bessie said.

That made them feel better. Bessie was about the only grown-up who ever admitted that other grown-ups might be wrong sometimes and children right.

"But what did she mean about a step-sister?" asked Cecily. "I know about step-sisters like in Cinderella, but I didn't know we had one."

"Why, of course you do, Cecily. It's your own sister, Miss Beatrice, who sent you your Swiss clock when you were small, and that lovely toy village to Clare."

They stopped to think about this. Half-memories were coming back, but it was all very confusing and a long time ago.

"If she's our sister, why don't we see her?" demanded Chris. "How can we have a sister we don't know? Who is she?"

"Why, your own daddy's daughter, of course. She'd grown up and gone away abroad to learn to be a singer before ever your father married your own dear mother. Now don't pretend you've forgotten he was married before, because you've seen Miss Beatrice's mother's gravestone in the churchyard. Helena Grace, that was what her name was."

It sounded all right, but they still weren't sure. Miss Pringle had spoken as though this Beatrice was rather a stern person. And why hadn't their father told them about her coming?

"What's she like?" Chris blurted out.

"Well, I was only a bit of a thing myself, not as old as you, when I saw her last; but I remember her pretty well for all that. She was the sort of person you do remember. Small, she was, and dark. More like Erica. And she always wore pretty clothes. People liked to hear her talk, because she made them laugh. And sing! She could sing like an angel! Play the piano, too. And the harp. There'll be plenty of music in the house when she comes."

The others went on pestering Bessie with questions, but Erica was silent. She was thinking about the new sister. It certainly sounded as if it was going to be all right after all. A grown-up sister who wore pretty clothes and made people laugh. A sister who looked a bit like Erica herself. Perhaps sister Beatrice would be fond of her specially, because of that, and perhaps she'd understand about her fidgeting and her tempers, and how she always really meant to be good. Yes, perhaps she'd understand.

Chapter 4 · Starch for Sunday

It was Sunday. On Sundays Erica lay in bed for a long time after she first woke. So long as she stayed in bed, she could pretend it was still Saturday, but as soon as she was up then it was really and truly Sunday – with Sunday clothes, Sunday behaviour and nothing but Sunday books to read. Erica preferred to lie in bed and think. She thought about her new sister, who had now come to live with them. Erica hadn't made up her mind about her yet; none of them had. Erica didn't know whether she admired her more or feared her more. She was so very quick and so very clever. She could paint, she could play the harp and the piano and she could sing. There seemed to be nothing she couldn't do. It was no wonder she was sometimes a bit impatient with a girl who couldn't do anything, not even pick up a china ornament without breaking it.

Erica's thoughts veered sharply away from that unhappy memory. She was anxious to think only nice thoughts about sister Beatrice because she did so much want to love her and be loved. She thought about her name – Beatrice Dorothy Gratiana. She savoured the dignified syllables, and thought how sad it was they were never used. The household called her Miss Stock, and her father called her Beatie. The children had been asked to say "sister Beatrice", but Molly, who still talked in a very babyish way, could not manage it at all. Beatrice had laughed in a kindly way at her attempts and had said that they had all better call her Beatie. So they did, but for a long time it seemed odd to be calling someone so much older than themselves by a pet name.

Erica had got this far in her thoughts when Bessie came in and told her briskly to get up. She had Erica's and Cecily's Sunday clothes over her arms and laid them very carefully on the ends of their beds. Erica began reluctantly to get dressed. The vest first, and then the chemise, which was another vest but made of white cotton. Then there was a white cotton bodice, followed by long white cotton drawers – very smart ones for Sunday, with Swiss embroidery frills round the knees. The drawers had to be fastened on to buttons on the bodice: four easy buttons in front, and four at the back which were very hard to reach. Then there was a white starched petticoat, with lace let into the bodice and two deep frills round the bottom edge. Long white stockings with garters above the knee came next, and then at last the dress. It was of white muslin, stiff with embroidery and starch. It looked lovely, but it was a terrible responsibility.

Erica was just cautiously pulling the dress over her head when Chris began shouting from the next room.

"Bessie! Come and help with my collar! I *can't* get it done up. Do come!"

"All in good time," Bessie called back. "I've the girls' buttons to do up before I can attend to you."

It took a long time to fasten all the buttons. Cecily had eighteen up the back and Erica twenty-two. The buttons were so tiny that even Bessie found them a fiddle.

"Stand still," she begged Erica. "How can I do you up while you jiggle about like a dancing bear?"

"I wish I was. At least I wouldn't have to wear a frock I hardly dare move in."

"Now just stop grumbling," said Bessie. "You be thankful your father can afford nice clothes for you. There's many a child would give their eyes for such a dress ... There now, that's done. Go and sit down while I do your brother's collar ... Careful now! You'll crush your dress. Smooth it out under you like Cecily, and for goodness sake sit *still*!"

Bessie went to Chris's room. He was still doggedly trying to get the stiff collar of his Eton suit done up. Each time he almost managed to get the second end anchored, the first end slipped out of his fingers and sprang away. He had tried again and again, and it happened each time. Even Bessie had to have three shots.

"Beastly thing!" said Chris angrily. "Why do I have to wear it?"

"It's done now," said Bessie soothingly, but she did not tell him that there was many a child who would love such a suit. She knew very well that no boy in the village would be seen dead in such a rig-out.

When Cecily and Erica and Chris were dressed, Bessie still had Clare and Molly to attend to. Cecily stayed to help her, but Chris and Erica went downstairs. On Sundays breakfast was half an hour later than on other days but, as Chris said, no one had arranged for them to be half an hour less hungry. The smell of frying bacon wafting up the back stairs made them hungrier than ever.

"Let's go to the kitchen," said Erica.

They went down the back stairs and into the kitchen. It was very full of people. There was not only Sarah, who did the cooking, and Kate the new kitchen-maid, but Alice too. Even William Long was there, drinking a large mug of tea. He was leaning on the back of a chair instead of sitting down, to show that he did not really belong in the kitchen. He had come up from his cottage to tend the horses and see if the carriage would be needed.

"Well, well, how nice," said Sarah when she saw Chris at the door. "Come in and sit by me, Chris dear. And you'd like a nice piece of toast, wouldn't you? Kate shall fry some."

"Erica, too," said Chris.

"Of course," said Sarah.

Erica did not think it was "of course" at all, for Chris was always the favourite. She did not resent it, for he was her favourite, too, and in any case he always shared with her any extra presents or things he was given.

The fried toast was delicious, crisp and brown and tasting sweetly of bacon. Alice thoughtfully draped a tea-towel over Erica's Sunday dress so that she could enjoy the treat without anxiety. After a while Alice looked at the clock.

"You'd better clear out soon," she warned. "Miss Stock will be down any minute."

A bell tinkled sharply, and they all looked up to see which had rung. There were two rows of bells over the kitchen door, each with its label. The one labelled DINING-ROOM was ringing. Alice got up and went out.

"Breakfast," she said when she got back. "Hop it, you two. She asked where you were and I said in the garden, so you'd better make it so."

There was no need to ask who "she" was. Erica and Chris went into the garden, Erica puzzled and uncomfortable.

"I wish I knew why Beatie doesn't like us in the kitchen."

"Oh, just silliness," said Chris. "I heard her telling Mrs Upthorpe about learning bad ways from the servants."

Erica stamped her foot so hard that the gravel hurt her.

"You couldn't learn bad ways from Sarah! Anyway, Beatie didn't say that, I'm sure. Mrs Upthorpe might because she's fairly idiotic, but not Beatie." Chris said nothing, and Erica's heart fell.

"Must we really not go into the kitchen? Sometimes it's the only place where anyone is, and Sarah's never cross like ... like other people sometimes are."

Chris looked at her scornfully. At times he seemed years older than Erica instead of a year younger.

"Of course we'll go on going to the kitchen. We've known Sarah and Alice and William much longer than we've known Beatie. Even Cecily can't remember when there wasn't a Sarah; and if you mean to turn your nose up at her just to keep in with Beatie, then I think it's pretty mean of you."

"Of course I wouldn't turn up my nose at Sarah! And it's mean of you to say I would!"

So Chris said he was sorry, and Erica said, "All right", but it wasn't really quite right. It didn't matter so much to him what his new step-sister thought of him. Everybody seemed to like him, but Erica was sure she was no one's favourite. Only, she did think that if she could learn to please Beatie, then perhaps Beatie would learn to like her as much.

Breakfast was the best part of Sunday, because of the bacon. The only trouble now was that it had to be eaten with Beatrice sitting at the top of the table watching everything they did. *Her* fork never clattered on her plate; *her* fried toast never shot on to the clean tablecloth, *her* egg yolk never splashed off her fork. This morning Erica was being very careful to hold her knife and fork properly, but she was so careful that she forgot to watch what her elbows were doing. One of them knocked her mug of milk across the table. Cecily had to jump up quickly not to get milk in her lap, and her chair fell over with a crash.

"Really, Erica," said her father, annoyed, "you'll have to eat in the nursery if you cannot do better than this."

"It was only an accident," said Beatrice. "Erica cannot help being clumsy. I expect she will grow out of it. Ring the bell for Alice, Cecily, please."

"I'm s-sorry," stammered Erica. "I ... "

"We quite understand," said Beatrice. "Get on with your breakfast."

Erica finished her breakfast in silence, while Alice mopped up the milk and put a saucer under the wet patch to save the polish. Erica was furious, but not because her father had spoken sharply. The vicar was allowed to be a little irritable on Sundays because of having so much to do, and his sermon to think about. It was her step-sister she was angry with; and yet Beatrice had done nothing except to say that it wasn't Erica's fault. Erica thought she must be a very wicked girl to be angry with such a kind step-sister.

After breakfast there never seemed anything worth doing to fill the gap until church time. Bessie had tidied up all the toys on Saturday night and shut them away in the chest, and even Molly knew that they must not be brought out again until Sunday was over. All the story-books, too, were lined up on their shelves. The only ones which might be opened were those on the "Sunday shelf". Erica looked at them. Some of them weren't bad stories. They all had a moral, of course, but you could skip that – particularly as it was usually at the end of the chapter, so that you knew when it was coming. Erica pulled out *The Fairchild Family* and began flipping over the pages, looking for the funny bit where Henry fell into the tub of pig-wash. Instead, she found the chapter where the family came into money. The children had made their beds in the morning just as they had done when they were poor. But their mother made them unmake their beds again, because the maids would despise them if they found they didn't know how rich people behaved. Erica slammed the book shut. Surely no grown-up could really be so foolish. She forced the book into the ordinary shelves. It wasn't fit to be a Sunday book, she thought. She went out into the garden and found Molly there.

Molly was standing absolutely still on the gravel path. Her little feet were carefully together. She held her arms stiffly away from her side so as not to crush her dress. She looked as good as gold, and completely miserable. Erica was quite sorry for her.

"Come and look at the snapdragons, and watch how they try to eat me," she said. "I'll put fox's gloves on my fingers first so that they won't hurt me."

Molly stared at her in amazement. She had great gold-brown eyes and masses of tawny hair. Beatrice said she would be a beauty, but Erica thought she looked a bit queer and not like other people's baby sisters. She was always kind to her, however. She led Molly across the lawn to where the snapdragons grew. On the way she snapped off five foxglove flowers and stuck them on her fingers and thumb. She pinched the snapdragons with the other hand and showed Molly how they seemed to nibble her gloved fingers. She sang Chris's snapdragon song.

"Snapdragon, I love you,
And I am above you.
Now I have picked you.
Rap, rap! Snap, snap!
I'm not afraid of you,
Dragon!"

Molly laughed, but she was half frightened as well, and backed away. Erica smiled and told her in fun that she was a baby. There was something in it, too. Everybody thought of Molly as a baby though she was now four, a whole year older than Chris had been when he made up his snapdragon song. You couldn't imagine Molly making up a song, but she was a dear all the same, and she thought Erica one of the cleverest people in the world.

"Dragons *and* foxes in the garden," she said wonderingly. "It's very 'stonishing."

After that came church. The four girls went indoors and were buttoned into long black boots. Then Bessie got out four lace hats. The others looked charming in theirs, but it did not suit Erica's brown face. Chris said it made her look like a goblin. Then there were silk gloves to put on. Erica loathed silk gloves. They were as slithery as the skin on hot milk, and yet when she moved her fingers they gave a horrid dry creak which was more feel than sound.

"It sets my teeth on edge," she complained.

"What nonsense you do talk!" said her step-sister briskly.

Beatrice wore silk gloves herself, but such charming ones that Erica thought they might be worth the discomfort. They were a soft pink and all ruched up the back, and they had eight pearl buttons at each wrist. Erica and Cecily were quite proud to walk with her to church, for no one else in the village dressed with such style. Her bonnet was a marvel of lace and flowers and she carried a pink-lined parasol. Her tiny feet in their pink kid boots were the envy and despair of Cecily: already Cecily took shoes two sizes larger.

When they reached the church, Beatrice folded the parasol with an elegant gesture and led the way in. She stopped at their pew and waited to let the others slide in before her. Chris and Cecily went first, because they could be trusted to behave. Clare sat next to Cecily so that Cecily could find the place for her in the prayer-book, and Erica and Molly sat at the end where Beatrice, in the outside seat, could keep an eye on them. Not that Molly was a restless child, but she sometimes fell asleep, and someone had to be there to stop her falling off the pew.

The five-minute bell, warning late-comers to hurry, had just begun to toll by the time they were all settled. Chris brought out his pocket bible and began to read. He had set himself the task of reading it right through from beginning to end and was finding it heavy going. Cecily sat staring up at the stained-glass window over the altar, thinking her own thoughts and perfectly happy to sit and be silent. Molly sat quiet and awed, like a wax doll which you know won't move because it can't. On one occasion, a sleepy wasp had crawled down inside the neck of Molly's dress and stung her twice, and she hadn't even cried. She said afterwards that she thought you weren't allowed to cry in church.

To Erica, church was agony because of not being able to move about. That Sunday she was particularly restless. She dropped her prayer-book and had to go grovelling for it. Her collection money slipped out of her hand and went rolling out into the aisle. Tom Upthorpe handed it back and winked at her, and Erica did not dare to look to see if her step-sister had noticed the wink. Beatrice did not say anything when they came out of church. As they passed through the churchyard she smiled at her friends and inclined her head graciously to the greetings of various villagers. Erica began to breathe again, but when she tried to stop and speak to her own friends as she usually did, Beatrice kept a firm hold of her hand. She set off home at a very quick pace and Erica had to go with her willy-nilly. Chris and Cecily exchanged a look and hurried after them. As soon as they were inside the vicarage gate, Beatrice dropped Erica's hand.

"You naughty little girl!" she said. "How could you behave so? To stare about and make all that noise instead of setting an example of good behaviour to the village children! One would think you would at least try to listen to your own papa's sermon!"

"But I listen much better if I can move a bit," said poor Erica. "If I'm having to think about sitting still, I can't listen at all. Truly I can't!"

"Really, Erica! Please don't talk such rubbish!"

"But I thought ... "

"Then you shouldn't think. You will go without pudding at

dinner. I am most displeased with you. And how many times have I told you not to argue?"

"Oh, Beatie, no! I didn't think."

"Then you should have thought," retorted Beatrice. "I am sorry the loss of your pudding means so much to you."

"It's not so much the pudding I mind," said Erica. "It's you being so angry with me, and ... "

But Beatrice had already shut her parasol with a snap and had gone indoors. The others gathered round Erica and tried to comfort her.

"It's not a pertiker'ly nice pudding," said Molly. "It's rice mould. Sarah told me. If it had been nice, she'd have said it was a wait-and-see pudding."

But, as Erica had said, it wasn't the pudding that mattered; it was her step-sister's unfairness. She had tried to explain, and she had said she was sorry. She had done all she could, and Beatie hadn't even listened.

"You were an idiot to argue," said Chris frankly. "If you'd just promised to keep still next time, she'd have forgotten all about it."

"But I wanted her to understand. I really can listen better when I wriggle. I thought she'd like to know."

"Well, you heard what she said. You shouldn't think."

"But the very next thing she said was that I *should* think. How am I supposed to know which she meant? It's not fair."

"Beatie never is fair," said Cecily coolly. "She says one thing one time and another the next, and she never even notices."

"She doesn't! You're a story!" said Erica perversely. However angry she was herself with Beatrice, she couldn't bear to hear anyone else speak badly of her. Cecily said nothing. She was very good at saying nothing. She said nothing in a way that told you more than whole speeches from other people. Erica looked at her resentfully, but couldn't think of anything to say. It is very difficult arguing with someone who hasn't said anything.

Beatrice had recovered her temper by dinner-time. There was a visitor, a Mr Plumpstead, who was the rural dean. He was a jovial, elderly man, who rather liked elegant young ladies, and Beatrice was always at her best with him. At dinner she set them all laughing by imitating how Mrs Upthorpe sang the hymns – very soulfully, but just a bit off key on the top notes. Even Mr Stock laughed, though he shook his head at his daughter's liveliness. When the pudding came, it was served in new bowls which none of them had ever seen before. Even Erica had a bowl, though without any pudding in it. On the bottom was painted a rose, a dark purple "double velvet", her favourite flower of all. As the others finished their rice mould, they each in turn found a flower painted on the bottom: honeysuckle for Father, a snapdragon for Chris, a primrose for Cecily, a daffodil for Clare and a daisy for Molly. There was even a bowl for the guest, with a chrysanthemum. It was Cecily who understood first.

"Beatie! You painted them yourself! You *are* clever!"

"By Jove!" exclaimed Mr Plumpstead. "Fancy that! Miss Stock, you're a regular Raphael!"

Beatrice blushed and smiled and said she was glad everyone liked their bowls. Erica exclaimed louder than anyone else. Unfortunately, this drew the attention of Beatrice, who surveyed her critically.

"Where is your hair-ribbon, Erica? Don't tell me you have lost it again?" Erica put her hand up to her head. The bit of tape which held her long hair up on the top of her head was still there, but the white bow which should have hidden it was not there.

"I don't know," she said helplessly. "I didn't notice it was gone."

"Such a price ribbon is, too," said Beatrice. "I wish now I hadn't chosen the most expensive length." She turned to Mr Plumpstead with a pretty smile. "I'm sure I don't know why it is, but once I've seen something really attractive, I can never be sensible and buy something cheap and ugly."

"Ah, Miss Stock, you have an artist's soul," said Mr Plumpstead. "Artists ... "

"But, Beatie," Erica broke in. "It's all right. Don't you remember? You bought the cheap ribbon after all. You said the expensive one would be a waste, because I'd be sure to lose it. And, you see, you were right!"

"Please do not talk nonsense, Erica," said Beatrice with a little laugh which deceived hardly anyone. "I should hope I know which ribbon I bought better than a little girl does."

Erica shut her lips tight. She looked very hard at the beautiful plate her sister had painted specially for her, and that helped her to say nothing. Beatrice frowned, but before she could tell Erica to hold her head up, she caught sight of Cecily's face and stopped. Cecily's eyes were full of grave wonder. Beatrice went rather red.

"I distinctly remember choosing the more expensive ribbon," she said sharply. "I hope you at least believe me, Papa?"

The vicar was not pleased with her for putting him in an awkward position in front of the rural dean. He looked at Beatrice and he looked at Erica, and decided that the important thing was to separate them.

"I do not think we should pursue the discussion any further over the dinner table," he said weightily. "The ribbon is lost and must be replaced. Erica, go and ask Bessie to find you another one before Sunday school."

Erica ran thankfully out of the room, but she did not go to look for Bessie. Cecily and Chris guessed where she would be. When dinner was over, they went to look for her. When things were a bit bad with Erica and she wanted to hide, she crept in under the asparagus plants. When they were really bad, she made for the corner of the garden where the horse-radishes grew. Their stiff, ugly leaves suited her better then than the feathery prettiness of the asparagus plants. Sure enough, Chris caught sight of her curled up among the horse-radishes.

"Come on," he said.

Erica crawled out and joined them. Her dress looked none the better for the earth on it, and her face was tear-stained and dirty. Fortunately the ground was dry, so Cecily was able to brush most of the earth off her. Chris lent his handkerchief and Erica scrubbed her face clean.

"You *are* silly," said Cecily, not unkindly. "Why did you have to say right out that it was the cheap ribbon Beatrice got for you? And in front of Mr Plumpstead, too! You know he's always telling us about his wife's grand relations. I don't suppose Mrs Plumpstead even *thinks* of buying anything but the best ribbon."

"Do you mean Beatie *knew* it was the cheap ribbon?" Erica's eyes were wide open with astonishment. "But ... but she said she *remembered* buying the expensive ribbon. That would be *lying*!"

"Oh, well ... pretending, anyway ... just so that Mr Plumpstead shouldn't look down on us for being poorer."

"Daddy knew she was pretending. That's why he wouldn't back her up," added Chris.

Erica was horrified. She had a very downright mind, and to her, pretending was the same as lying, and lying was not a thing she could think that Beatrice Dorothy Gratiana could ever stoop to doing.

"She ... she'd just *forgotten* which ribbon it was she'd bought," she said defensively. "Anyone might."

"Have it your own way," said Cecily mildly. "Though I can't think why you want to stand up for her so. She doesn't stand up for you much in return."

"That's not true! She does!" Erica was looking a little white.

"It doesn't always feel like that," said Chris doubtfully.

Erica drew herself up to the fullest height she could manage. "You do not in the least know what you are talking about," she said very clearly and distinctly. She walked away from them with a stiff dignity. They had watched her in silence as she went indoors with her head high and her back very straight.

"I *hate* Beatie!" said Chris suddenly.

"Oh, hush! I'm sure you ought not to say that."

"Why not, if it's true?" Chris was impatiently kicking at a stone at the side of the path and wriggling it out with the toe of his boot. He did not look at Cecily.

"It isn't true, though," said Cecily shrewdly. "You don't really hate her. She's good fun sometimes, you know she is."

"Perhaps. When she's in a good temper."

"And it *was* good of her to come and look after the house. She might have been a famous singer by now, with lots of money to buy *any* kind of ribbon. Everybody says we ought to be very grateful."

Chris thought about this. After a moment his stone came loose, and he gave it a terrific kick. It sailed through the air and hit the fence with a satisfying plop.

"Oh, well ... we're going on holiday next week. I'll think about being grateful when we come back."

Chapter 5 · Horse-tram to school

That autumn, after their holiday, Chris started at school. It had always been understood that he would go to school as soon as he was seven, so that he could work for a scholarship, first to a Grammar School and then to the University. No one had thought of the girls going to school till Beatrice surprised her father by saying she thought Cecily and Erica ought to start at the same time as Chris. Mr Stock was old-fashioned and would have preferred his daughters to study at home with their governess, as his own sisters had done when they were young. However, he never argued with Beatrice about her arrangements for her sisters, so to Erica's delight, a school was chosen for her and Cecily.

Appleby Hall was in the centre of Gloucester, and there was some argument at first about how they were to get there. The horse-bus went three times a day to Gloucester and back, but the first bus in the morning left too late to get them to school on time. Their father wanted William Long to drive them in each day, but Beatrice said it would be absurd to get out the horse and carriage for three children, and besides, by the time William got back to his proper work, half the morning would be over. In the end Mr Stock had to agree to them all walking the two miles to the outskirts of Gloucester, and getting the horse-tram there. He was not very happy about the girls walking so far and tried to say they were too young, but he was overborne by Beatrice.

"Erica is eight-and-a-half and a very strong child. If Chris can walk so far at seven, then I am sure she can."

Erica felt like hugging Beatrice, but was afraid she would not like it. She quite forgot her quarrel with her, and once again thought of her as the best of sisters. She was quite sure that she would prefer the excitement of the horse-tram to a dull, decorous ride in the carriage, and in the event she was right. It just suited her restless nature to have to get up in the half-dark of a winter's morning, to race two miles along the frosty roads and to scramble on to the tram shouting noisy greetings to her friends.

About school itself she was not so sure at first, for it was all very strange to her. She was put with the other eight-year-olds in Class I. Cecily was in the next class, which was called Transition, though as a matter of fact the two classes, despite their different names, sat in the same room and had the same teacher. Erica and the other younger ones sat at long yellow tables in front. The Transition girls sat behind them in high wooden desks which towered above the little tables. Erica did not find the work difficult, but at first she didn't know what to make of the rest of the school at all. Even the little babies in the kindergarten seemed to know their way about better than she did. They knew what all the bells meant, and where to go when they rang. As for the big girls at the top of the school, she was almost frightened of them. They already wore their hair turned up and their skirts right down to their ankles in a grown-up way. They were full of scorn. "Doesn't that new girl know she mustn't run in the corridors?" they asked. Or, "Really, Erica Stock, you ought to know by now that you mustn't talk after the dinner-bell goes."

Of course she did in the end learn all the rules, or at any rate learnt the really important ones, like not talking outside the staff-room, not bringing sweets into the classoom and not going out into the street without your hat and gloves. If you broke those rules, she was told, you were sent to Miss Grossard, the Head Teacher, and that was very awful. Erica could believe it. Miss Grossard was tall, and wore her grey hair piled on top of her head so that she looked taller still. She wore pince-nez and grey silk dresses, and she was altogether very grand and gracious. Erica first met her about two weeks after she came to the school, and for a very serious reason. She had been accused of stealing.

The day had begun like any other day. Bessie came upstairs at half past six when it was still dark. She woke Chris first and then came into the girls' room. She lit their bedroom candle from the one she was carrying and set it on the mantelpiece. Then she put a big brass jug of hot water on the floor by the wash-stand and covered it with a folded towel so that it wouldn't get cold too quickly. Then she went into the night nursery to see how Clare and Molly were.

Erica wriggled out of the bedclothes. It was so cold in the bedroom that her breath froze in dragon snorts in front of her face. Frost flowers gleamed on the window in the flickering candle-light. She flung the bedclothes right back and scrambled out on to the cold floor. Cecily was nothing but a mound under the blankets. Erica gave up looking for her bedroom slippers and skipped across to the wash-stand, where there was a small square of mat to stand on.

She lifted the heavy ewer of cold water out of the basin and set it on the floor. She took the towel off the brass jug and poured a careful half of the steaming water into the basin. The other half was for Cecily.

"Erica," called Bessie from the night nursery. "Don't let Cecily stay in bed till the jug's cold. Tell her I'm not going all the way down to the kitchen again to boil her any more."

"All right, Bessie," said Erica.

She had made a discovery. The cold water in the ewer had frozen in the night. She cracked the ice with the end of her toothbrush. She tiptoed across to Cecily's bed. She drew back the coverlet till she could just see Cecily's fair curls and the frilly collar of her nightgown. Very gently she let a small piece of ice fall into the gap between the two.

Cecily was out of bed in no time at all. She stood in the middle of the floor and shrieked, till Bessie came running in from the other room. Cecily went on shrieking, so Erica had to explain. Bessie laughed.

"Is that all? Now stop making that noise, or you'll have Miss Stock sending to know what was wrong. I thought you were dying at least."

"So I might have died. People do die of shock," said Cecily, but she stopped shrieking. "Erica shouldn't have done it."

"No more she shouldn't," agreed Bessie cheerfully. "But seeing she's got you out of bed for once, there's no harm done."

Erica had been beginning to feel anxious, but she cheered up at that and let Cecily wash first while the water was still hot. Then there was breakfast in the nursery. They used to have breakfast in the dining-room downstairs, but Beatrice had said it wasn't worth while asking Alice to light the fire there so early. Alice said she'd rather light any number of fires than carry bacon and egg upstairs for so many. But Beatrice said there was no need for Sarah to make bacon and eggs so early either. Bread was much more wholesome for children. They didn't mind in the least: the nursery was much warmer than the dining-room, and Sarah's idea of providing bread for breakfast was to bake as many brown scones with raisins in them as they could eat.

Cecily and Erica and Chris left the house at half past seven as usual, and they were safely in school sitting down to their lessons by nine o'clock. The first lesson for Class I was Geography. The only girl who wasn't listening to Miss Young was Mamie Marden. Everybody knew they had to be kind to Mamie and that she didn't have to do the same things as they did. She was very pretty with blue eyes and fair hair, but she wasn't at all clever. She was still trying to learn her alphabet although she was already nine. In the classroom she sat at the end of one of the yellow-varnished tables and played with the money in her purse, taking it out, polishing it, counting it and putting it back, and then taking it out all over again.

That morning, in the middle of the Geography lesson, Mamie burst into tears. They all turned and stared, for Mamie had never been known to cry in class before.

"My shilling!" wailed Mamie. "It's gone! My beautiful shilling that Uncle Harry gave me."

They turned out her desk. They turned out her pockets. They turned out her purse. There were a penny and two halfpennies and two farthings and a silver threepenny bit in the purse, but no shilling at all. Miss Young began to look very serious. Mamie was quite sure the shilling had been in her desk when she went out to be excused, and now it was gone. Miss Young made them all sit down, and spoke very quietly but very solemnly.

"I am afraid some girl has stolen poor Mamie's shilling."

She paused to make sure they were all listening, but indeed they were hardly breathing, so anxiously were they listening.

"A shilling is a great deal of money," Miss Young went on. "You could buy very many sweets and nice things with a shilling." The girls nodded in agreement. A shilling was indeed a great deal of money. It was more than the richest of them had for pocket-money, and many times more than most of them had.

"Perhaps one of you was tempted. Perhaps you thought that, because Mamie does not quite understand what money can do, it does not matter so much taking from her. But, children, it matters much more. It is as though you had stolen from a blind child or a crippled child."

She paused again. Some of the girls were already crying.

"Dear children! If any one of you has taken Mamie's shilling, I beg of you, tell me now, at once. Let Mamie have her little treasure back. Say you are sorry and you will be forgiven."

There was dead silence. No one moved. Even Mamie had stopped crying. Miss Young waited for a long moment, and then she spoke again. Now her voice was very sad as well as gentle.

"Since we have a thief in the classroom, every girl must open her desk. Every girl must turn her pockets inside out, and I must look for the shilling till it is found. I am sorry."

Miss Young walked slowly along the rows of tables and desks. Each girl had turned her pockets inside out. Some had pockets in their jackets, some in their blouses, most in the side seam of their long navy-blue skirts; but, wherever the pocket was, inside out it had to be. At last it was Erica's turn. She had only one pocket, the one in her skirt. She held on to the top tightly with both hands and would not let go.

"I didn't take Mamie's shilling. Please don't look," she said.

Miss Young still spoke gently. Erica was very red in the face and was looking guilty. But many of the girls had looked just as red and guilty, though there had been nothing at all in their pockets.

"I have to look in everyone's pocket," Miss Young explained. "I don't think you stole the shilling. I can't think that *any* girl in my class is a thief. That is why I must look in everyone's pocket. Just to be fair. You do see, don't you?"

But Erica was too alarmed to see. She couldn't think anything but that Miss Young must not on any account find what was in her pocket. She held on more tightly and wouldn't turn it inside out. Miss Young begged and ordered her, but still Erica held on. Cecily was called to come down from her desk and reason with her sister, but it was no good. Erica just looked at her with desperate eyes.

"Oh, Cecily, don't! Tell Miss Young not to look in my pocket. Please!"

"Oh, Erica!" said Miss Young.

She sounded really sorry, and so she was, for she had rather liked her new pupil. The class monitor was sent to fetch the Head Teacher. In a little while Miss Grossard sailed in, and everyone curtsied.

"Let Miss Young look in your pocket. At once!" she said.

Erica let go of her skirt. That was one of the rules she *had* learnt – that you obeyed the Head Teacher. The tears rolled helplessly down her cheeks, but she let Miss Young take everything out of her pocket – a marble which belonged to Chris, half of her tram ticket, some biscuit crumbs and a bag of sticky bull's-eyes.

"Is that everything in her pocket?" asked Miss Grossard in astonishment.

"Absolutely everything," said Miss Young.

Of course, they all wanted to know why Erica would not

open her pocket, since she had not, after all, stolen the shilling. Erica hung her head. She could hardly speak for tears.

"They t-told me n-not to bring s-s-sweets into the class. I thought Miss Young would be angry. I thought she w-would tell them at home and I'd be in trouble again."

"But, you funny little thing," said Miss Grossard, too puzzled to be angry, "you made us all think you were a thief. Surely that was worse?"

"But I *told* her I wasn't a thief. I *told* her the shilling wasn't in my pocket." Erica sounded aggrieved. "She didn't have to look."

"But, Erica ... " Miss Grossard looked at Erica's perplexed face and gave it up. "Oh, well. All this isn't getting us any nearer to finding Mamie's shilling."

"If you please, Miss Grossard," said one of the girls. "Mamie is playing with her shilling."

It was quite true. Mamie was happily polishing her shilling again. When they asked her where she had found it, she smiled brightly and said she had found it in her purse; but they had turned her purse upside down, and the shilling had not been in it. They never did find out what she had done with it or how it came back to her. Nor was anything done about Erica's bag of sweets. She shared them round at play-time with the girls she liked best.

It was Bessie who made Erica understand. Bessie always liked to hear about school. She laughed heartily at the story of the shilling.

"How could you be so daft as not to turn your pocket inside out like the others?" she asked. "How could your poor teacher know whether you'd stolen it or not when you wouldn't let her look?"

"But I *told* her, Bessie. I told her ever so many times. And I don't tell lies, you know I don't."

"As a matter of fact, you don't," agreed Bessie. "At least, not nearly as many as some little girls. But how was your teacher to know that? They don't know anything about you at school. Not like me, who's known you since you were a baby."

To Bessie's surprise, Erica's anxious face suddenly lightened.

"I hadn't thought of that! They don't know *anything* about me really, do they? They don't know how I fidget, or how I forget things. Or about having a temper. I might be as good as Cecily, and patient like Chris, for all they know."

"That's right. And if you're careful about the fidgeting and forgetting, they never will know."

"Oh, how wonderful! All the bad stupid things I've ever done wiped right out! Like when the rain came and washed away all the hop-scotch lines we'd chalked on the school path, and left it clean and shining!"

Chapter 6 · Teasing

Erica took to school completely from that moment, and the school, on the whole, accepted her. She acquired a best friend, Amy Briggs, and a worst enemy, Edie Summers. Edie was very clever and she had been top at everything until Erica arrived. Now she often had to take second place, particularly in History and in English. She pretended that she didn't mind, but she did mind a good deal and she began to work very hard to get back to the top. The one subject she never had to worry about was arithmetic, for Erica did not even try, but made silly guesses at the answers and moved happily down to the bottom of the class.

Erica continued to admire Miss Young and was always looking out for ways to please her. When the end of the Easter term was near, Miss Young taught them a poem about spring flowers which was to be recited on Parents' Day. She wanted them to have bunches of suitable flowers to hold, and asked who would be able to bring some. Erica was on her feet at once.

"The garden's full of flowers where I live, and the fields, too. I could bring enough for everyone to have an *enormous* bunch."

"You'd forget to bring them on the right day," said Edie.

"I should not!" declared Erica.

She actually didn't forget, perhaps because Cecily knew what she'd promised and reminded her to pick them the night before. When they got on the tram the next day she had a bunch so big she could hardly see where she was going. Some of the passengers laughed. They knew the three Stock children quite well now, for they were businessmen going into Gloucester to their offices and travelled on the same tram each day.

"Well, well, is it a wedding?" asked one jovial old man. Erica explained that they were wanted at school, the flowers were.

"Aha, a scholar! Now then, young lady, let's see if they teach you well at this Appleby Hall. Just you tell me – if a herring and a half cost three halfpence, how much would one herring cost?" Erica didn't want the man to think Appleby Hall didn't teach well, so she really tried to work it out.

"I'm afraid I can't do it," she said politely after a bit. "But it's not because I'm not properly taught. It's just that I'm stupid at sums."

"Well now, that's honest at any rate. I tell you what, young lady, I'll ask you each day and when you get it right I'll give you a threepenny bit."

Cecily looked worried. She was always a bit shy and never chatted to people on trams like Erica did.

"You mustn't take money from strangers," she told Erica after they got off the tram.

"I shan't have to," said Erica cheerfully. "It's the end of term. He'll have forgotten about it by next term."

Only he didn't forget. The very first day of term he waved to her as she got on the tram and asked her how much a herring cost. Erica still didn't know. After that, whenever the man and his friends saw her, they said, "Hello, young Herring-and-a-Half!"

It got boring, and in the end Erica asked her father to tell her the answer. He explained it carefully, and Erica really thought she had understood. The next day, almost before anyone had had time to ask her how much a herring cost, she shouted out,

"Twopence!"

There was such a roar of laughter that she knew she had got it wrong again. Cecily went quite red with embarrassment, but Erica merely laughed. She was so happy in those days that she didn't mind anything very much. She cheerfully forgot her homework. She forgot to bring her music to music lessons. She forgot which was her right hand and which was her left. She muddled up the spellings she learnt and put *soldier* when she meant *shoulder* and *century* when she meant *sentry*. She never seemed to have a pencil or a pen or an india-rubber just when she needed one.

"It's a good thing your head's fastened on, or you'd be going to school without that next," said Bessie tartly.

Erica only laughed again. She was always laughing now, and the anxious frown which Bessie disliked so much was hardly ever there. She loved work and she loved play, and she loved to be in the centre of any mischief that was going. She even loved quarrelling with Edie.

"We hate each other, but nothing's half so much fun the days she isn't there," Erica explained to Bessie. "Whatever she does I try to do better, and whatever I do she tries to do better."

She was sitting in the nursery at the time, watching Bessie bathing Molly in the big hip-bath in front of the fire. Cecily was there, too, getting on with her sewing and listening to what they were saying. She frowned at Erica.

"I don't know about doing better than Edie. It seems to me most of the time that any bad thing she does, you do worse."

"You only know that because Mavis Bell sneaks to you," said Erica angrily. "All the girls sneak to you because they think you like it."

"I don't like it," said Cecily.

"No, I know you don't," said Erica with a sigh. "But they think you do. No one minds what I think."

Cecily went on with her sewing, and Bessie lifted Molly out of the bath and on to the towel on her lap. Erica lapsed into thought. It really was an odd thing about Cecily. She wasn't particularly clever or particularly amusing, and she didn't specially try to make friends, but somehow she always had a crowd of girls round her. They fought to walk with her, they sharpened her pencil, they brought her flowers. Mavis Bell even went half a mile out of her way coming to school each morning just to meet Cecily off the tram and carry her books for her. Silly, Erica called it, but she was a bit jealous all the same. She had plenty of friends herself, but they didn't want to carry her books or give her flowers!

Perhaps it was because Mavis was the most devoted of Cecily's followers that Erica didn't like her, or perhaps it was because Mavis really was a rather silly girl in some ways. For one thing, she boasted. She kept telling everyone what a big house she lived in and how important her father was.

"Is a treasurer a very important person?" Erica asked Beatrice one day.

"It depends what he is treasurer of."

"Of the missionary society in the village where they live."

"My dear child! There's nothing important in that. Anyone could do the work."

Beatrice always seemed to know which people were important and which weren't, so Erica believed her, and despised Mavis even more than before.

One day Mavis came to school in a new straw hat with a wreath of artificial flowers round it. She said it had been bought especially for her in London and had cost a great deal of money. Erica asked if she could look at it, but Mavis put it away quickly in a paper bag.

"To keep the dust off it," she explained. "The flowers are so delicate, they would break if they had to be dusted."

At play-time Mavis began to boast again about her hat. The girls were mostly very impressed, but Edie and Erica wanted to know why Mavis was allowed to wear it for school if it was such a very precious hat.

"My mother believes in wearing beautiful things *all* the time," said Mavis scornfully. "It's very commonplace to put beautiful things away for best so that no one sees them."

That annoyed Edie and Erica so much that they slipped

back into the cloakroom and peeped into the paper bag. With a crow of delight Edie drew out a perfectly ordinary straw hat. Jones, the linen-draper's in the High Street, sold dozens of them at half a crown each. Beatrice had nearly bought each of her step-sisters one because they were so cheap, but had decided in the end that they were just a bit too vulgar. Erica put the tawdry thing on her head and danced out into the playground.

"Look at my hat!" she called. "Isn't it a *lovely* hat?"

Mavis ran at her with a cry of rage. She snatched at the hat and crammed it all anyhow on her own head.

"Oh, *Daisy Bell has her new hat on!*" chanted Edie. "Look at Daisy Bell!"

In a moment the class had closed round poor Mavis. They held hands and danced around her. They took up Edie's song. Everybody knew the tune, and the words didn't take much altering to fit.

> "Mavis Bell has her best hat on,
>   her new hat, best hat, new hat on!
> There's a wreath of flowers round the crown,
>   round the crown, round the crown.
> It cost at least ten shillings!
> Isn't it a fine one, fine one!"

Round and round they danced, pointing their fingers at Mavis and yelling with laughter. As soon as they reached the end of the verse they began again.

> "Mavis Bell has her best hat on ... "

Suddenly the song broke off. Mavis could bear it no more. She sank to her knees in the middle of the dancing ring. The flowered hat fell sideways over one ear. She hid her face in her hands and sobbed. One by one the class stole away. Some pretended to laugh. Serve her right, they said. Teach her not to swank, they said. But there wasn't any heart in it. Only one child stayed behind. It was Mamie. Poor stupid Mamie who didn't understand anything except that someone was crying. She tried to comfort Mavis. She picked up the hat which had fallen to the ground and tried to straighten the crooked wreath.

"Don't cry, Mavis," she said. "Put your pretty hat on. Please don't cry."

Amy and Edie and Erica watched Mamie in silence. They were ashamed of themselves for teasing Mavis, and ashamed of being ashamed.

"I hate a cry-baby," said Edie fiercely. "It was only a game. Why couldn't Mavis laugh at it? I'd be ashamed to cry just for a game like that. Wouldn't you?"

Erica said, of course she would, but she felt very uncomfortable inside herself. She tried to forget that awful picture of Mavis falling to her knees with the little straw hat falling absurdly over her ear; and by being very noisy and silly all afternoon she almost managed to forget. On the way to the tram stop she and Cecily had to pass the end of one of the poorer streets of the town. She glanced down it as they hurried along, and there she saw a dirty little girl queening it in front of an admiring circle of other ragged children. She had on a bedraggled pink satin dress and above was the wreck of what had once been a half-crown flower-wreathed hat. Erica shut her eyes quickly till they were right past the end of the street.

Though Erica was really sorry for making Mavis cry, it didn't cure her of teasing. For she never meant any harm by it – or at least not very much – and she never went on long enough to make anyone cry again. But it was such fun to be in the centre of a laughing crowd. No one was as quick as Erica to think of silly names to call people or to make up nonsensical jokes about them; and no one was quite quick enough to catch her out in return.

Then one day Vera Davenport came to school in red knitted stockings. No one had ever seen such stockings; they weren't the fashion. Everyone wore black stockings for every day, and white ones for best. Vera was a quiet, shy girl, not a boaster like Mavis; so there was no excuse for teasing her. There was nothing really wrong about the red stockings, either. But when Erica came rushing into the cloakroom, late as usual, and saw them, she gave a great shriek.

"Oh! Your legs! They're on fire!"

After that everybody had a lot of rather fatuous fun pretending to jump away from Vera as though they were afraid of being burnt, or asking if they should get a bucket of water to throw on her. Vera did not seem to mind very much. She was always a rather awkward and silent girl, and she just smiled and looked more awkward than ever; and anyway it was soon time to go into the classroom. When it was play-time, the girls began rushing up to Vera again and screaming that she was on fire. Amy and one or two others wouldn't join in, and the joke might have been dropped quickly; only Erica, who was in a rather senseless mood, pretended she was a fire-engine and circled round Vera and acted at whipping up her horses and ringing the fire bell. Clang! Clang! Clang! Soon half the class was rushing round the garden clanging imaginary bells. Vera stood quite still. If Erica had looked, she might have seen that Vera had gone rather white, but Erica did not stop to look, and Vera had too much pride to cry openly.

That was on Friday. On Saturday Beatrice called Cecily and Erica to the morning-room at home. There was a brown-paper parcel open on the sofa beside her.

"Look what your Great-Aunt Rose has sent," said Beatrice. "You must both write and thank her. Erica, you must bring me your letter so that I can see you haven't made any really foolish spelling mistakes."

Erica did not hear her. She was staring in horror at the parcel. Inside were four pairs of stockings, two bright blue and two bright red.

"They're too nice for school," she said in a small voice. "They're for best, aren't they?"

"For best? Of course not. Stout knitted stockings like these will be just the thing for school. You had better wear the red ones with your tartan dress on Monday."

Erica was so desperate that she actually dared to say that no one else wore stockings like that at school and that the girls would laugh at them. Beatrice drew herself up to her tiny height.

"If they laugh, they will show their ignorance. These bright colours are very fashionable. The children of all the best families in London are wearing them."

Erica didn't ask her step-sister how she knew. If Beatrice took it into her head that something was or wasn't done in "the best families", then that was the end of it. Erica crept silently upstairs to the nursery. It was empty. Molly and Clare were outside playing in the garden, and Bessie was down in the kitchen. Erica climbed on to the window seat and sat staring out into the yard. She could hear someone whistling between his teeth as he curry-combed the pony, and the swish of William's scythe as he mowed the lawn. She could hear Molly's excited laughter as Clare pushed her in the swing. Everybody seemed busy and happy except Erica herself.

"Why, whatever's come over you, Miss Erica?" said Bessie.

Erica started. She hadn't heard Bessie come up the back stairs and hadn't known there was anyone in the room. Bessie spoke of Miss Cecily and Miss Erica now, when she remembered it, because Miss Stock had told her to. She wore a starched apron and an absurd starched cap, too, but she was still the same Bessie. Erica hid her face in the stiff apron and sobbed out her story. She longed for just one shred of comfort, but when she had finished, Bessie pushed her away.

"I'm surprised at you, Miss Erica, I really am. I never thought you were an ill-natured child. You that was so angry with those lads for only tying an empty tin to a puppy dog's tail and then laughing when he frightened himself with the noise."

"That was different," said Erica angrily. "Those boys were really cruel. We didn't *hurt* Vera. It doesn't hurt just to be laughed at."

"Then that's all right," said Bessie. "You can go to school in those red stockings and let them laugh."

Erica was very silent on the walk from the village on Monday morning and very silent on the tram. Yes, how the girls *would* laugh! And she couldn't really blame them – after all that joking about Vera's stockings, to have to turn up in an identical pair! All the girls she liked least would snigger at her, and nothing she could say or do would stop them. Or would it? Erica came to a halt in the middle of the road and was nearly run down by a baker's cart. Cecily screamed, the horse reared and the baker's boy swore, but Erica hardly noticed.

Everybody was already in class when Erica came dancing in, holding her skirts well up to her knees so that everybody could see the red stockings.

"Look! Just look!" she shouted. "Look, everyone! Red stockings! *Much* brighter than Vera's. A dreadful great-aunt knitted them and she'd be furious if I didn't wear them, so you'll have to get used to them. Isn't it awful?"

Then everybody exclaimed and sympathized, even Vera. They laughed, of course, but in a friendly way without sniggering. They even said they didn't think the stockings were so bad after all; and some of the girls said they were going to ask their mothers to buy them red stockings.

When the class filed into the hall for prayers, Erica's heart was still pounding so that she hardly had breath to sing the hymn. When the hymn was over and Miss Grossard began the morning prayer thanking God for his blessings, Erica joined in with real fervour. That morning she felt she really had something to thank God about. She also wanted to apologize for calling the red stockings awful; Great-Aunt Rose would have been shocked indeed if she had heard her.

"My dear," she used to say in her stern voice, "if you use the word awe-ful to describe the petty things of life, what word will you use to describe the Day of Judgment?" Erica privately thought that, if she were there to see that day, she would have other things to think about than what to call it, but of course she never said so to her great-aunt.

After prayers Miss Grossard spoke to the school. She wanted all the girls to promise her that they would go straight home by the main road and not turn down any side streets.

"There have been some cases of diphtheria in the poorer streets. A child died only this morning not half a mile from this school."

That evening Cecily and Erica stopped and peeped fearfully down the side-street which opened between two tall houses in the grand street where they caught their tram. It was the very side-street where Erica had seen the little girl in her satin finery and her half-crown hat. It was a poor enough street, though nothing like the crowded alleys which were huddled together in the centre of the town. Outside one of the houses was a group of people, silent and still. As the two girls watched, they saw a black coffin carried out of the house to the hearse waiting in the street. There were two black horses with waving black plumes and mourners in tall black hats which were wreathed in black crêpe; they looked rather grand in that drab street.

"It's a very small coffin. It must be a child," whispered Cecily.

"I do hope ... " began Erica, and then stopped. She could not explain to Cecily but she hoped very much that it was not the little girl in the pink dress. She gazed anxiously at the children in the crowd but could not recognize anywhere the perky face she had seen under the straw hat.

The next week the school was closed. There were two hundred cases of diphtheria in the town, and it was not safe for the pupils to come too near the areas where the infection was centred. They had better, said Miss Grossard, remain in their own homes, and go out only into the fresh country air, and pray to God to keep them safe.

"That's all very well for Cecily and me," objected Erica when they were explaining to their step-sister what had happened. "But what about all the children in the back streets of the town who can't escape into the country and who catch diphtheria? Perhaps they prayed too."

"You must not question God's ways," said Beatrice severely. "He knows what is best for all his children."

So Erica tried to believe her, because that was what everyone told her, but she wished she could get the memory of that small black coffin out of her head.

Chapter 7 · A golden holiday

"We're going to Weston-super-Mare for our holiday," Molly announced one day during tea at the Upthorpes.

"Super-Mare is Latin and means on-the-sea," added Erica with a careless air. She was immensely proud of knowing two Latin words.

"I thought it meant on-the-mud," said Tom Upthorpe teasingly.

"You are very wrong, I am afraid," said Molly with all the condescension required from the sister of a Latin scholar to a mere school-boy.

"Wait till you try digging in the sand at Weston. Then you'll know I'm right," said Tom.

Molly looked at him reproachfully, and turned to Mr Upthorpe.

"Perhaps he does not understand that I used to live at Weston."

Tom laughed delightedly. He was very fond of little Molly Stock with her baby face and her solemn grown-up speeches.

"And how old were you then, Miss Molly?"

"Well, actually, I'd only just been born," confessed Molly. The whole table laughed; they could not help it. Molly went very red.

"Have some ice," said Tom kindly.

"Certainly not," said Molly.

She watched rather sadly as everyone else was offered a sort of pink and white pudding, and none came to her. She didn't know what it was, but it looked lovely. However, she was quite used to being told that nice things weren't for little girls; so she didn't complain but ate as much jelly as she could manage.

"Did you have a nice time at Effie Upthorpe's birthday party, dear?" asked her father when they came home.

"Tom wasn't nice. He asked me if I wanted to eat rats."

"Oh, Molly, he didn't!" said Erica indignantly.

"He did," said Molly. "And also you all had lovely pink and white stuff and nobody asked me to have any."

Her beautiful eyes filled with tears. The vicar asked Erica a little crossly what the pink and white stuff was and why she had not seen that her little sister was given some.

"It was called ice-cream, Daddy. It's perfectly heavenly. You make it in a special tub with ice all round the tin. Letty showed me. A man came all the way from Gloucester with blocks of ice in a cart. Where do you think he got it from in the middle of summer? Letty and I couldn't think."

"Erica, please answer my question," said her father. "Why did Molly not get any?"

"Sorry, Daddy, I was truly just going to tell. Molly said she didn't want any. Tom asked her."

"He didn't!" sobbed Molly. "He asked me if I wanted rats!"

"He never! He said, 'Have some ice' as plain as anything. I heard him."

"Oh, very well, mice, then," sniffed Molly. "I thought it was rats." There was a moment's puzzled silence, then Erica gave a shriek of laughter.

"Not 'some mice', silly! 'Some ice'."

But Molly still did not understand, and cried harder than ever. So her father kissed her quickly and said he'd ask Aunt

Libbie to buy her ice-cream in Weston, because he was sure there would be a shop there which sold it. Everyone was very intrigued at the idea of a special shop to buy ice-cream, and even Molly stopped crying.

The next day they all set off to Weston-super-Mare with Bessie to look after them on the journey. They were to stay with Great-Aunt Libbie Milsom and her daughter, Aunt Mary. They had looked after Molly for a whole year just after her mother died. The others had once stayed there, too, but Chris and Clare had been too young to remember. Erica said she did, but Cecily really did, though what she mostly remembered was being unhappy because her darling mother had died. Altogether, none of them wanted to go to Weston very much except Molly, who was looking forward to her ice-cream.

"Your Great-Aunt Libbie is very old," Beatrice told them. "You must be very quiet and good and not disturb her, and not bring sand and dirt off the beach into her beautiful house."

"Of course not, Beatie," they said.

"And Chris, if you collect seaweed or shells or anything like that, you are not to take them into your bedroom."

"No, Beatie."

"And, Erica, will you *please* remember that nice girls do not whistle, or climb trees?"

"Oh, yes, Beatie, I'll remember."

"Most unfortunately your Aunt Mary will be away," Beatrice went on. "However, your great-aunt's companion Miss Cuxford will be there. She will tell you if you are too noisy or if you are doing anything your Great-Aunt does not like. You will obey her as you would me."

"Yes, Beatie," they said, very depressed.

Afterwards they had an indignation meeting in the nursery.

"What's the good of a holiday if we've got to be good and clean and quiet all the time?" demanded Chris.

"That Miss Cuxford needn't think I'm going to obey her unless I choose," said Erica.

"I expect she doesn't even know where to buy mice-cream," said Molly, who still hadn't quite sorted out the ice and the mice.

Even Bessie was angry. She thought she ought to have been trusted to keep the children well-behaved by herself, and not be put under a mere companion.

It was getting dark when they arrived at the station at Weston. There didn't seem to be anyone there to meet them, and they didn't quite know what to do. The busy porters paid no attention to Bessie's shy attempts to find someone to get their trunks. They stood in an unhappy huddle on the emptying platform, and they almost wished they were back at home. Then they heard a voice behind them.

"My dears, I'm so sorry I missed you. That foolish porter sent me to the wrong platform. Never mind, we'll soon find a cab, and then we'll drive straight home and have a nice supper before bed. You must all be starving."

They turned to stare at the big smiling woman, and suddenly everything was all right after all. Miss Cuxford – for it was the dreaded companion herself – found their luggage and seemed to know just how to get porters to do what was wanted. In no time at all the luggage had been tied on the roof of a cab, and the porter was holding the door open for them to get in. It was a bit of a squeeze, Miss Cuxford was so very wide. Molly had to sit on her lap: Bessie was afraid she would cry, for she was very choosy about who she would take to. But Molly settled comfortably and began to suck her thumb.

"It's as though she remembered me," said Miss Cuxford delightedly. "But she can't really. I don't suppose any of you do, except Cecily."

"I do," said Chris unexpectedly. "You had a work-box that played a tune when you opened it. I'd forgotten till just this very minute, and then I remembered. And we used to call you Cuxie, didn't we?"

"Chris!" said Cecily anxiously. "You mustn't call people nicknames."

"Oh, but please!" said Miss Cuxford. "I hope you'll still call me Cuxie. I'd like it."

Molly took her thumb out and looked up with sleepy affection.

"Cuxie, dear," she said. She put her thumb back in her mouth and went to sleep.

The next morning Erica woke with a start. The room was so full of light, she thought she must have overslept. She couldn't think where she was. Then she remembered. She got out of bed and hurried to the window, hoping to see the sea. Instead, there was only a perfectly ordinary road with ordinary houses opposite. Or perhaps the scene was not perfectly ordinary, for everywhere was the same over-bright light which had first woken her. Erica turned back into the room and started to dress, putting on her clothes anyhow because she was trying not to wake Cecily. She turned the door-knob softly and went towards the stairs. As she passed Chris's door, it opened.

"Sh!" said Erica.

"Sh, yourself!" Chris whispered back.

They heard the clatter of fire-irons. Somewhere the kitchen-maid was raking out the stove, perhaps, but no one else was about. The front door was unbolted and they were able to slip out unheard. They found their way down steep streets to the empty sands, still wet from the receding tide. They found fishing boats high and dry and rock pools with coloured sea-anemones. They gathered shells and pebbles, and trod on stranded seaweed to hear the bladders crackle under their feet. They had such an absorbing hour on the deserted morning beach that they thought of nothing else. Then hunger drove them back home.

"They'll be pretty cross with us," said Chris uneasily as they turned into the road on the brow of the hill.

The first person to see them as they pushed open the garden gate was Cuxie, who was cutting flowers. She did not look displeased, but you never knew.

"I'm afraid we're a little late for breakfast," said Chris politely.

"I don't think so," said Cuxie. "In fact, breakfast's not quite ready yet. I hope you're not too hungry. I know how it is about waking up so early in a new place."

They were half-afraid she was being sarcastic, for such common sense seemed too good to be true.

"Perhaps I'd better go in and wash," said Erica cautiously. "I'm a bit sandy."

"Are you?" said Cuxie mildly, not looking up from the

flower she was snipping. "What about going in by the back door, then it won't matter."

That was the beginning of the most golden holiday they remembered. No one nagged them or minded if they got dirty or tore their clothes. No one said that children should be seen and not heard. When it rained, the big cupboard in the corner of Great-Aunt Libbie's room was opened and everyone got out whatever they wanted to do. There was backgammon and ludo and word-making-and-word-taking and chalks and a paintbox and lots of paper. There were books and an enormous jigsaw map of England which took them three rainy days to finish.

Cuxie never seemed too busy or too tired to join in. Great-Aunt Libbie herself did not play with them, but she liked to have them in the room and never minded the noise. She seldom moved from her large armchair but sat there, generally with a Bible open on her lap, in a black silk dress with a lace cap on her white hair. The Bible was in very big print because of her short sight, and even so she had to have a magnifying glass. Sometimes she put it down and looked at the children over the top of her spectacles; and she looked longest at Erica. Erica couldn't play any game calmly, least of all backgammon. She shrieked if her man was "blotted" and had to wait his turn. She fidgeted until her turn came again and then shook and shook the dice-box, begging it to throw a deuce-ace for her. If the two-and-one did fall out of the big leather dice-box, she nearly overturned the board in her joy.

"Erica," said Great-Aunt Libbie after studying her for a long time one day, "you are the queerest girl I ever saw."

Sunny days were even better. They mostly went to Anchor Head to scramble about on the rocks or bathe. Sometimes Bessie and the maid, Marjory, took the older ones among the crowds on the Big Sands to watch the Black and White Minstrels. When they bathed on the Little Sands, they just undressed under coats, but on the Big Sands there were bathing-machines. You went inside to change and it smelt of salt and wet clothes, and there seemed to be sand everywhere. Then you heard the man outside say "Giddup!" to the horse, and the bathing-machine went rocking and swaying over the hard sands to the water's edge. When the horse had been led away, you opened the door and stepped straight down into the water. Some people thought the bathing-machines were old-fashioned, and weren't a bit ashamed to walk right across the sands with nothing on but their bathing-costumes. Very skimpy costumes, too, some of them. Grown women in costumes that scarcely came down to their knees, and even with no sleeves at all! Cecily and Erica had very pretty costumes which Beatrice had provided, but they had proper sleeves and skirts and also frills on the ends of the legs to cover their knees.

Day followed happy day until it was August, when Great-Aunt Libbie and Cuxie were to go away for a holiday themselves and Beatrice was coming down to look after them. Erica did not let herself think about it until the day before, and then, with all Great-Aunt's luggage in the hall in a huge leather trunk, she had to admit that there were going to be changes. She sat on the stairs in the cool, dark hall to think things over. Cuxie came out of the dining-room and asked if there was anything wrong. Erica shook her head, and Cuxie just stroked her hair gently as she went past her up the stairs. Cuxie was so wide that Erica could not help smiling at the way she nearly filled the staircase, and the choking feeling inside her grew a little less. She thought she would go and join the others, but when she stood up, she saw there was a big smear of paint on her dress because she had forgotten to put on her pinafore to help Chris paint his new model sailing boat. Cuxie hadn't said anything and perhaps hadn't noticed, but Beatrice could see the least spot of dirt right across a room. Erica suddenly fled upstairs. She meant to go to her bedroom, but Cuxie might hear her and she went on up to the top of the house, her steps sounding on the uncarpeted stair.

She paused at the top to look about, for she had never been right up there before and was interested in spite of her gloom. The landing was small and had only a piece of coconut-matting, and the three doors leading off were painted a serviceable brown. As she looked, she heard someone coming up the attic stairs.

"Well, well, well," said Bessie. "Little Miss Nosey Parker, eh?"

"Oh, Bessie, don't tease," begged Erica.

Bessie looked at her more closely and said resignedly, "What is it this time? Quarrelled with Cecily? Broken something? Lost a game of your precious backgammon?"

Erica was indignant. Bessie ought to know she wasn't upset by fiddling things like that now!

"I wish she wasn't coming tomorrow!" she burst out. "I wish she was never coming!"

Bessie looked at Erica thoughtfully and then smiled.

"You'd better come and tell us about it, I suppose. When it comes to worries, they're better out nor in. That's what our mam says, and she ought to know." She opened one of the brown doors, and Erica followed her in. Bessie shared the room with Marjory. It was a very small room for a large double bed, and the ceiling sloped down so much that a grown person could only stand up straight on one side of the bed. The room was very hot and had a mixed smell of serge and button-up boots and lavender bags and the shiny American cloth on the dressing-table. Bessie opened the skylight, which was a relief.

"We daren't leave it open if we're not here," she said. "It makes the place terrible hot, but if it came on to rain the bed would be soaked before we could get up here." She poured some water out of the little jug on the table at the foot of the bed.

"Come here and let me wash that face of yours, or they'll all see you've been crying."

Erica said she didn't care, but Bessie washed her face all the same, and it was soothing to have your face washed like a baby, even if the towel was harsh.

"That's better," said Bessie. "Miss Cuxford wouldn't think you were nice at all if she knew you were crying because your own sister was coming."

"I've tried and tried to please Beatie, but she's *never* pleased," said Erica, making an effort to explain. "Whatever I do, she always looks as though it ought to have been something else."

That probably wasn't the real reason why she was crying. She was probably crying for the older sister that never was, the one who would love and understand her and be her friend.

Perhaps, deep down, she was crying for her lost and now forgotten mother.

"I wish Beatie had never come to us. I wish we'd never heard of her, and you could have gone on looking after us," she finished mournfully.

"Now, that's silly talk, Erica dear," said Bessie. "You know I won't be able to look after you for much longer. When my George gets his Sergeant's stripes, I'll be leaving Woodhuckle to marry him."

She looked across at a framed picture propped on the wash-stand. It showed a pink boat on a very blue sea with a flag almost as big as itself standing out from the mast; it wasn't painted but stitched in thick wool. Erica knew George, a great tall man with side-whiskers and a droopy moustache, looking magnificent in his scarlet coat. Bessie said soldiers got so bored in barracks they did anything to pass the time, even sewing and knitting. George gave Bessie the picture before his regiment went to Ireland.

"Now, there's no point in you sitting there feeling sorry for yourself," went on Bessie in a heartening tone. "Even if you can't be right down fond of your sister, at least you can be *proud* of her. It's not everyone that has a sister as clever. Seems to me sometimes there's *nothing* she can't do. She sings, she plays the piano and paints pictures like an artist, and she writes things that they publish and that people pay down good money to buy."

"She's written a book," Erica admitted. "Cuxie told us. It's to be printed, and have her name on the front and lots of pictures."

"Well, there you are," said Bessie. "I don't suppose any of the other girls' sisters write books. Perhaps their mothers will read it, and when you go to tea you'll see it lying about and you'll be able to say – quiet like, you know – 'Oh, yes, my sister wrote that.'"

Erica giggled and began to feel better.

"Besides, your father's coming in a few days – and your cousin Henrietta. You'll like that."

Erica went downstairs again much more cheerfully, but that evening she broke something for the first time since she came to Weston. Chris had shown her how, if you swung the big dressing-mirror right over flat, you could peer down into it and see the sky reflected like a great lake, and the white clouds like islands floating on its surface. Erica tried to show the upside-down islands to Clare. The heavy mirror swung out of her hold and knocked the pot-pourri bowl on to the floor. Great-Aunt Libbie had been very forgiving. She expressed great interest in the sky-sea and the islands, and said there was a shop in Weston which mended china beautifully.

"Cheer up," Chris said to them afterwards. "Just think how awful if it had happened tomorrow. Beatie wouldn't have kissed you and told you not to cry. She'd have scolded you till you did!"

"I deserved to be scolded," said Erica nobly. "I felt a – a worm for being forgiven like that. I'd rather have been scolded."

"Would you?" asked Clare innocently. "I'd much rather be kissed than scolded."

Erica stopped looking noble and laughed.

"Well, so would I really, I expect," she confessed.

When Beatrice arrived next day, it seemed that Erica had been worrying about nothing. Beatrice was in a holiday mood, pleased with everyone and everything. She kept the house in such a bustle of laughter and amusement that Erica wondered how she could ever have dreaded the coming of someone so charming. She had almost worked herself back into her first admiration of her step-sister by the time Mr Stock and their cousin, Henrietta James, came to join them in Weston.

Henrietta was the only child of their mother's eldest brother. Her widowed father adored Henrietta and always did exactly what she wanted. Most people did. She did not wheedle or make a fuss; she looked at people with her big forget-me-not blue eyes – and got her own way. She might have been unbearable with so much spoiling, but somehow was not. She was generous and gay and full of laughter. They all liked Henrietta.

Then, out of the blue, a terrible thing happened to her while she was with them. They had spent the afternoon scrambling about the rocks near Anchor Head, and at tea-time they collected their things for the long walk home. Cecily and Chris went ahead, talking and laughing as they trudged up the cobbled slope towards the Marine Parade. Henrietta unexpectedly chose to scramble along the top of the sea-wall which climbed right up from the shore. It wasn't particularly difficult, for the top of the wall was wide enough and not rough. But near the top there was a long drop to the shore below, and not everybody liked it. Erica had been up that way herself, but she was surprised to see Henrietta try it.

Of course, Erica went up that way too. She danced along happily, only thinking hungrily of her tea. Looking up ahead, she saw Henrietta had stopped, and so she stopped. Henrietta looked back over her shoulder laughing ... suddenly Erica began to run. Henrietta was no longer laughing. She had gone pale and she was swaying. Erica reached the spot too late. Henrietta was already falling. She seemed to fall and fall, while all time stood still.

Then Henrietta was lying still on the shore below, and people were screaming and running towards her. Erica did not remember getting down there, but somehow she was on the beach being jostled by the crowd and not knowing what she ought to do.

"Lend me your bucket, little girl," said a man. "There's a child fallen and hurt herself."

"I know," said Erica. "She belongs to us."

The man was dipping the bucket in a rock pool and did not hear. Someone picked Henrietta up and laid her on a coat on the sand. Her face was white, and blood ran slowly from a gash on her forehead. A woman sprinkled water on her from the bucket.

"She's dead, ain't she?" said someone in the crowd, and a child screamed. Erica thought it was Clare, but everything was a muddle. All she could recall afterwards were sudden sharp pictures which didn't join up – Henrietta falling – Henrietta lying on the rocks – finally, Henrietta sitting up with her head resting against Bessie's shoulder.

"Tell all these people to go away," said Henrietta very clearly.

Then she was lying white and still again, and a man was saying loudly, "Get her to hospital," and Bessie was saying, "No, no, no."

Then Erica was walking up from the beach with Clare holding her hand very tightly. Ahead of them was a man in a blue shirt who had been mending the road; his shirt showed the sweat stains where it pulled across his great shoulders. He was carrying Henrietta, whose legs and arms dangled helplessly.

Then all the children were sitting miserably in the drawing-room on their own. They wanted to be useful – to run for the doctor, send a telegram to Henrietta's father, go for their own father, who was over in Kewstoke – but no one wanted them to do anything, and they hadn't the heart to read or play or even talk. Outside there were running feet and busy voices.

Hours later, it seemed, Beatrice was in the room questioning them. Her voice was high-pitched and quite unlike itself. Clare and Molly were too scared to answer, and Cecily was stammering. No, Bessie wasn't with them; she had gone first with Clare and Molly. No, she hadn't waited for Henrietta, who was looking for Erica's hat. She next saw Erica on the wall, but not Henrietta, because she had just fallen. Suddenly Beatrice was shouting.

"Erica, Erica, Erica – it's always Erica! How many times have I told you not to go on that wall, but do you ever do what I say? You wicked child, how dared you lead your cousin into danger?"

"I didn't! I didn't!" Erica was shouting too, in her desperation. "She went on the wall first!"

"Nonsense! Henrietta didn't do things like that!"

"But she just *did*. And then I started after her. She looked all right. She turned round and laughed and then ... "

Erica broke off, seeing again Henrietta's laughing face distorted with terror as she fell. She heard Cecily trying to speak, and then Beatrice's voice once more, high and quick and angry.

"If Henrietta dies, it will be your fault, Erica! She would *never* have gone up that wall if you had not led her on!"

Beatrice went out, and as the door shut behind her, Erica

sank to the ground and lay in a huddle on the carpet, her nose full of its dusty smell. She pressed her hands over her ears but couldn't shut out Beatrice's voice and the memory of what she had just said. She found herself sobbing loudly.

"Don't!" said Chris. "Please don't!"

"Go away! Go away!"

In the end they all did go, leaving her sobbing in the silence. After a long time she stopped and got to her feet. Very softly she opened the door and crept upstairs to the front bedroom and looked round the open door. The blinds were down and Henrietta lay on the bed in the half-light, watched quietly by a uniformed nurse. The tick of the clock on the mantelpiece was the only sound. Erica crept away again downstairs to the empty, sunny sitting-room. She crawled in under the sofa, forcing herself right to the back, and curled up into a tight ball of misery; she did not even cry.

After a while there were voices in the dining-room next door, and the chink of plates and a laugh from Molly, quickly hushed. They were having tea: as the cook had said, it wouldn't help poor Henrietta much if they all starved. Bessie came in once looking for Erica, and called, but Erica did not move or answer her.

"I expect she's under the sofa," said Molly helpfully.

"Best leave her, then," said Bessie. "I should think she's asleep by now."

Tea was cleared. There was the sound of the doctor's carriage and his voice in the hall talking to Beatrice, and then the horses' hooves clip-clopping away once more.

Much later, she heard her father's voice in the hall on his return from Kewstoke. There was another long pause as he went upstairs. Finally she heard a babble of voices in the next room as he entered and everybody started talking to him at once. Then she heard his voice, suddenly clear.

"Where's Erica?"

Chris answered. Beatrice broke in. Cecily said something, but Beatrice's voice seemed to talk her down. A slow tear or two slid down Erica's dusty cheeks. Then the sitting-room door opened and her father came in.

"Erica, my dear, where are you hiding?"

He did not sound angry, but Erica still could not answer.

"Come out, Erica. I want to speak to you." So she crawled out. Her father stretched out his hand but she did not take it.

"Will she die?"

"No, no, indeed! Thank God, it is not as bad as that. The doctor tells us that she was saved because she has such a tiny frame that she fell lightly She has concussion, but there are no bones broken."

"Then I haven't killed her?"

"Killed her? Gracious, no. What put that idea into your head?"

Though there was now nothing so terrible to cry for, Erica burst into tears instead of answering. Her father didn't argue or ask what was wrong. He simply picked her up in his arms and carried her to her room. He helped her to undress and to get the sitting-room dirt off her face and hands. Then he tucked her up in bed and bent to kiss her good night.

"You haven't done that for ages," she said. "Not since Beatie came."

"Poor Beatrice!" said Mr Stock.

Erica, who was recovering under his kind treatment, felt it was more poor Erica than poor Beatrice, but she was too sleepy to argue. She closed her eyes. Her father was sitting by her bed and he was talking to her, but the sound of his voice was only lulling.

"What a dear child Henrietta is! Her father's only daughter, too, and entrusted to our care. No wonder your poor sister was frightened when she thought Henrietta might be going to die ... and when people are frightened, they say things they don't mean. We all do, and then we are sorry afterwards."

But Erica was asleep.

Chapter 8 · Poor Miss Traill

By the next day Henrietta was well enough to understand what was being said to her. She was upset and indignant when she heard of Erica being blamed for her fall.

"I'm older than Erica! I don't go around copying her. I got on the wall because I wanted to and for no other reason at all!"

Neither Erica nor any of the others had been allowed by the doctor to visit Henrietta yet, but they knew what she had said because the nurse had told Bessie, and Bessie had told Erica in the hope of cheering her up.

"So you don't need to go about looking as though you were to be hanged tomorrow," she added bracingly. "Miss Stock knows now you weren't to blame."

Erica waited for Beatrice to apologize for the things she had said. She would have forgiven her straight away, not being one to bear a grudge for long, but Beatrice did no apologizing. She behaved as if all the terrible things she had said were not worth remembering. Erica could not understand it at all. The hours she had spent weeping after Beatrice had said Henrietta might die and it would be her fault were the most terrible hours she had spent in her life. It never entered her head that her step-sister – taken up with worrying over Henrietta and with arranging about telegrams and doctors and nurses – had scarcely noticed her distress. For the rest of the holiday Erica went about full of resentment towards Beatrice. Unfortunately, Beatrice merely thought she was being sulky. Perhaps if Erica had cried or complained she might have found out what was really wrong, but Erica would not let herself make a fuss, and the misunderstanding was never sorted out.

When the long holiday came to an end at last, they all went back to Woodhuckle. The vicarage seemed strangely big and echoing as they rushed round revisiting all their favourite corners. Outside, a rag doll was still lying upside down under the apple tree where Molly had dropped her and forgotten her. The sunflowers Chris had planted before they went away had grown so tall that their heads came up to his bedroom window. There was a new family of piglets in the sty and ten new chickens in the orchard.

The first day home Sarah made them a magnificent blackberry tart, and Chris ate so much that he felt quite peculiar. Only, the next day it turned out that it wasn't the blackberry tart making him feel queer, but the measles. Two days later Clare got them, then Molly, and last of all Erica and Cecily. Bessie got quite thin and tired, looking after them all.

They appreciated being nursed as long as they were really ill, but as they began to get better they grew bored. But they were not even allowed to read: Dr Manders was most strict about that. He said they might ruin their eyesight for ever if they read before they were right over the measles. He even made Bessie put a thick pink shade over the light in case the glare of the oil lamp was too bright. The shade made the light so dim that they really couldn't see to read, even when Bessie wasn't there. They played all kinds of baby games in an effort to keep themselves entertained. Even Cecily was reduced to dolls' houses and dressing-up and Strip-Jack-Naked, as though she were no older than Molly.

One rainy day the drain under the window blocked up and

a deep pond filled the whole yard. They began throwing out Molly's bricks to watch them float. Then someone had the clever idea of fetching their sea-side buckets and a ball of string and starting a competition to see who could scoop up the most water. It looked easy, but wasn't. Sometimes you got no water because the bucket wouldn't go under. Sometimes when you had drawn it almost to the window, the string would slip or the bucket would catch something and turn over and the water go cascading down again. They spent a glorious half-hour leaning out of the window and screaming with laughter at each other's failures.

It was unfortunate that Beatrice should arrive back home in the carriage at the noisiest moment, when Chris had landed a full bucket of water on the window-sill and spilt it inside all over Clare. It was still more unlucky Beatrice had with her old Mrs Daviot – Old Nosey Parker Daviot, as the Upthorpe boys called her. The moment Mrs Daviot had left, Beatrice swept upstairs. Such behaviour! Shouting and laughing and hanging out of the window for anyone to see! She was ashamed of them! They must all go without pudding and write out a hundred times, "I must not be vulgar".

"It's a very funny thing," said Clare sadly when Beatrice had gone. "Whatever I like doing best, I mustn't."

Beatrice decided that they were getting completely out of hand and that they must immediately start lessons again. Chris was lucky; he had begun the measles first and was finished with them first, and so was able to go to school. Cecily and Erica, who were still in quarantine, had to go back to lessons with Miss Pringle. When she was too busy with Clare and Molly, they had to study French with Beatrice instead. Beatrice was too quick and impatient to make a pleasant teacher, but otherwise they enjoyed being able to make a start on French.

"If we really learnt it," said Erica hopefully, "we might be able to understand when she talks to Daddy in French so that we shan't know what she's saying."

"But she talks French so terribly fast," said Cecily.

"Yes, but we might learn to understand Daddy's answers. He speaks much more slowly and the way he says it isn't so

French. Besides, half the time he sticks in English words when he's forgotten the French ones."

Cecily looked a little more cheerful. They both disliked Beatrice's habit of talking secrets in front of them. She was always telling them it was rude to whisper in company, and yet she never seemed to think it impolite to talk French in front of people who didn't understand it.

Chris was enjoying his second year at school a great deal. He had done so well in the tests at the end of the summer term that the headmaster himself was impressed. Chris had to take him a letter on his first day back at school; it was from Dr Manders, to say he was no longer infectious. The headmaster read it and then looked rather suspiciously at Chris.

"Been having a good time, I suppose, eh, Stock? Didn't think to do any work while you were lolling in bed enjoying the measles, eh? Or did you?"

"Oh, yes, sir," said Chris enthusiastically. "I've been working at History. I am writing the Life of King Henry the Eighth."

The headmaster was a bit taken aback and stared down at the eight-year-old scholar. There was a slight twinkle in his eye which Chris did not notice.

"Are you indeed? And what does your father think of your Life of King Henry the Eighth?"

"To tell you the truth, sir," said Chris very seriously, "I don't think my father knows much about that period."

Fortunately for Chris's dignity, the headmaster managed not to laugh until after the earnest young historian had left the room, but he began to take notice of him. When Chris started Latin and did very well, the headmaster even sent for him once or twice to translate in a senior class, to show up the dense ones there. It was a good thing Chris was liked or he might have had a bad time. As it was, several boys paid him pennies to do their prep for them.

Erica listened enviously to Chris's stories of school and dreamed of equal triumphs for herself when she went back to Appleby Hall – she hadn't the slightest intention of working hard for Miss Pringle, not even when bad work meant an hour's needlework as a punishment.

"I reckon it's as much a punishment for me as you," said Bessie. "I've got better things to do than watch you make a botch of everything you touch." Bessie herself sewed beautifully; tucks and button-holes grew under her fingers in no time, and her hem-stitches were tiny. "Don't push your needle in as though you were poking the fire!" she begged. "And look, you've unthreaded your needle *again*! Seeing what a work it is to get the thread through again, I'd think you'd be more careful!"

In fact, Bessie usually rethreaded the needle for her in the end because she couldn't bear to watch, but one day she got really angry with Erica.

"I don't believe you even *try*!" she exclaimed. "I'm not going to let you out into the garden until you've threaded that needle by yourself, now! You ought to be ashamed of yourself!"

Erica really felt Bessie was right and meekly picked up the needle; but the more she tried, the more she couldn't do it, and she didn't know why she couldn't. "Born clumsy," old Mrs Daviot had told her grumpily. The thread went to one side of the eye and then to the other, and then it doubled itself up. Bessie gave her a bigger needle.

"Not that it'll do much good," she said. "Even if you threaded it, you couldn't sew with such a skewer."

Erica was in such a state she couldn't thread even the big darner she'd been given. She sucked and smoothed the thread until it was black, and still it wouldn't go through. Outside she heard Chris calling in the sunshine.

"I can't! I can't!" she moaned.

Then Bessie's hands came over her shoulder. Her own trembling hands were steadied in Bessie's, and slowly they were brought together and the thread slipped easily through the eye.

"There!" said Bessie. "You can do it if you try. Out you go into the garden."

Erica knew perfectly well who had really threaded the needle. Dear Bessie, she thought gratefully as she ran out to join Chris; dear, dear Bessie.

The other person who was particularly kind to Erica at this

period was her father. Ever since the day of Henrietta's accident, when he had been so helpful, he seemed to take a new and special interest. It had always seemed that only Chris had the right to go into his father's study unasked, but now Erica dared to feel that she too was welcome. She and Chris did their homework in front of the fire on the mat, away from the noise upstairs – and away from Beatrice, too, who seldom came into the study.

Beatrice did not often interfere in the garden, either, and Erica was happy for long stretches helping her father there with weeding and tying up. She puddled each seedling in with plenty of water, as she had been shown, and firmed it with hand and heel.

"We'll make a gardener of you yet," said William Long once. "You aren't afraid to dirty your hands!"

Erica was not used to being praised for being dirty, and she was charmed. Being untidy in her clothes was another thing which suited her, and she liked rushing about with Chris and the Upthorpe boys. That autumn they were mapping the course of Woodhuckle Brook, Chris and Tom doing the scientific measurements. But everybody joined in inventing names for the banks and pools and tributaries. Letty Upthorpe and Cecily were interested chiefly in the pretty places, and so there were Cecily's Honeysuckle Bower and Letty's Wonder Island; but Erica liked to see her name on the dangerous parts – Erica's Leap, Erica's Mud Trek and Erica's Tree Crossing. The last cost her a ducking in one of her best flannelette dresses.

Occasionally the Bantock boys from Houghton joined them. Beatrice thought they were delightful children to have for friends because they lived in the Manor House and their father was a Justice of the Peace. She never heard their language when they were by themselves or knew about the sort of games they got up to. They played Cherry-Knocking and an even more inane game in which, instead of running away when you'd knocked at someone's door, you had to stand there and ask "Do you take in washing?" Sometimes you had a polite answer and sometimes a rude one, and sometimes an angry swipe. Whatever it was, the Bantock boys just laughed and ran away; the angrier people were, the funnier the boys thought it.

Erica hadn't the courage to say so, but she didn't think it was particularly funny, because she was friends with children whose mothers did take in washing and knew that they pretended they didn't. Taking in washing was what you came to when your luck was out – if your man fell ill or lost his job, taking in washing might be the only thing between you and the work-house. Chris knew too, and after a while he said firmly he wasn't going to play any more. The Bantock boys chanted, "Cowardy, cowardy custard! Eat a pot of mustard!", but Chris just shrugged and somehow the game was not played when he was in the group.

Before half-term Cecily and Erica, as well as Chris, were back at school. It was lovely to be on the old horse-tram once more, and even Cecily was excited enough to shout a noisy greeting to each friend who got on at a stop. On the first morning Erica met Miss Young in the corridor.

"I'm not in your class any longer," she said. "I wish I were."

"Oh, no," said Miss Young. "It's nice to move up. You'd be bored staying with me." She paused, with an odd expression on her face. She glanced quickly along the empty corridor and then bent and kissed Erica's cheek. "Work hard in your new class, my dear. That's something you can always do."

By the end of the first day Erica thought she understood why she had been given that unexpected kiss. Miss Traill was a very different teacher from Miss Young. She meant well, perhaps, but her lessons were dull and deadly. She couldn't keep order, either, so that it was often quite difficult to hear even if you were trying. Consequently, Erica did not try very hard. It was more fun to fool about with her friends; and teasing a teacher was better than teasing another girl and did not make you feel so guilty. As Edie Summers said, teachers ought to be able to look after themselves, and if they couldn't, it was their own fault. They led Miss Traill a terrible life between them. Edie probably teased her most, but Mavis Bell was almost as bad. It was watching Mavis that first made Erica uneasy. Now that everyone was careful not to tease Mavis, it seemed mean of her to try so hard to tease the teacher.

One day Erica was made to stand out in front of the class for fidgeting. There was nothing new in that, for she often fidgeted deliberately merely in order to stand up for a change. Then she could see out of the high windows and watch what was going on in the road. This morning, however, she was not standing by the window but by the teacher's desk. She looked at Miss Traill and saw tears behind the thick lenses which distorted her eyes and made her look plainer than ever. She stared at her lined and sallow face, and at her tired, drooping mouth, and at her thin figure under the skimpy dress. Miss Traill's dress was so old that it was even made with a bustle, though bustles had been out of fashion for years and years. It wasn't even a big handsome bustle such as Beatrice had worn with such style when she was younger. It was a half-hearted little bustle which jutted out behind and waggled awkwardly when Miss Traill walked.

A day or two later Edie and Mavis invented a new game. Mavis would put up her hand to ask about something in her work. When Miss Traill walked across to see what it was, Edie would walk behind her, balancing a ruler on her bustle with one finger. Of course, the other girls giggled, but when Miss Traill turned round to see what was the matter, Edie was standing there with a perfectly solemn face holding her exercise-book in her hand and pretending she needed help. Then, a little later, it would be the turn of Edie to get Miss Traill to come over while Mavis pranced behind her with the ruler. Miss Traill knew she was being made fun of, from the giggling which went on behind her through the lesson, but she never found out what the joke was.

One morning soon after, when they went out at the play-break, the class were laughing their heads off over this game, all except Erica and her close friend, Amy Briggs. The two of them sat in the corner of the garden under the big chestnut tree and talked earnestly. The result was that after the play-break, when they were sitting waiting for Miss Traill, Erica got to her feet. Her knees were knocking a bit and her cheeks were very red, but she spoke out loudly.

"I don't believe we ought to tease her so much," she said. "It's mean. She can't help being like what she is."

"Oh, stuff!" said Edie. "Of course she can, and if she can't, she oughtn't to pretend to come and teach us."

"She has to come," said Erica. "Amy told me. You tell them, Amy."

But Amy was too shy, and Erica had to go on; she didn't mind, for it was a fine romantic story.

"Miss Traill has to work to keep her family from starving," she said dramatically. "She has an old widowed mother, and a brother who has consumption and can't work. So she has to pay the doctor's bills, and buy special nourishing food for her brother. Everything depends on her!"

Erica's story was not well received. Most of the class groaned, and Edie made noises as though she was being sick.

"Tell us another," begged Mavis. "All that stuff about saving her starving family – you read that in a Sunday school book!"

Erica's cheeks flamed redder than ever, but she stuck to her point, and her next remark was not quite so romantic but more her own.

"I don't care what you say, Mavis Bell! It's all true, and I still think it's mean to tease her like this. If Miss Grossard knew she couldn't keep us in order, she might send her away, and then they'd all starve."

"And a good thing, too," said Edie robustly. "It's cheating for her to take money for teaching us when she can't teach. My father pays for me to have good teachers here, not an old thing who couldn't teach a lamb to say baa!"

At this point Miss Traill came back, and Erica sat down rather thankfully. She felt she had made a fool of herself and done no good to Miss Traill. What was more, after what she had said, she couldn't join in any more teasing herself. To keep herself from boredom she began to work, and shot ahead of Edie. Then Edie had to work, too, and so there was only Mavis to lead the teasing. But Mavis wasn't very popular and wasn't somebody people wanted to copy. So, after all, Erica's interference did not help Miss Traill, though not in the way she had meant.

Edie and Erica kept more or less level in their marks through the rest of the year. At the end it was Edie who had the larger total, but she had to lose too many on account of all the "order marks" she had been given for bad behaviour in the first term, and it was Erica who had the form prize. Erica thought Edie would never forgive her; but fortunately, when Erica went up to get her prize from the mayoress, she tripped over her trailing shoelace and fell flat on the dusty platform. Edie laughed uproariously and said it served Erica right; but it cleared the air and they were friendly again.

Chapter 9 · The safety bicycle

Shortly after Chris went back to school he was given his first bicycle. It was almost the first bicycle in the village, too, and a young man called Sam Barker had to be paid to come out from Gloucester to give him lessons. Chris's bicycle was one of the new safety ones with a chain, and both wheels the same size, but Sam still rode a penny-farthing. The others always gathered round to watch enviously, and after the lesson was over Sam would hoist one or other of them on to the high saddle of the penny-farthing to give them a ride.

"I want a bicycle of my own," Erica declared at dinner the day after one lesson.

There was dead silence round the table while everyone waited for the answer. If Erica got a bicycle, Cecily ought to have one. And if Cecily got one, then Clare and Molly would be entitled to one as soon as they were old enough. They were disappointed: Beatrice gave one of her irritating trills of laughter.

"If wishes were horses ... or bicycles in this case ... beggars might ride. Will you pay for it out of your pocket-money?"

"You know I can't," said Erica resentfully. "You've stopped it for three weeks because I broke the china lion in the drawing-room."

"It would take more than three weeks' pocket-money to buy a bicycle. Have you any idea what they cost?"

"Yes," said Erica promptly, "and I asked Sam about it, and he said you could get a second-hand one really quite cheap now. I shouldn't in the least mind if it was second-hand."

"Oh, well, if you don't spend any pocket-money at all, you'll be able to buy one in a few years' time," said Beatrice lightly.

At this point their father, who had seemed lost in his own thoughts, joined in, to everyone's astonishment.

"I do not see why Erica should not have a bicycle of her own, if Chris is to have one. Indeed, it is quite the thing nowadays for girls to ride. I saw the dean's two daughters on their bicycles only last week, and very charming they looked in blue bicycling-suits and little sailor-hats."

Erica would not have been more astounded if the last trump had sounded. She'd had some hopes of getting Beatrice on her side, because Beatrice always liked to be up to date, but she had thought that dear Daddy, with his old-fashioned notions, would take a lot of persuading. Clare was surprised, too, and dropped a spoonful of apple tart on the floor, but Beatrice never even noticed.

"My dear Papa, the dean's daughters do *not* look charming! Such blowsy girls, with their hats askew and their skirts dragging in the mud, or very likely catching in the back wheel and toppling them off, which is a thing that happens, I understand. I suppose you do not want Erica to break her neck?"

"Certainly not," said Mr Stock. "But I hear that a special guard can be affixed to the back wheel to obviate that danger."

All of them, even Beatrice, quite gawped at their father: he really was a most remarkable man! You would think sometimes that he knew nothing except about the Bible or what St Paul was doing in the year A.D. 40, and then he would come out with something completely modern and practical like that!"

"Besides," the vicar went on, beaming, "if Erica had a bicycle, she could do my errands much more quickly."

"But the cost!" exclaimed Beatrice defensively.

"More expensive than purple muslin hangings?" said her father quizzically.

Everybody laughed except Beatrice and Erica.

The summer before, Beatrice had banished the damask curtains and the Turkey-red carpet from the drawing-room and had had the whole room redecorated. The walls were papered in a white and green ivy pattern, and the new carpet had pastel flowers woven on a beige background. The windows were hung with purple velvet over-curtains and yellow muslin under-curtains. Most dashing of all, the high double-mantelpiece was swathed in purple muslin, and it cascaded down either side of the fireplace. The room had been the wonder of the village, but the purple muslin had soon vanished. One unexpectedly cold day in June, Alice lit the coal fire, and the inevitable happened. A gust of wind blew the muslin into the fire and the hangings went up in a sheet of flame. Erica had rushed from the room, and when she returned, Beatrice and Cecily had torn down the remains of the hangings and were stamping on the smouldering material. Erica explained that she had gone to get a jug of water to throw on the flames, but it wasn't true. She had run away because she had been frightened, and she was very much ashamed of the episode.

Though she was afraid of fire, she was in general fairly brave. Her father had said that she could have her bicycle as soon as she had learned to ride; so, when no one was about, she fetched Chris's bicycle from the coach-house and set off. She found it difficult to get on because of her long skirt. However, by standing on one of the big tubs by the front door – to the great danger of Father's Agapanthus lilies – she was able to get her foot across the bar and start. Naturally, she fell off almost at once, but she picked herself and the bicycle up and started again: if Chris could do it, then she could. Her knees were grazed by the gravel, and her heart was racing from fear in case anyone saw her and tried to stop her, but she would not give in. When Mr Stock came driving back, it was to see Erica riding round the carriage sweep – out of one gate, along the road and back through the other gate. She nearly made the horse shy, but she got her bicycle the next week.

Beatrice may have been defeated over the bicycle, but more usually she got her own way. It seemed to the children that her way was too often the way least comfortable for them. Really well-made clothes and well-fitting shoes turned out to be "too expensive". So did most toys and games, and their new ones were those given by other people as presents. Molly was still nursing Erica's old legless doll with one eye – admittedly she was very fond of it. The other thing that tended to be "too expensive" was interesting food, especially for the children.

"I wouldn't mind so much," said Chris, "if she didn't say so many good things to eat are bad for us. If they're really bad for people, she shouldn't give them to visitors the way she does."

Chris, as usual, had put his finger on the spot. They didn't mind just the going without. They knew their father's stipend was very small, and that they would not have managed on that alone without the little money of his own which he had. So they were able not to be jealous of children with better clothes and more toys. But showy meals for visitors and no cooked breakfasts for the family did hurt. Even Sunday bacon and eggs came to an end for the children – and what was more, they had to pretend they didn't like bacon and eggs. When visitors were staying, the children would be asked if they wanted bacon and egg and were expected to say, "No, thank you".

One visitor who wasn't taken in was Mrs Fulmort, a cheerful, plump woman, who had come with Dean Fulmort. He was to preach about the missionary work he had done in East Africa, a place where such work had not long begun. Mrs Fulmort's round eyes grew rounder as each young Stock dutifully said "No, thank you" to the offer of eggs and bacon.

"What extraordinary children!" she exclaimed. "Mine gobble up eggs and bacon whenever they get the chance."

Chris and Erica avoided each other's eyes and Molly gave

a nervous giggle which earned her a furious glare from Beatrice, who was vexed. Only Cecily remained calm, for Cecily always knew what to say.

"Alice will be bringing hot scones for us soon. We like them."

"I see," said Mrs Fulmort. But there had been such a twinkle in her eyes as she said it, that Erica was sure she had noticed more than she was meant to notice. She said as much to Cecily in the garden after breakfast as they were waiting for church time.

"It serves Beatie right," she said. "She oughtn't to make us say we don't like bacon when we do. It's lying."

"It's not lying," said Cecily. "It's a ... a social convention. Like getting Alice to tell callers she's 'not at home' when she doesn't want to see them."

"That's lying, too," said Erica uncompromisingly.

"You're impossible! You'll never learn manners," said Cecily loftily.

"Good," said Erica. "I don't want manners if they mean always telling fibs."

"Don't worry, you're a long way off," retorted Cecily. "And wait till your Fulmorts see how you wriggle in church. They won't think so much of you then." But Cecily was wrong this time.

After church, when they were all sitting round waiting for dinner, Mr Fulmort was full of enthusiasm for "this little dark-eyed girl" who had sat so still and enthralled through his sermon.

"Erica, do you mean?" asked the vicar, trying to keep the astonishment out of his voice. He drew her forward.

Mr Fulmort beamed at her with pleasure. "Come and sit beside me, Erica, so that we can talk."

Erica went and sat gingerly beside him, looking so nervous that her brother and sister grinned secretly at each other.

"It was a great treat to me to see your eyes raised with such interest," said Mr Fulmort. The serious sincerity of his voice prevented his words sounding patronizing. "I so seldom meet a young person nowadays who feels the same enthusiasm for the noble work of the missionary that I myself have felt since

I, too, was a child. Do tell me what first awoke your interest? How long have you wished to be a missionary?"

"But I don't want to be a missionary," Erica blurted out. "I'm not interested in them at all."

There was dead silence in the room and the kindly smile faded from Mr Fulmort's face. He looked forlorn and hurt, like a puppy slapped down when it wanted to be friends. Erica went scarlet, tried to stammer out an explanation and could find no words. Mr Fulmort did not try to talk further, and Erica had to comfort herself by making up a conversation in bed that night in which she always said exactly the proper thing. Curled up and alone like that, she often had the most intellectual conversations. So she explained to Mr Fulmort (even though he wasn't there) that though she never happened to have thought of being a missionary, she really had been listening hard to his sermon. She and her brother Christopher had been *most* interested (her dream voice said, really quite truthfully) to hear how a missionary learnt to speak the language of strange tribesmen when he hadn't known a single word before and the tribesmen didn't know any English. Both Christopher and herself (she went on, not quite so truthfully) would welcome a visit to East Africa but did not feel they were quite good enough yet to be missionaries.

She pictured Mr Fulmort being enormously impressed with her intelligence and truthfulness; and he invited her and Chris to come and see him at his Mission Station. While they were there, Chris discovered the *real* source of the Nile, and Erica wrote a dictionary of the most difficult African language there was. It was sad to wake up and remember that none of this was true, and that she was just a school-girl who had been stupidly rude.

It was a relief next morning to get out of the house to run some errands for her father. They could wait till later, but she preferred to avoid saying goodbye to the Fulmorts. She took the go-cart because there were quite a lot of things to carry. Beatrice had given them the go-cart in one of her impetuous fits of unexpected generosity. It had two wheels, and shafts, and was big enough even for Cecily to sit in. Someone had to be the donkey, of course, except downhill. But after Clare had nearly run herself under a passing gig and Chris had upset Letty Upthorpe into a cucumber frame, interest in it cooled down; and now it was mostly used for practical jobs like taking heavy parcels along into the village.

Erica muttered to herself as she pushed it along through the spring morning:

"Hap'orth of dolly mixture for Clare, hap'orth of bulls-eyes for me, and a sugar mouse for Molly. Milk pudding for Mrs Marston. Broth for old Mrs Prudhoe. Ask young Mrs Prudhoe why Martha wasn't in school. Fetch the shoes from the cobbler, and then go and ask Mrs Poine why the new baby hasn't been christened."

She paused with a worried frown on her face. She was sure there had been something else – her face cleared and she ran happily on:

"Ask Billy-Bob if he can pump the organ next Sunday, and say please will Miss Emmeline Browne be well enough to come to choir practice on Wednesday."

Erica was beginning to feel pleasantly important as she trundled along, and running errands for her father was one of the things she liked doing best. He said she was as good as a curate any day, and as Woodhuckle couldn't afford a curate, she really was useful.

"I'm too old to go running from one end of the parish to the other for every forgotten message," he said to Mr Upthorpe. "But here's Erica longing to rush about, and the farther I send her, the better she likes it."

First she went to Mrs Tiddie's. There were only two shops in the village: Joe Barnes, where you could buy sides of bacon and candles and sacks of meal or seed potatoes, and Mrs Tiddie's. This was the post office, and it also sold sweets and some groceries. Mrs Tiddie had only opened the shop a year before, when her husband died, but now Erica could hardly remember the time when there was nowhere nearer than Gloucester to buy sweets.

The shop was tiny, and its window was tiny too, and so full of boxes and jars that hardly any light got in. It seemed tinier than usual today because fat Mrs Barnes was sitting there, and she had Toddy Barnes with her, the youngest and solidest of her eight children. She was about to get up and go as Erica came in; she heaved herself to her feet and groaned as she bent to pick up her big, untidy basket.

"That looks terribly heavy," said Erica, "and you've Toddy to carry as well. Couldn't I put it on the cart and push it home?"

"Well ... well, I wouldn't say as I'd not be grateful. These hot days do seem to *draw* a woman so."

Erica seized the basket and staggered outside with it to the cart.

Mrs Barnes turned doubtfully to Mrs Tiddie. "Mightn't there be a bit of a pother if Miss Stock sees?"

"Never you mind for that," said Mrs Tiddie comfortingly. "What the eye don't see no one don't bother about, and Miss Stock's drove into Gloucester with the reverend and his wife that were staying with them. I saw her go by, bowing gracious to me like a duchess, which she's got more the manner of than some I could mention!"

So they laughed and Erica was allowed to run the basket home, with young Toddy sitting up on the cart and shouting with delight as the cart bounced over the uneven road. With Mrs Barnes and Toddy safe home, Mrs Marston's milk pudding was the next thing. Beatrice had objected, but Mr Stock was firm.

"We always do send milk puddings to women in childbed, if they're in need, and Mrs Marston isn't less needy because her husband's in jail for a month for poaching."

When Sarah's beautiful creamy pudding had been handed over to Mrs Marston, who seemed genuinely pleased (which was pleasant for Erica too), the next visit was to the Prudhoe family. Beatrice thought well of them, for the children bobbed her a curtsy when she passed, and the cottage was spotless. In fact, it was washed so often that it never seemed quite dry even in summer. As for the five little Prudhoes, they looked as if they had been boiled in the copper along with the clothes. Their faces were pink and shiny and their stringy hair almost colourless. Erica found Mrs Prudhoe scrubbing the kitchen floor, and the two littlest Prudhoes marooned on top of the table to keep them out of the suds. Martha, who was eleven, was peeling potatoes at the stone sink.

"Please, Mrs Prudhoe," said Erica, "Daddy wants to know why Martha hasn't been to school."

Mrs Prudhoe put down her scrubbing-brush and sat back on her heels. She had string-coloured hair like her children but her face was string-coloured, too, not pink and shiny. Erica did not like her much, or the whine in her voice.

"You tell the reverend I haven't got the pennies to send them," she said. "Tuppence a week each is a mortal amount of money."

"Please, Daddy says they've got to go to school all the same. It's the law."

"There was no such law when I was a little girl," said Mrs Prudhoe. "I stayed at home and helped my mam, same as our Martha should. What's a great big girl want with more schooling? She can write her name and say her catechism and she can figure real well. What else will she ever need?"

Erica knew she was not to argue, and only repeat what her father had said.

"Please, Mrs Prudhoe, she's got to stay at school until she's twelve or else till she can read well enough to please the Inspector."

"Then why can't them dratted teachers learn her to read," said Mrs Prudhoe, getting emotional. "It's what they're paid for, isn't it?"

"Well, they can't teach her if she's not there to teach," said Erica mildly. But Mrs Prudhoe burst into noisy tears, and Martha, who had been gaping, burst into tears too, and the little Prudhoes on the table joined in.

"If the law says I've got to send a lazy great girl to school, then the law ought to find the tuppence!" cried Mrs Prudhoe.

Erica had run out of replies, so she opened her bag of bulls-eyes and offered it round. Everyone took a sweet, including Mrs Prudhoe, and there weren't many left.

"May a blessing light upon you for thinking of the fatherless!" said Mrs Prudhoe. Some people did think they ought to make remarks like that to the vicarage children, and Erica hated it. There didn't seem anything to say, but luckily the Prudhoe baby at this point choked on his bulls-eye and went quite purple in the face, so that Mrs Prudhoe had to turn him upside down and slap him on the back till the bulls-eye fell out. Then another little Prudhoe seized it and popped it in his mouth, and the baby yelled with such fury that he went purple again. Erica backed out of the door unnoticed.

Half way along Church Lane she noticed she still had the broth she should have left for Granny Prudhoe. Old Mrs Prudhoe was bedridden and often had broth from the vicarage because she had no teeth and couldn't chew. Erica ran back with the jar and cut across the back garden, her feet making no sound on the earth path. As she came up to the back door she was stopped in her tracks by a bellow of rage from inside, very different from Mrs Prudhoe's usual whine.

"And *why* can't yer learn to read so's yer can leave school? Pounds I must have paid out for yer, and not a hap'orth of good to show!"

"I *'ate* school!" Martha's voice was as shrill as her mother's. "I can't learn that stuff! It's difficult, I tell yer. You just try reading and see if it's easy!"

"Oo says I can't read, you brass-faced young varmint? If that little nosey parker from the vicarage can read, so can you!"

Erica turned and fled, and she did not stop running until she was in the lane. Her heart was knocking against her ribs, but she told herself she simply must take the broth back for old Mrs Prudhoe, or Beatrice would be very cross. But for once that did not seem so dreadful as being shouted at by Mrs Prudhoe with her stringy hair. She decided to leave the broth till last and to do her other errands first: you never knew, the end of the world might come before she had finished, and then at least she wouldn't have to face Mrs Prudhoe.

She called at Rose Cottage, and Billy-Bob said he'd come and pump the organ on Sunday. Then, at Jessamine Villa, Miss Emmeline Brown explained that she would not be able to come to the choir practice on Wednesday. She gave Erica a long lecture on proper conduct in the young and a small caraway biscuit. It was much too horrible to eat, and the bits got between your teeth, so Erica hid it under a stone as soon as she was out of sight of Jessamine Villa and set off on her last call, to Mrs Poine. Half a mile along the road to the church she turned up a lane. The Poines's cottage was the last before the lane petered out into open fields. It was small and dark and in a bad state; rags were stuffed into broken panes, and in the garden there was little but nettles and fools' parsley. Mrs Poine was sitting on a kitchen chair outside the door with the baby on her lap. Despite the sunshine, she looked pinched and ill, and though her eyes were shut, she did not look as if she was sleeping but she did look as if she had been crying.

She opened her eyes as Erica approached and greeted her with a wan smile. Erica explained her errand, saying, "I only came because Daddy was wondering when you'd be bringing her to be christened."

"Poor thing, she's never thriven," said Mrs Poine, looking down at the baby on her lap. "She don't cry, but she don't seem to suck either. Sometimes I do think it's because she's never been christened as she ought; but times I think it's because I'm so fretty myself."

Erica rather thought christenings weren't to make babies suck better, but decided she'd better consult with her father before she said anything.

"Do let me tell Daddy you'll bring her next Sunday," she answered at last.

"I know I ought," said Mrs Poine. "But I 'aven't a thing fit to wear myself, and ... "

"I'm sure Daddy wouldn't mind," said Erica, trying to be reassuring.

"Oh, he wouldn't notice, bless him, but ... " she broke off again. "I did think my Sararann might have helped me with a new dress for the baby, now she's out at service, but there ... "

"And didn't she? What a shame!"

"Oh, it weren't her fault, poor girl. She tripped over a ball that boy at her place left on the stair and broke two dishes, and they stopped it out of her wages. Two whole months' money, it took."

There was nothing more to say, it seemed to Erica, and she asked if she could see the baby. It was the right thing to do, because Mrs Poine looked quite pleased and carefully turned back the corner of the shawl. Erica knew you were supposed to say how pretty a baby was, but this baby was so thin and its face so dry and mottled that it was the ugliest baby she had ever seen, and she stared in silence. The baby opened its eyes, but they did not see her. They were dark and dull, as though the baby was already tired of life. Erica looked unhappily at the mother, but she was smiling down tenderly at the shrivelled little face and hardly looked like worn Mrs Poine at all, but almost beautiful.

Erica found herself suddenly wondering whether her own mother had ever smiled down at her like that. She couldn't usually remember her mother's face at all; she had tried sometimes, but she knew that it was the oil-painting in Father's study she was really seeing. But now, in the weedy, sunlit garden, it came back to her that when she was still tiny, she used to sit on her mother's bed and watch her mother doing her hair. She would brush it forward over her face so that everything was hidden, nose and eyes and all. The Erica of long ago was a bit afraid, until her mother's hands parted the long black hair and there was her own face smiling down at her, as Mrs Poine was smiling now. Erica bent forward and kissed the ugly baby.

"I think she's a lovely baby. What are you going to call her?"

"I've hardly dared to think," said Mrs Poine, "in case she doesn't live to need a name. I've so little milk she dwindles day by day. Maybe if I could eat more – but I don't fancy taters and turnip, even if we had plenty of them."

Erica's eyes grew bigger. She knew families sometimes came down to turnips only, especially at the end of the week, but she hadn't thought of people who hadn't enough of those.

"Mrs Poine," she said suddenly. "I quite forgot. My father sent some veal broth for you. It's in the go-cart."

"You don't mean it!"

"Yes I do," said Erica, stoutly putting Mrs Prudhoe out of her mind. "I'll get it right away." She went and lifted the jar out of the bottom of the cart and thrust it at Mrs Poine.

"Heat it up straight away," she said. "Then you can have some before ... well, I mean, then you can have some."

Erica had time to reflect as she pushed the cart home.

Suppose Mrs Prudhoe asked about the broth she'd been promised? Suppose Mrs Poine returned the broth-jar at a time when Beatrice saw? As she went in by the garden she saw her father at the far end doing some weeding. On an impulse she went down to him. He gave her a look and stuck his weeding-fork in the ground.

"What's wrong?" he said. Stumbling over it, Erica told her tale.

"I told Mrs Poine to drink it straight away," she finished, "so that Ben shouldn't get it. Beatie says it's no use giving things to the Poines because Ben sells them and drinks the money at the pub. Well, he doesn't drink the money exactly, of course."

To her relief her father laughed. "I'm *glad* you gave Mrs Poine the broth. I hadn't realized things were so bad again up there."

"And Mrs Prudhoe?" asked Erica timidly. "It was her broth, you know."

"Bother Mrs Prudhoe," said the vicar. "She should be glad to help someone worse off than herself."

"I don't think she will be," said Erica.

"No, she won't be," said Mr Stock. "She is *not* a nice woman, and I don't believe she needs half the things she gets out of ... " He broke off hastily. "I tell you what we'll do, we'll go and ask Sarah privately if she happens to have any soup left. Then Billy-Bob can run down to Mrs Prudhoe's with it. He's here helping his father."

They went to the kitchen, and Sarah did have some more soup, and she put it in a jar, and Billy-Bob took it down to the village. And Beatrice never knew.

"So that's us out of the soup!" said Erica's father.

Chapter 10 · "Pigs, Miss!"

"What were you and Daddy laughing about?" demanded Cecily when Erica came upstairs.

"Daddy made a pun," said Erica. "I didn't know he could. I thought it was only Mr Upthorpe who made puns."

"How silly you are," said Cecily fretfully.

Erica remembered not to answer back. Cecily was feeling poorly that day and cried if you teased her in the slightest. By the next day she was feverish and Dr Manders was sent for. He put his top hat on the table and came to sit by Cecily's bed. Cecily told him crossly that there was nothing wrong with her at all. He paid no attention but took his stethoscope out of his top hat and listened to her chest. He told her to open her mouth and say "Aah", and he peered down her throat.

"Horrid!" he said. "Shut it up quickly."

That made Cecily laugh, but when he threatened her with a week in bed she stopped laughing and said she could not possibly go to bed for a week because there was no one else to take her Sunday school class.

"Give them a holiday," said Dr Manders. "They'll like that."

"Not *my* class," said Cecily. "They like coming."

That was true, too. The boys tried to come into Cecily's class and, what was more, they were never naughty with her, or at least hardly ever. No one quite knew how she managed it, but even Alfie True, one of the worst-behaved boys in the whole village, was as good as gold. In fact, if anyone else tried to misbehave, he could be relied on to punch their heads. Some of the other teachers, like Letty Upthorpe and Miss Emmeline herself, were rather jealous of young Cecily because their own pupils were not so easy to manage and didn't get so many rewards for good attendance. So Cecily was proud of her pupils and very upset that they might be scattered among the other classes on the coming Sunday. Her father said amiably that he'd have to invite somebody else to take the class, but whoever he suggested, Cecily said they wouldn't do at all. Her father couldn't understand, and mentioned it to Beatrice in the sitting-room.

"Cecily is afraid that her class might like another teacher just as well," said Beatrice drily. "She prefers to think that no one else can manage her children. I am afraid she is becoming a little conceited about it."

Erica had been sitting near by, half listening and half learning some poetry, but she put her book down at that.

"Cecily isn't conceited," she said sharply, and the more sharply because there was something in her step-sister's remark. "She just wants to be sure her class is taught properly because she thinks it's important. She'd like anyone to take her class if she thought they'd take it the proper way. She'd even let me."

"Very well," said Beatrice, taking her up on it. "We'll ask her just that."

They went up to Cecily's bedroom; and Cecily cheered up at once and said, of course – Erica would be just the person to take the class. Erica had not really taken the idea seriously and was horrified.

"But, Cecily, I couldn't. I never meant ... Oh dear! What have I let myself in for!"

Even Beatrice relented and was a bit sorry, and she told Cecily she'd only suggested Erica for a joke. Erica, at ten, was much too young to take a class. But Cecily was taken with the plan.

"She's often looked after the little ones. You know she has," she urged. "She's good with them too, and they like her."

Erica couldn't deny that. She loved the babies' class and they loved her. They came running to meet her on the way to Sunday school, tried to sit near her and liked to get hold of her hand. They brought her small bunches of wild flowers picked on the way – daisies or Stars of Bethlehem or dandelions with oozing stalks.

"But, my dear Cecily," – Beatrice was still amused – "you see very well that poor Erica does not want to take the class."

Erica certainly hadn't wanted to, but she didn't like the way her step-sister was laughing, either. Why should the idea of her taking the class be so very funny?

"I don't mind taking the class at all," she declared more firmly than she felt. "At least, if Cecily really wants me to, I don't mind."

So Cecily prepared the lesson with great care and tried to make sure that Erica would give it the way she wanted. She even invented questions that might be asked, so that Erica would be ready with an answer for everything any of the children might ask about the lesson.

When Sunday came, Erica's heart was beating hard as she knelt with the others to pray in the big schoolroom. She was thinking it was absurd to suppose she could teach boys like Alfie True and Billy Barnes, who were taller and stronger than she was, or girls like Elsie Tiddie, who (though she was only eight) could peel the potatoes, wash the dishes, bath the baby and scrub the floor – all things that seemed terribly skilled. Erica was not spoiled, but she lived in a big household and never had to make the tea, even, or do cleaning. In her home Beatrice rang the bell for things like that.

All too soon the hymn after the prayers reached the "Amen" and was finished, and the different classes filed off behind their teachers. There weren't enough classrooms for Cecily to have one, and she taught her class in the little dark lobby where the children hung their coats on weekdays. Even on a Sunday it still had a queer smell of corduroy and wet leather boots. The eight boys and girls sat on top of the boot-boxes, and Erica sat in front of them on a chair from one of the classrooms. The children on the boot-boxes were giggling to each other. Alfie was trying to tip Tommy Long on to the floor. Someone was throwing pellets of paper. Someone else was whistling. In a moment Mr Edwards, the Sunday school superintendent, would have to come in from next door to restore order, and Erica would be shamed for ever.

"I want someone to come and hold this picture up," she said loudly.

Elsie Tiddie stopped pinching Katie Brewer and Alfie left Tommy on the floor. Both made a rush for the picture and Elsie got it. Alfie tried to snatch at it, but Elsie wasn't having any of that.

"Oo, miss! She kicked me!" cried Alfie.

"Don't tell tales, Alfie," said Erica. Then quickly, before Alfie could retort, she added, "Yes, I dare say she did kick you, but it's not brave to tell on a girl. If you're good, you can hold up the next picture."

So Alfie sat down, and then all the other children sat down, too, and it was possible to get them listening. Erica pointed to the picture Elsie was holding.

"Who can tell me what that is?" she asked.

"A caterpillar!" chorused the class.

Erica nodded approvingly. She did not let on how relieved she was that they had recognized it. She and Cecily had spent a long time drawing and chalking that big caterpillar, but they hadn't been very happy about it. Chris said it looked more like a mouldy sausage.

"Now, who can tell me what happens to a caterpillar?"

There was dead silence until at last Tommy Long waved his hand. He was William Long's grandson and the brightest in the class.

"My grandad says they eat and eat until they burst!"

The class laughed loudly, but Erica frowned at them.

"Tommy is very nearly right," she said reprovingly. "They do eat and eat, but when they are big enough they shut themselves up in a sort of case, and then that's called a chrysalis. Come and show us *your* picture now, Alfie."

The chrysalis was rather better drawn than the caterpillar because Cecily and Erica had copied it out of a book. Alfie was so interested in it that he forgot at first to turn it round so that the others could see it. After puzzling over it he gave a smile of triumph.

"I seen things like this 'ere, Miss. I seen lots of 'em on the garden fence at home. Christles, did you say? I'll tell my dad. Only, there's not any caterpillars inside. I've squashed lots of 'em and there's nothing but juice."

"Chrysalises, not christles," said Erica, correcting him in what she thought was a superior sort of teacher's voice. "And you shouldn't squash things. It's cruel."

"I don't see that," argued Alfie. "My dad allus tells me to kill caterpillars 'cos they eats the cabbages, and these things is only caterpillars gone wrong."

"Not gone wrong," said Erica, glad to see a way out of the argument about being cruel. "A very wonderful change is going on inside the chrysalis; and when it's all ready, the chrysalis bursts open, just like Tommy says. Now, can anyone tell me what comes out?"

"Pigs, Miss," said Billy Barnes.

"That's silly," said Erica severely. "How could a little caterpillar change into a great big creature like a pig? Let someone else tell me."

The others started making wild guesses. They all knew in fact what caterpillars turned into, but the introduction of the unknown word "chrysalises" had confused them. So Erica unrolled her third picture and held it up. It was her masterpiece. It had started off to be an ordinary Cabbage White butterfly, but enthusiasm had run away with Cecily and her. The butterfly finished up with more colours than a Red Admiral, a Peacock and a Purple Emperor all put together. The class gave oohs and ahs of admiration. A little doll-faced girl jumped up from her boot-box and ran forward to kiss the picture. She kissed it over and over again.

"It's so pwetty," she lisped.

Erica didn't know what she should do. She thought Katie a

silly affected little thing, but after all it wasn't wrong for her to say the picture was pretty. Elsie Tiddie solved the problem for her. She got hold of the back of Katie's skirt and pulled hard. Katie sat back down on the boot-box with a bump.

"Don't act so daft! Look at your face, it's all over chalk."

Erica couldn't help feeling pleased that the situation had been dealt with. She told Katie in as kindly a way as she could to wipe her face. Elsie unpinned the bit of rag which had been pinned to the front of Katie's dress as a handkerchief and held it out for Katie to spit. Then she scrubbed her face clean with the rag and pinned it back on.

"Go on, Miss. Never you mind Katie. She can't help being a show-off."

Erica wondered if a good teacher ought to tell Elsie off for rudeness, but decided not; besides, she rather agreed with her. She went on with the lesson.

"Now we've learnt how a creeping caterpillar changes into a beautiful butterfly with wings," she said. "Tell me what great change will come to you and me one day. Yes, Billy. You may answer."

"Pigs, Miss," said Billy. He had not been listening at all. "Our old sow 'as ten little 'uns. Borned yesternight, they were. They 'as *such* tiny little eyes, Miss!"

"That's very interesting, Billy, but you haven't answered my question. Let's see if someone else can. What shall we all be one day if we're good?"

"A lady, Miss, what never 'as to do any work," suggested one of the Prudhoe twins hopefully.

"*Us* won't never be ladies," objected Alfie. "Us'll be men what smokes and comes 'ome full on a Saturday night. Yes, that's what I'll be, Miss. A real man what flings 'is money on the table and says it's all 'e's earned that week, swelp me Gawd."

"I hope you'll be a much better man than that when you grow up," said Erica, shaking her head. She was beginning to be afraid she'd never get the answer she wanted, and she gave the broadest hint she could. "What shall we all be when we die?"

"Worms," said Elsie in a matter of fact way.

"Worms will eat your body," agreed Erica, to a chorus of ughs and ohs of horror.

"They shan't eat mine," said Tommy fiercely. "I'll kitch 'em all and give 'em to the birds to eat."

"You couldn't kitch 'em all," stated Billy.

"I could so!"

Erica broke in hastily. If she didn't get the answer soon, the bell would go before she'd reached the point of the lesson.

"It doesn't matter if the worms do eat your body, Tommy. Your body is only like the caterpillar. When your body dies, your soul will fly away like the butterfly. You will be a lovely white angel with shiny wings and a crown."

The class considered this. They had more often been warned they would go to hell for being wicked than promised heaven if they were good. Heaven, they supposed, was for the good children in the Sunday tracts rather than for them.

"Shall us be allowed to play games?" asked Alfie.

"I ... " Erica hesitated. Cecily had not prepared her for this question. She decided to be honest. "I don't know, Alfie, but there will be no more pain."

"It's apples as gives us pains, our mam says," offered Billy. "Shall us have plenty to eat?"

"You won't need to eat, but you will have a harp and sing beautiful tunes and always be near to God."

"Then I don't want to be an angel," said Alfie firmly. "God be awful strict. He be allus keeping his eye on you, Miss, waiting to burn you up in hell."

"But, Alfie, if you were in heaven, you *couldn't* be burning in hell!"

Fortunately the bell went at this difficult theological point, and the lesson was over. Erica stood up feeling very shaky and hoped she wasn't going to cry. She found Elsie beside her.

"That was a real nice lesson," said Elsie, and sounded as though she meant it.

"I'll tell my dad about them christles," promised Billy. "He says I don't never listen in Sunday school, so now I'll show him."

"You'll tell Miss Cecily I was good, won't you?" said Alfie, last of all.

"Yes, I will, Alfie. I'm sorry it was only me this time."

"That's all right," said Alfie magnanimously. "You did it pretty well for a little 'un. But tell Miss Cecily to come back next week."

Cecily was sitting out of bed in her dressing-gown when Erica got back. She'd been given jelly and sponge cake for tea and had kept most of it for Erica as a reward.

"How did it go? Was Alfie good? Did Mr Edwards have to come in and keep order?"

"No, not once. He had to go into Letty's class, though. I heard Martha Prudhoe say so. And Alfie says I didn't do badly; but he wants you back next week."

"Thank you ever so much!" said Cecily, beaming with approval and with pleasure at knowing she was missed. "You *are* a dear to have done it. I knew you'd manage, but I'm sorry if you hated it."

Erica thought about the lesson. There had been bad moments, of course, but she had liked bits of it, too. The feeling of being the one sitting out in front, the one who knew – well, more or less – and who could help other people to know, was thrilling in its way. She suddenly laughed.

"As a matter of fact I didn't hate it. I didn't do it right, not the first time like that, but when I'm older I think I might like to teach. It's more difficult than I thought, but more interesting, too. I'm afraid I didn't really make them understand about our souls being like butterflies, though."

She paused, and then added more hopefully, "But at least Billy Barnes knows it's butterflies that come from chrysalises, not pigs. I suppose that's something!"

Chapter 11 · Homework by candlelight

On her twelfth birthday Cecily twisted her long fair hair into a loose knot on the top of her head and pinned it there with Alice's hairpins. Chris dared her to go down to drawing-room tea like that, and so she did. Mrs Heatherington-Hearnley and her son Edward, neither of them favourites of the young Stocks, had come to tea; they belonged to what Beatrice referred to as "one of the better families". Mrs Heatherington-Hearnley was large and over-dressed and even Beatrice admitted she was rather slow. Edward had just left Marlborough, where he seemed to have learnt nothing except to despise boys who hadn't been to Marlborough; he was waiting to go on to the army. He sat on the sofa and sucked the end of a gold-headed cane.

Beatrice welcomed the three children with her company smile, which got a little mixed up with a quick frown for Erica's untidy dress and for Chris letting the door bang. Then she caught sight of Cecily's hair.

"But, my dear, how charming! Did you invent the style

yourself? So few English girls have any natural feeling for doing their hair. Don't you think so, Mrs Heatherington-Hearnley?"

Mrs Heatherington-Hearnley said "Oh, quite" in a vague way, but Mr Edward stared.

"Most charming, eh, Miss Stock? I mean to say."

All through tea he tried to make conversation with Cecily. She gave him little help, just saying, "Yes" or "No" or "Is that so, Mr Edward?" Erica and Chris watched with growing amusement, and when the guests had gone Beatrice turned on them.

"So unmannerly to giggle and splutter into your teacups like that! Even those two Munter girls Cecily has grown so fond of do not laugh in that uncouth way."

"They would if they saw someone making sheep's eyes at Cecily the way Edward did," declared Chris.

"And Cecily wouldn't even talk to him!" added Erica happily. "She looked at him exactly as Perkins does if you give him cat's-meat when he has smelt fish in the house. Now, Cecily really was bad-mannered!"

"Nonsense," said Beatrice, quite red with annoyance. "Cecily was behaving very properly. A girl should have a great deal of reserve when she's admired by a nice young man."

"Edward is not a nice young man," said Cecily distinctly. "He is an idiot. Ugly, too. And he has a stupid laugh."

So then she was in trouble as well, and they were all sent off to the nursery, which Beatrice said was the right place for such silly giggling young children.

Upstairs, Cecily pulled out the hairpins and let her hair tumble about her shoulders. Then they played a noisy game of hunters and bears with Clare and Molly. Four got under the table growling, and the fifth was the noble hunter who came to shoot them and got eaten instead: very good mindless fun.

"Gracious, what a noise!" said Bessie, coming in with a pile of darning. "I'd have thought you were too old for that sort of game."

"We're not old at all. We're silly giggling young children. Beatie's just said so." With that Cecily threw the stick she'd been using for a gun violently at the wall and dashed out. Bessie continued searching through her work-box for the needle she wanted and paid no attention.

"What's the matter with her?" asked Erica.

"Growing up," said Bessie briefly. "You'll understand better when you're older."

"No, I shan't," contradicted Erica. "I'm never going to want silly idiots like that Edward goggling at me."

"Well, that's a good thing, Erica, because they won't. You're not the type."

Erica laughed as loudly as Chris at this; but that evening, when she went to bed, she put the candle on the dressing-table and stared for a long time at her reflection in the mirror. The sallow, oval face stared uncompromisingly back out of the dark glass. She saw dark, almond-shaped eyes, a too decided nose and a long firm mouth. She moved the candle this way and that, trying for a more flattering light, and the shadows flickered grotesquely across the mirrored face. She gathered up her silky dark hair in one hand and held it on top of her head; but the candle-lit face looked more pinched and sallow than ever with the softening hair scraped back. She scowled, and then suddenly burst out laughing. Immediately the mirrored eyes gleamed and the thin face softened into charm, but she was already turning away and did not notice. She blew out the candle and jumped into bed.

Downstairs Beatrice was playing the piano, a sad and complicated piece which floated up to the bedroom as something thin and far-away and soothing. Erica snuggled up comfortably with knees almost to her chin and her nightgown tucked round her feet. She pulled the bedclothes over her eyes, and her sleepy brain began weaving the story with which she often thought herself to sleep. Nothing much ever happened in the story, for she was always asleep too soon; but it did not matter much, since she was always the heroine. Or the hero – she was never quite sure. The lost heir to the kingdom, Prince Eric ... no, Princess Erica. That night she stood on a wind-swept cliff staring down at the great castle on the shore. A castle which was hers by right, though wrested from her by the foul usurper. It had belonged to her ancestors from time immemorial, and she knew every room and corner. She knew the secret entrance which was hidden beneath the sea except at the lowest ebb of the tide ... Now the magic shore was flooded with the light of a vast harvest moon. It shone into Erica's eyes ... so bright that it hurt ... brighter than any moon ...

And then it wasn't the moon at all, but the morning sun glittering in at her. Erica was out of bed and scrambling into her clothes almost before she was awake, for it was Monday morning and the beginning of term. Bessie had put out their school dresses – red-and-black checked wool with black sashes – with the famous red stockings which still weren't worn out. Their new black boots were very thick and sensible for winter.

"They make my feet look huge," complained Cecily.

"And heels!" said Erica. "I hate heels. You can't run in them."

"They're not really high. Rose Munter has a lovely pair of beige boots with proper high heels and little blue buttons. Beatie said they weren't suitable for school." She primmed her mouth. "She was quite right, of course."

"She meant too dear, and she bought these because they were cheaper. That's why they are so ugly." Erica slipped her foot in and grimaced. "And fit so badly, too."

"Beatie says shoes for five cost an awful lot. Perhaps she really didn't have enough money," said Cecily fair-mindedly.

"Catch her wearing clod-hoppers like these!" said Erica sarcastically.

Erica didn't really mind much about the boots. She was enjoying school and she would have worn herring-boxes like Clementine so long as they got her there.

After Assembly, Miss Grossard told everyone to sit down, for on the first day of the autumn term she read out all the girls' names and their new classes. Miss Traill's girls all hoped they were not going to stay, but one by one they heard their names and went off after Miss Traill. Erica found she was still sitting in her seat and looked round wildly; she could not think how she had come to miss her own name. However, Edie was still in her seat, too, as well as Millie Dewar, whose father kept the grocer's shop near the cathedral.

Then Miss Grossard read out Miss Grant's class; the twenty names included Edie Summers, Millie Dewar and Cecily and Erica Stock. They marched to their new classroom, where the line broke up suddenly as they all made a rush to occupy the desks they wanted; all except Erica, who didn't quite realize what had happened.

"Sit down, everyone," said Miss Grant.

They stopped talking and sat down at once. In Miss Traill's class you obeyed or not, as the fancy took you. Erica slipped hastily into the nearest empty desk.

"And now I want the girls from Miss Traill's class to stand up so that we can get to know them. I want you to be helpful to them in case they find the work difficult at first."

At last Erica understood. She had jumped a whole class and caught up with Cecily in one of the best forms in the school. Miss Grant was handsome and amusing and quite awe-inspiringly clever, and she had been to Oxford and was a Bachelor of Arts! Erica's thoughts were still in a whirl and she found she had missed the beginning of the timetable Miss Grant was dictating. Latin and Geometry and Algebra and Literature – subjects whose scope she hardly knew and whose names she certainly couldn't spell. She looked timidly round at the others. They were mostly eleven and twelve years old – no older than Cecily if she had stopped to think – but they seemed alarmingly grown-up with their skirts to their ankles and their loud, assured voices.

At the mid-morning break the new girls stood awkwardly together in the garden, watching the others shyly but not liking to join any of the knots of girls unasked. Erica began to eye the yellow leaves fluttering down from the poplars.

"Let's catch Happy Months," she suggested.

"They'll think it babyish," said Edie, but Millie said she didn't care, and they started to leap after the falling leaves. It wasn't easy in the erratic breeze.

"What are you playing?" asked Moira McKechnie, the dignified class prefect.

"Happy Months," panted Erica. "One happy month next year for every leaf you catch before it touches the ground."

She missed a leaf and it was neatly fielded by Moira herself.

In a moment Moira was racing after another, dignity forgotten, and the whole class were soon leaping into the air and cannoning into each other. Miss Grant, crossing the garden with a pile of exercise books, stopped to watch and was almost knocked over by Erica, dashing head down after a low-flying leaf.

They rushed round to see if Miss Grant was all right and to pick up her exercise books; they all wanted to carry them to the staff-room. Miss Grant smiled her slow and charming smile.

"Thank you, I am unhurt. Erica Stock shall carry the books for me ... as a punishment."

"I don't call that much of a punishment," said Moira.

"Perhaps Erica does; she didn't offer to carry them. I think she wants to finish collecting her happy months."

"Oh, no!" stammered Erica hastily. "I mean, I didn't ask because I thought it would be cheek. I mean, being new."

Miss Grant laughed and handed her the pile. They walked in silence across the autumn garden, Miss Grant thinking her own thoughts and Erica turning great things over in her mind, too.

"My brother Chris means to go to Oxford and get his degree," she said suddenly. "Of course, it's easy for him; he's a boy. Anyway, he's terrifically clever, much more than me."

Miss Grant looked down at her for a moment but said nothing.

"I must be *fairly* clever, mustn't I?" said Erica, made anxious by the glance. "They wouldn't have put me – I mean, not swanking – they wouldn't have put me in your class if I was completely stupid, would they?"

"No, I don't suppose you're completely stupid," said Miss Grant with a slight smile. "What then?"

"Well, I was wondering ... " Erica hesitated, and then brought it out with a rush. "Do you think I could get a degree, too?"

To her relief Miss Grant took it seriously.

"It might be a bit of a struggle, Erica. Nearly all university teachers are men, and many are very much against women students. It's getting easier, though, and I really don't see why you shouldn't manage, if you are prepared to work, and if ... "

"Oh, I'd work all right," interrupted Erica. "I like work."

"And if your family will find the money to pay for you," continued Miss Grant. "Not all families are as ready to pay for a girl's education as for a boy's, and scholarships for girls have hardly been thought of yet."

"Oh," said Erica, dampened. She remembered that money *was* sometimes short at home anyway. Another thought struck her and she cheered up. "There's another seven years at least before I'll be ready to go to university, isn't there? I'll worry about the money then!"

They had reached the staff-room, and Erica handed Miss Grant her books and ran back. The others were still catching leaves in the sunshine, and it seemed incredible that so little time had gone by.

"Come along!" called Millie. "You haven't very long to catch your twelve."

Erica bounded forward. "Not that it matters," she thought to herself. "I don't need leaves. I'm going to be happy anyway."

She often woke early in the morning and got up and lit her candle to do her homework in her bedroom, wrapped in the eiderdown. Cecily, who had done all hers the night before, would mutter sleepily and turn over to shut the light from her eyes. Erica worked alone in the little circle of candle-light until the winter sun rose and it was time to dress. Then there was breakfast of hot scones and jam and milk. That was the year the milk was diluted with hot water because Beatrice had been impressed by an earnest book on nutrition, which said that milk was indigestible if it wasn't watered down a bit. Bessie sniffed and said privately that her mother didn't hold with such fads and no more did she. Erica quite liked the tepid chalky drink; you had to drink more, but it helped the scones down faster, which left more time for finding all the things she had lost, before tearing down the path after Cecily and Chris. Before school there were noisy scenes in the school garden, using the old swings on the tree or playing Prisoners' Base.

In the dinner-hour they made quick visits to other girls'

homes. They might visit Millie's mother behind the shop, or the mother of Myfanwy Rees at the small dairy where there was a china swan in the window and a real cock crowing in the yard at the back. If there was time, they might go all the way to the level-crossing to admire Lily Hodgson's new baby sister and to watch her father swing open the crossing gates to let the express thunder by. Erica chattered away about her friends when she was back at home, and told about the sign over the door at the dairy with S.P.Q.R. on it. Mr Rees said it meant, "Small Profits, Quick Returns". Erica was proud of this inside information about business life.

"I don't think I'd talk so much about Lily and Myfanwy when Beatie is about," said Cecily.

"And why not?" Erica was truculent.

"Beatie doesn't like us to be too close friends with shop-keepers' daughters."

"Well, I'm not a snob, even if you are."

"You know I'm not a snob," said Cecily. "But there's no point in going out of your way to annoy Beatie."

Erica wouldn't listen to her, and said proudly that she had no intention of being deceitful. Fortunately, nothing awkward did happen and she wasn't put to the test.

The work at school was fairly hard, but work was what you expected there. Erica seldom thought about lessons but just did them as they came along. She did them well, too, for she hadn't forgotten her talk with Miss Grant. Her first term's report was good enough to make Beatrice put aside a painting and read it right through.

"I always knew you couldn't be such a scatter-brain as you seemed, Erica," she said as she read. It was a back to front sort of compliment, but it was a compliment. Erica watched a little anxiously as Beatrice came to the last lines of the report.

" ... So we are pleased to find evidence of an acute and inquiring mind, even though her written work is often marred by carelessness. She must pay attention to her spelling. *Some approximation to the accepted spelling of proper names is necessary in a candidate for higher education.*"

Beatrice laughed, in a warm and genuinely amused way; she asked just what sort of higher education Appleby Hall was planning for her. Erica was so pleased that she blurted out her ambitions just as though her step-sister was the best friend she had in the world. She felt a qualm after she had done so, but Beatrice remained friendly and interested.

"Don't you think girls can have as good brains as boys?" asked Erica shyly. "It *is* nonsense, isn't it, that girls can't study as well as boys?"

"Haven't I always said so?" said Beatrice. "I had to fight for my own education in music. The number of people who tried to tell me that no woman's brain could stand the regular application and competitive examinations! I told my mother it was complete rubbish! I've more skill in art and music than nine out of ten men I meet."

"I haven't!" said Erica. "The only thing I can draw is boxes and the back view of cats!"

Beatrice gave her friendly laugh, and Erica was encouraged to go on.

"But I *can* get top marks in English and things, and I thought ... well, Miss Grant ... well, she doesn't see why I shouldn't get a degree like Chris in the end. There are colleges for women now. Only, she said most families won't find the money to send a girl to college."

"These school teachers!" said Beatrice with a touch of scorn, though she was still in a good mood. "They cannot imagine a family with minds above money. Does this Miss Grant of yours think you are the child of some uncultured tradesman or shopkeeper?"

Erica hesitated. It was so unusual to have her step-sister so closely interested in her, but she wished she wouldn't speak like that about Miss Grant. Beatrice swept on without noticing.

"How delightful if I had a sister as well as a brother at Oxford! May I come and visit you there?"

For a moment it was the realization of Erica's old dream of a loving, understanding sister. Her go-to-sleep story that night was not of Princess Erica. It was of Miss Erica Stock welcoming her sister to Oxford against a vague background of ancient buildings. (They had to be vague, for she had never been to Oxford or Cambridge either.) There was an admiring buzz of conversation from the assembled students. "That's Erica Stock, B.A. That elegant lady is her sister, the authoress and painter and singer, you know." Of course Erica Stock's sister would be someone special. Lucky Erica! Clever Erica! And Erica drifted off happily.

Chapter 12 · The baroness

The next day was the beginning of the Christmas holidays. Erica came down to breakfast full of smiles and was greeted by a smiling Beatrice. The two of them actually had a long and amiable discussion about decorating the church for the festival, without Erica being rude or Beatrice nagging. It seemed like the beginning of better times, and the friendliness lasted throughout the holiday. For one thing, Beatrice was in a good humour because her great friend the Baroness von Düring was coming to stay. The baroness had once been her childhood friend, with not much to recommend her but a pretty face and a great admiration for clever Beatrice Stock. Then she had married an elderly German, who had unexpectedly fallen heir to his cousin's title. She had at once risen from "poor Eliza Carter" to "my dear friend, the baroness". Now she lived in a romantic castle in Thuringia in central Germany.

Such a baroness, too! Such silk dresses, and such a gush of perfume when she entered a room! Such charming ways, too –

and such laziness! The whole family were hardly enough to run her errands. Even Erica's tireless feet faltered at the end of a day of dancing attendance on her. If she merely wanted to sew on a button, someone had to find the button and the thread and the needle, and hover round as she sewed in case there was anything else to fetch. She never got up for breakfast, and Alice was not best pleased at having to light fires in her bedroom and carry a tray up and down each morning. Erica offered to do it, but she wasn't to be trusted with the best Worcester breakfast china. But she would follow behind Alice, for there was often some extra little thing which the baroness felt she would just fancy. Then Erica would dash downstairs for it and be back in no time. The baroness would thank her charmingly and perhaps invite her to stay and chat while she ate.

Erica wanted nothing better. She was fascinated by the baroness, though no one could understand quite why.

"All that lace underwear, and the silk petticoats you go on about!" protested Alice. "Why, they aren't even clean! Black with dirt round the bottom edge, believe you me!"

"They can't help getting a bit dirty," said Erica defensively. "They're so beautifully long they have to trail in the dust behind her. Like a queen's train. I expect, if we knew, the bottom of the Queen's dresses get pretty dirty!"

"Her room smells," said Cecily roundly.

"I think it smells lovely," said Erica. "Almost as good as a hot-house. I love it."

She did love the change. The other bedrooms in the vicarage smelled of polish and cold winter air, for their windows were hygienically open top and bottom. Baroness von Düring hated draughts and never had a window open or let in even a hint of air to blow away the mixed smells of powder and eau de cologne, bath salts and scent, and more beside.

"A smell to hide a smell," said Alice crudely, but Erica would not allow that it was so.

"Does she use rouge?" asked Clare in hushed tones. "Bessie says she does."

But Erica, who was usually famous for letting things out, managed to say nothing at all.

Erica was learning a lot from the baroness, including some discretion. Beatrice had preached to her repeatedly about tact and things that "weren't done", and Erica had shrugged it off as hypocrisy. The baroness merely made it charmingly obvious that she trusted Erica, as one woman to another, not to give the game away. Erica fell for it completely, and would have suffered anything rather than hint at what she had seen. It was a real self-sacrifice, too, for it would have been very good fun to whisper the truth and startle friends like the Munter girls or Letty. For there were no two ways about it – the baroness painted her face. Erica had watched, and she had even held up the mirror for her. The first time she had undoubtedly been taken aback. The baroness had looked up and seen the dark eyes staring at her in curiosity.

"My dear girl! Surely you have seen someone make up their face before?"

Erica shook her head wordlessly. Ladies in Woodhuckle never even used powder – or if they did they kept it the darkest secret. Beatrice had a small enamelled box of dusty rounds of paper with which she took the shine off her nose if need be. But she called them *papiers poudrés* and did not admit that the French word had anything to do with powder.

The baroness had smiled at Erica a little maliciously. "Ah, yes ... I too thought I should never come to it. When I was your age I was shocked, just as you are."

"No ... " began Erica, and stopped.

"Well, perhaps not shocked," conceded the baroness. "But very sure you would not do such a thing yourself."

"I don't suppose I'd ever bother," said Erica frankly. "It takes so long, and I'd never be pretty, not like you and Cecily."

The baroness put down her hand-mirror and for once actually paid attention to someone else's face. Erica found herself blushing under the appraising stare.

"No," said the baroness slowly. "No, you're not pretty, but there's something about you ... Even if you don't grow prettier ... yes, I think you will always find a few people who prefer your sort of plainness, who will turn from Cecily to smile at you."

Erica shrugged her shoulders and laughed, though secretly hoping to hear more. However, the baroness was once more absorbed in her own face. She had become bored with Erica and soon sweetly dismissed her.

Erica went downstairs unresentfully, having no illusions about the baroness's attitude towards her. She would be sent for when she could be useful, and sent away again when no longer needed.

"She's a beastly, selfish cat!" said Chris, indignant at seeing his sister put upon. "Why on earth do you run about for her? She isn't even grateful. She calls you a funny little thing, and goes on raving about Cecily."

"Don't I know it!" said Erica with a giggle. "She thinks Cecily is the prettiest and best brought up English girl she's ever seen, and she's going to tell her son Harry to marry her!"

Chris didn't believe her, but it was true. The baroness had discussed it quite seriously with Erica, not seeming to think it an unsuitable subject for a child of eleven. That was one thing Erica liked about her. She spoke so casually and openly about things that Beatrice and Mrs Upthorpe only whispered about: things like making up your face for men to think you pretty, or planning to marry someone rich because that was more comfortable than being poor. Such talk was an eye-opener to vicarage-bred Erica. Though she knew she disapproved strongly, she was undoubtedly fascinated. It was like coming suddenly on a window which looked out on a landscape she never knew existed.

Wanting to know more about the ways of this strange new world, she asked what would happen if Harry decided that he didn't wish to marry Cecily. The baroness said that no one could be forced, but she rather thought her son would be relieved to have a good-looking and nice-mannered wife found for him without being put to too much trouble. So Erica asked what would happen if Cecily was unwilling. The baroness smiled at that.

"My dear Erica! Harry will inherit the title and the castle as well as a very respectable income. I do not think he need fear that many young ladies will turn all that down."

Erica said she was sure Cecily would never do anything she didn't think right.

"Then doubtless she would decide it was right to marry so good a catch," said the baroness with a rather hard little laugh.

The baroness stayed a long time after Christmas, and the new term had begun before she began to prepare for her return to Germany. Erica spent all of a weekend helping. She brought dresses from the cupboard and underclothes from the drawers, and toiled up and down stairs finding suitable paper to wrap them. She ran to Mrs Tiddie's to match small buttons. She helped to pack and unpack and then repack again, till at last all was ready and the baroness was leaving. She kissed Erica goodbye and added that she must come and stay in her castle one day. Erica looked at her with glowing eyes, for she had taken it into her head that the castle in Thuringia must be the most romantic place imaginable – probably in a lonely mountain forest and high above the looming gorge of a thunderous river. Even Prince Eric wouldn't have sneered at it.

The school year was running cheerfully on, with Erica continuing to do well and enjoy herself too. But there was a nasty episode at home at the end of the spring holiday when the puppy fell ill. He belonged to the family and they thought him a dear, though he kept them in their place by firmly preferring the people he knew in the kitchen, being always ready to eat anything that was going. One day, though, he disgraced himself by being sick in the hall. After that he crawled about shivering, with his hind legs dragging. In the end, Alice wrapped him in a piece of blanket and took him down to her brother at the smithy who was good with animals, and he began to recover slowly.

On the second day of the summer term Miss Grossard announced that all girls should provide themselves with indoor slippers which had low heels. It was to do with high heels being bad for growing feet or growing backs or something; but Cecily and Erica were too alarmed to listen properly. Beatrice had only just bought them indoor slippers with high heels, on an impulse about introducing them to fashion, and had then complained strongly about the cost. Things were going to be difficult.

They were. When the two of them told Beatrice, she got on her high horse and said Miss Grossard was making a fuss about nothing. Their new slippers were good-looking and entirely proper things to wear, and they were to go on wearing them. In a week or two almost everyone had low-heeled slippers and it was announced that anyone continuing to be without them would be given "order marks".

"Whatever shall we do?" asked Cecily.

"We can't do anything," said Erica, "except just get order marks."

So when Monday came they wore their high-heeled slippers and got order marks. These weren't anything new to Erica, but Cecily sat through the class with bowed head and pale cheeks. That afternoon, back at home, they both asked Beatrice again and tried to make her understand, but Beatrice wouldn't listen.

"Couldn't you even get Cecily a pair?" begged Erica. "She does mind dreadfully about the order marks." Beatrice said it would be quite unacceptable, and when Erica tried to press her, she cut her short.

"I haven't time to argue. If I don't finish this vase quickly, the plaster will be too dry."

They were in the downstairs room where Beatrice was occupied with her latest craze. She bought enormous pottery vases and decorated them with white plaster garlands of leaves and fruit and flowers and great swags of plaster drapery. Like all Beatrice's work, they were beautifully done. Erica had admired them, but now she scowled.

"If you didn't buy so many vases, you could get Cecily some slippers!"

"How dare you!" Beatrice flushed scarlet. "I've never heard such impertinence! If that's the sort of manners you learn at school, I'm sorry I ever sent you there. You and Cecily are growing shockingly wild. The girls you meet must be a very common class!"

"They're not common!" Erica was shouting back, oblivious of the open door. "They're nice girls! And how can I be growing wild when you always said I was wild before I went to school? You're unfair and beastly and ... "

There would have been a lot more, but just then there was the sound of someone coming in the back of the house. It was Alice's brother Fred bringing back Jo. Mr Stock happened to come out of his study along the corridor at the same moment.

"Here he is then," said Fred, nodding at the puppy. "I think he'll do now all right. Very thin, o' course, and nervy like, but he'll plump up."

"What do you think was the matter, Fred?" asked the vicar.

"Dunno for certain, but it looked to me as though he'd been eating lead paint. Anyone been doing any painting lately?"

"No," said Mr Stock, "not round the vicarage."

Fred was looking at one of the vases on the floor in a dark corner of the corridor. Half the plaster fruit and flowers were gone at the back, and if you looked more closely, there were small teeth-marks. Jo had evidently developed a taste for the plaster decoration.

"Oh," said Beatrice, following Fred's gaze. "But I had no idea that plaster had lead in it."

"Ah. A lot o' them fancy plasters is stiff with lead," said Fred knowledgeably. "Dangerous, I call it. I wouldn't use them myself."

Beatrice managed to thank him cordially for all he had done for Jo, but she was distinctly ruffled to think that the children would consider her responsible for Jo's illness. Her temper was not improved at supper that evening when she found Clare's eyes on her in a long, long look of sad reproach.

Next morning at school, Cecily in desperation went and knocked at Miss Grossard's door. Miss Grossard's eyebrows rose when she saw that Cecily was still in high-heeled slippers.

"Oh please, Miss Grossard, I can't help it! I haven't any others, and my step-sister says I must go on wearing these because they're nearly new. *Please* may we go on wearing these slippers? I don't want order marks!"

Miss Grossard was silent for a long moment. "I will write to your step-sister and ask her to let me know what the difficulty is," she said at last.

"Thank you," said Cecily in a small voice and hoped she sounded grateful.

Cecily took Miss Grossard's letter home that evening, but she had little hope. Erica, on the other hand, had faith in Miss Grossard and was sure everything would now be all right. She gave Mrs Upthorpe, who had come to call, a lively description of an excitement they had had that day at school. Miss Grossard had allowed Myfanwy Rees from the dairy to bring her baby sister to school so that Mr and Mrs Rees could join the special excursion train trip to Bournemouth. And only think, they had never had a holiday from the shop since they had been married fifteen years before! Mrs Upthorpe tut-tutted in a kindly way and hoped the poor things had enjoyed their outing. Beatrice listened in silence. Erica did not notice her silence, any more than she noticed Cecily's frantic signals to her to be quiet about the dairy family.

The next day Beatrice drove into Gloucester. She went in the glory of her new Berlin silk and a black mantle with a fringe six inches deep. She wore a straw hat with row upon row of purple violets nestling among black velvet leaves. Miss Grossard happened to see the carriage drive up with William Long perched on the high iron seat; and she saw Miss Stock get out and adjust her silk gloves and ivory-handled umbrella. Till then she had been expecting to compromise. She was a fair-minded woman, and she knew some clergymen might find even a small extra expense difficult. Miss Stock's appearance put the thought out of her mind.

It was a meeting of rival queens, but it lasted only about five minutes. Nobody ever learnt exactly what was said, but at the end of the exchange Miss Stock swept downstairs to her carriage somewhat flushed. Miss Grossard's table bell rang sharply, and Prissy Underwood, as monitor for the day, was sent with a message to Miss Grant.

"Cecily! Erica!" Miss Grant's calm voice passed on Prissy's flurried message. "Change your shoes and collect your hats and coats. Your sister is driving you home."

They put on their outdoor things and happily said goodbye; it was rather fun to go home early for once. Outside, Beatrice was sitting bolt upright in the carriage with an expression of acute distaste on her face, ignoring the small children of the street who were crowding round the carriage, trying to pat the horse and jumping off and on the step.

"Get in at once!" said Beatrice. "I never saw such dirty, common children!"

They scrambled in. Cecily, not understanding which children Beatrice was referring to, laughed and said, "They're always hanging about outside the school, hoping to get a sweet or something."

That evening Beatrice came into the room upstairs and told Cecily and Erica that they would not be going back to Appleby Hall. The two girls had been happily sitting reading, and they jumped to their feet in dismay, half thinking they must have misheard.

"Why?" gasped Erica. "What for?"

For a moment it looked as if Beatrice was not even going to explain, since she was turning to the door. She seemed to think better of it and came back into the room.

"I had no idea what the school was really like. You have been mixing with girls from any sort of home, and some of the teachers are most unladylike. As bad manners are the chief things you seem to have learnt there, you will have to have lessons at home in future."

There was a silence, while Beatrice fidgeted with the bracelet on her wrist in a would-be casual way and waited for them to say something. They neither spoke nor moved.

"Well, if you have nothing to say ... " Beatrice spoke angrily, knowing she was acting unforgivably but unable to admit it.

"But you were so pleased I was doing well." Erica found her voice at last. "You said girls should be ... be educated just as much as boys. You said ... "

"My dear Erica, I know very well what I have said without you telling me. No more argument, please. Your father and I both think you will be able to do better at home."

Erica took a step towards her, and then another. She opened her mouth to speak, but the words choked her.

"You ... you ... "

She turned and rushed out of the room, almost colliding

with Bessie, who was just coming in. Down the long dark passage she ran, and into her own room. She flung herself on her bed and sobbed.

Cecily found her there in a forlorn heap on the counterpane at bed-time. When Cecily came in, she woke up and blinked in the candle-light.

"What can we do?" she asked. Cecily shook her head; she had been crying herself.

"We'll just have to hope it isn't Miss Pringle again."

"I don't mind who it is," said Erica sullenly. "I'm not even going to try to learn if I can't go to school." She started to cry again. "I can't *bear* to think of Edie and Millie and everyone having fun, and me not there. I can't *bear* it." She added without much hope, "Perhaps Daddy will make Beatrice change her mind."

"He won't even try," said Cecily gloomily. "He never interferes with what she decides for us. He can't know what's best for girls, she says, and he believes her." This was very unfair and not even true, but Cecily was very depressed indeed.

Chapter 13 · The front stairs

Although nearly a year had passed since the two girls were taken away from their school, Erica still woke early from force of habit despite the fact that there was no longer homework to finish. One morning, when she was nearly twelve, she woke up as usual when the drawing-room clock beneath her struck six. There were two empty hours to get through before breakfast. She sat up in bed and looked hopefully out of the window. It was raining, and it must have been raining for hours, for the garden was sodden and the drive full of puddles. A missel thrush was hopping among them with a snail in his beak. She knew where he was going. There was one particular flagstone on the edge of the drive where there were always fragments of snail shells. The thrush stopped by it and began his tap-tapping. She knew it would go relentlessly on until the shell broke; it was a sound which she hated more than most. She got a book out from under her pillow, pulled the bedclothes tight round her ears and began to read. She became so absorbed she did not hear Bessie come upstairs or Cecily at last heaving herself out of bed. In fact the first thing she noticed was that she was being roughly shaken by Bessie.

"Get up at once, you lazy thing!"

Something had gone very wrong with Bessie these last few weeks. She no longer sang about the house and she seldom smiled. She had sharp words for the slightest wrong-doing, and Erica wasn't the only one to resent it.

"I don't see why I should get up just to please you," she said now. "There's plenty of time before breakfast." She tried to go on reading, but Bessie whipped the book away with one hand and pulled the bedclothes off with the other.

"You get up when you're told, and go and help your sisters dress. I haven't time for their tantrums this morning."

Erica picked up her clothes and stalked past her into what they still called the night nursery. Clare was sitting on the cold floor in her nightdress crying, and Molly, wearing nothing at all, was lying on the bed drumming her heels.

"Shan't! Shan't! Shan't!" she was screaming non-stop.

"What shan't you?" asked Erica with mild interest.

But Molly had forgotten what had set her off. She only knew the world was wrong and she hated it.

"Shan't tell you! Shan't do anything! Shan't! Shan't!"

"Tell you what," said Erica. "Let's play shipwrecks."

Clare stopped crying and Molly's heels slowed and stopped too. Shipwrecks had the charm of the utterly forbidden, ever since Clare had fallen off a table and sprained her ankle playing it.

"We'll get into trouble," said Molly.

"Only me," said Erica, "because I'm older and they'll say I made you do it. Shut your eyes." She swept up her sisters' clothes and began to scatter them around the room, anywhere which was high or difficult to reach.

"*All* the floor is sea," she announced. "And any shipwrecked mariner who puts even a toe in the sea has to take off whatever they put on last and give it to me to hide somewhere else."

She had spread the clothes about with ingenuity. To get her vest Molly had to leap from her own bed to Clare's and then on to the table, and from there to a chair which she had to rock across the room till she could reach up from it to the top of the wardrobe. Clare's petticoat was on the curtain rail, and she had to leap from the end of Molly's bed on to a chair and try to snatch the petticoat as she jumped. Soon the room which had re-echoed with crying was full of laughter which grew louder and louder until the door suddenly opened and Beatrice walked in.

"Erica! I might have known. Go back to your room!"

So Erica went and dressed and started to go downstairs, but it was definitely not her day. Half way down she was stopped short by a wrathful shout from Bessie.

"Back stairs, Miss Erica! How many times have you been told, not the front stairs!"

So she had ignominiously to go back upstairs, along the corridor and down the other stairs. The rules, which were sometimes confusing, seemed to have become very strict. Children must always use the back stairs, except on Sundays when they were on *no* account to use them because their noisy feet disturbed their father resting in his study near by between services.

Erica looked forward with no enthusiasm at all to the lessons with Miss Pringle which began not long after breakfast. Miss Pringle had never been an interesting teacher, and she seemed to the girls duller than ever since they had been to Appleby Hall and found what lessons could be like. Besides, she now had to teach Clare and Molly. Clare was clever for her eight years, while Molly was still fighting b-a-t, *bat* and c-a-t, *cat*. Miss Pringle often gave the older ones long sums to do to keep them occupied while she dealt with these two. Cecily just steadily got them right, but Erica's calculations went on for pages and got further away from the answer. When Erica was very young, her mother had begun to teach her arithmetic with the help of a box of coloured Sonnenschein Squares. There were squares for units and rows of squares for tens and large squares for hundreds, and they were fun. She was beginning to understand when her mother fell ill and died; and now nobody seemed to be able to get her to grasp the idea of sums at all. Certainly Miss Pringle couldn't.

On that particular wet day the work seemed not much

flatter or more interesting than usual. But it was Wednesday, when the two of them spent an hour with their father learning French. They loved him very much, but they had to admit that as a teacher he was as uninspired as Miss Pringle. He gave them a very detailed French Grammar, and with the most friendly affection he got them to learn off a page a day by heart, with every rule word for word, and the exceptions to the rules in the small print at the bottom of the page as well. His French seemed to have very little to do with the French they had met at school. There, on the very day Beatrice had taken them away, they had just begun a new book. On the first page there had been a bright picture of a cart with a wheel off, and under it the words, *Un accident est-il arrivé à la charrette?* – Has an accident happened to the cart? Erica, ploughing through lists of irregular verbs, thought wistfully of that cart and wondered if she would ever know.

At the end of the morning, feeling hungry, she rushed upstairs to wash and was sitting at table immediately after the bell was rung. But dinner was late; or at least Alice brought it in on time, but Beatrice sent a message to say she must finish a drawing of some roses while the light was right and wouldn't be a minute. Their father sent the roast away and they looked at the tablecloth, crumbling bits of bread and fiddling with their knives and forks. At last, about twenty-five minutes late, there was a click of heels and Beatrice came in, full of smiling apologies.

"I'm so sorry; you must be starving. Ring the bell, Clare dear, you're nearest." But the vicar looked from her smiling face to his sullen children, and was suddenly angry.

"Beatrice, it is twenty-five minutes past one. Yesterday it was nearly as late, and the other day it was half-past one. It is inconsiderate to me and unkind to your sisters."

Two spots of bright colour – small warning flags of anger – showed in Beatrice's cheeks, and the children watched apprehensively. Clare, who was terrified of rows, clung to the bell, too alarmed to ring it.

"Really, Papa! I'm sure you exaggerate! I've never kept you waiting as long as half an hour, have I, darlings?" It was an unwise remark. The older ones kept silent, but Molly was too young to be careful, and too hungry.

"Yes, you do keep us waiting," she retorted. "Sometimes you're hours and hours late, and I'm always hungry. Why can't you begin your painting earlier and then you can finish earlier?"

Beatrice was too astonished to answer for a moment, and suddenly her father laughed.

"Out of the mouths of babes and sucklings! Beatie, give that child some food quickly as a reward! She's hit the nail squarely on the head. Isn't it what I'm always saying? Anyone can finish a job, but it's a wise workman who can begin on time!"

Beatrice just managed to control her temper. She shrugged her shoulders and gave a half-smile. "Clare," she said sharply, "haven't you rung that bell? What a child you are for wasting time!"

Everyone breathed again, and Alice came back with the roast.

Afterwards the four girls sat listlessly about upstairs. The rain had come sheeting down again, and no one had the energy to put on coats and goloshes and go out. They sat there and wished something would happen.

"Not that anything ever does happen in this house," said Cecily.

"Except horrible things," said Erica. She wasn't usually as peevish, but she often did feel queasy and at odds with the world these days. Old Mrs Daviot observed her pinched and sallow looks and told Beatrice authoritatively to put her on Parrish's Food. So Beatrice did, but it didn't seem to do a great deal of good.

The next day something horrible really did happen. The first they knew of it was the sound of crying from the kitchen. It was so loud that the family heard it as they sat at breakfast.

"Is that *Bessie* crying?" asked Beatrice in great surprise. "Is she ill?"

"It's her young man," explained Alice. "He's gone and got married."

"Married?" exclaimed the vicar. "But Bessie has been discussing the calling of the banns with me. He can't be married."

But he was. A young widow in Ireland had made a dead set at the handsome corporal, and George had not had the strength of mind to resist her or to tell Bessie what had happened. He let three months go by in silence, and that was why the children had been finding Bessie's temper so unusually sharp. Then a letter had come in the post to say he was now married.

"You're well out of a bad bargain," said Sarah in robust consolation. "Better find him out before marriage than after it's too late."

Bessie only cried louder. She didn't want to find him out at all. She had lost more than her dream of a brave and noble soldier. Being Bessie, she had been putting all her generous loyalty and ingenuity into planning for the future she now would not see. Everybody was sorry for Bessie and angry at George. Mr Stock went to fetch her mother and said that of course she must not think of coming back to work until she felt she could. So Mrs Hunt took Bessie home, and Alice took her place with the children for the time being.

It was very terrible, but perhaps a bit romantic as well. They talked of it in whispers and privately gave themselves airs over their friends who didn't have someone who had been jilted. They went and peeped at George's cross-stitch picture and wondered what would happen to it. There was even a pleasure in thinking out the kind things they might say to Bessie when she came back, to show that they cared.

But when Bessie did come back, they didn't have the courage to say any of them. It didn't seem to be their Bessie at all. Her laugh was gone, and her colour was gone and – most disconcerting of all – her voice was gone, and she could only speak in a whisper. Beatrice explained it was the shock, and that her voice would return when she was happier. They were to pretend not to notice. But that was difficult, and the more they tried to be ordinary with Bessie and not mention George and the things that interested them, the more they found there wasn't anything at all they could say.

Besides, Bessie often didn't seem to be listening, or was impatient and irritable. Clare and Molly would run away, and that made Bessie crosser because she had no voice to call them back. Erica began to keep out of her way, though she ought to have known from her own experience that bad temper and unhappiness went together. But Erica was the one who was missing the old Bessie most, and she grew irritable herself and started to think she was ill-used.

One afternoon about three months later she was sitting hunched up in the rocking-chair feeling particularly ill-used. Chris had gone off with his friends and Cecily was getting ready to go to tea with Rose Munter, who hadn't invited Erica. Clare and Molly were laughing in the passage, and Erica scowled at the closed door. Clare opened the door and looked in, but went away again.

"Let's not go in there," Erica heard her whisper to Molly. "She'd want to know what we're doing."

"Oh yes," said Molly. "Let's keep it a secret."

Erica thought how selfish they were to keep secrets, and how unkind of Cecily to go to tea without her and cruel of Chris to forget her. The door opened once more, and this time it was Alice come to ask where something was. Erica tried to answer her, but the sob in her throat prevented her.

"Why, Miss Erica, I do believe that black dog's on your shoulders again!" Erica looked away. Jokes about black dogs were for babies.

"Poor Erica!" said Alice in a kind voice. "Here, let me take him off for you." Alice crossed the room swiftly, made as though to lift the imaginary creature off her and pretended to throw him up the chimney. "There you are! There's the horrid beast gone! Mind it doesn't come back!" She smiled at Erica's astonished face and was gone.

When Alice had left, Erica sat up with a very startled expression. She knew perfectly well there wasn't a black dog. And yet her shoulders, which had been quite aching with her misery, now felt light and free. It was ridiculous; quite ridiculous. Before she could think any more, she heard Chris's voice under the window.

"Erica! Come quickly, we want you."

"Coming!" she called, and ran joyfully downstairs to the garden.

Clare and Molly came back into the room after she had gone. No wonder they wanted to hug their secret to themselves, for it was a great project they had in mind. After listening to the annual Missionary Sermon, they had decided they were going to convert the world. They had realized they were perhaps a little young to achieve this all at once, and they had decided to get some practice by converting the village first.

"How shall we do it?" asked Molly. She always expected Clare to produce the ideas, though she was often bolder in carrying them out.

"We'll colour all those Texts that Miss Emmeline gave us, and then we'll drop them in different places for people to pick up."

"How will that help?" asked Molly, willing but puzzled.

"Why, don't you see? Someone might be just walking along. Quite a wicked person who had never thought about God or anything like that." Clare's blue eyes glowed with fervour; she was beginning to forget this wasn't just a story she was making up. She could almost *see* the wrong-doer swaggering along, twirling his cane and fingering his black moustache. Clare had gathered that villains tended to have canes and black moustaches. "And then, you see, he'll see a *charming* picture lying on the ground!"

"Yes, because I'll paint it really beautiful!" agreed Molly.

"And he'll pick it up," went on Clare. "He'll pick it up and look at it, and then he'll see the Text and it will make him think about his sins for the first time in his life!"

Molly, too, had been brought up on Sunday school stories in which things like that were happening all the time, so she had no objections to make. They went and fetched the pile of Texts. Each had a few words like *Love one another* or *Even unto us* or *The end is nigh*. The first letter was decorated and there would be flowers or a dove in one corner. They spent a happy hour colouring them, then put on their hats and went to find a few places where sinners would be likely to be passing.

As they walked through the centre of the village Clare began to have doubts. Molly kept saying, "Shall I drop one here?" and Clare would say, "No, not here ... there are too many people about," and Molly would argue, "But we want people about, to pick up the Texts and be converted"; and Clare would say firmly, "But not people who know us," forgetting how many did. In the end they went up Gypsy Lane past Hoylands farm, looked furtively round and dropped one each. Coming back down the lane they were emboldened to drop two more near the farm gates.

"Hey, Missy! You dropped summat!"

The farm man they hadn't seen had picked up the cards and was holding them out. There seemed nothing to do but take them and thank him.

"Wouldn't you like to keep them?" said Clare suddenly, pushing them back at him. "They're for ... for ... they're quite pretty."

He looked surprised, but then said, "Well, I can give 'em to my little 'un. She likes pictures." He put them in his pocket without looking at them, nodded cheerfully and went on his way.

"Perhaps he'll see them when he gives them to his little 'un," said Molly hopefully. "And there's always the two we did drop."

"So long as someone from the Working Party doesn't find them," said Clare.

The Working Party met regularly at the vicarage and chatted as their fingers were busy with calico vests for paupers and flannel petticoats for orphans. It was the busy-ness of the Working Party's tongues which the children didn't like. If conversation flagged, there was always one or other of the Stocks to tell about, especially Erica, who was very good for disapproval. She rushed round on her bicycle more like a tomboy – riding with no hands, or hanging on the back of the horse-bus, and even trying to get her feet on the handle-bars. She whistled, she strode about with her hands in her pockets and her hat falling off the back of her head. She was noisy and untidy and she was far too quick with an answer. Erica was very good value for clucking over. The trouble was, Beatrice listened to it all, thanked the gossips for their concern, and poured it all on Erica's head afterwards.

Beatrice's At Homes were even worse than the Working

Parties, because the children – at least, Cecily and Erica – were directly involved. Beatrice loved wearing attractive dresses and presiding over the tea and cakes. Of course, Alice had dusted and polished, William Long had brought the flowers and Sarah had baked and had cut the bread and butter into slices so exquisitely thin they curled of their own accord into rolls. But it was because Beatrice was so lively and amusing that people loved the parties. "I cannot remember when I last enjoyed myself so much," they said as they got up to go.

She liked to have her sisters in pretty dresses making themselves useful handing round cups and plates of cakes. She thought it was good training for their entry into society later. Clare and Molly would soon be seen giggling or whispering and would be told to run along upstairs, dears, but Cecily and Erica had to stay. They both loathed these parties, but Cecily had a quiet dignity of her own which floated her through. Erica never ceased to feel self-conscious and awkward, especially when people asked kind condescending questions about her age and what she was learning. She blushed and her anger got into her fingers and made her even clumsier: she would tilt a plateful of meringues on to the floor without meaning to, and if there was a stool or a low table, she would stumble over it.

"It's her age," the kind visitor would say in an understanding tone to her sister. "She'll grow out of it." If she managed to avoid these disasters, she was in trouble for talking too much or too little.

"Like a mute at a funeral," Beatrice said indignantly after one party. "Mrs Hartland took a lot of trouble to talk to you, and you just stood there with your mouth open like a stuffed fish."

Erica tried to laugh, but no girl likes being told she's a stuffed fish. But if witty Mr Upthorpe or jovial Mr Munter got chatting to her, then there would be bother over talking too much or laughing too loudly. Or it would be, "When you sit, there's no need to *thump* down," or "Can't you *walk* across a room, the house isn't on fire," or "Please, please, don't *scream* at the ball when you're playing croquet". She began to think what she had not thought when she was younger – that there was something in it, that she really was graceless and ought to do something about it.

So she was even grateful when Beatrice said, "Dancing classes. That's what she wants, to learn some poise."

She was a little doubtful if she would ever learn dancing, but Chris said encouragingly, "Of course you will. Look how well you polka." That was true. When they pushed the furniture back upstairs, and Miss Pringle played the polka on the piano, no one danced with such life as Erica.

Dancing at Miss Burnett's Academy was so different it didn't seem like dancing at all. You moved your feet, not because of what the music demanded, but because of what the elder Miss Burnett called out. Right foot so, left arm so, left foot so. At the beginning of the class there were things called "Positions", when the boys stood in one row and the girls in another, and Miss Burnett called out the Position, and everybody except Erica did it. Then Miss Burnett came along and put her feet and her hands right, while the rest of the class groaned. Erica felt hot all over, and on the third Saturday she actually cried. She was so ashamed she fled behind the coatrack. The younger Miss Burnett coaxed her out, but did not find what was really wrong. The truth was – and Erica would have died rather than admit it – that at twelve she wasn't always sure which was her right hand and which her left, at any rate not when she had to decide in a hurry in the middle of a dance.

Beatrice happened to ask that afternoon if she was enjoying her classes, and Erica lied that she was, but Bessie, who happened to overhear, didn't believe that. She said as much when she came into her bedroom that night with clean clothes. "What went wrong today? You'd been crying, hadn't you?"

Erica tried to explain about the right and the left, and Bessie smiled ruefully. "All those hours I spent teaching you! I thought I'd managed!"

"Oh, you did, Bessie!" Erica assured her. "Only I have to make my mind up so quickly in the dance, and if I *begin* to go wrong, the whole class gets embrangled, and everybody's furious."

"Why can't you remember your right hand's the one you hold your knife in?"

"There aren't any knives at the dancing class," said Erica coldly. "I did try to work it out from the fireplace being on my left. But when we turn round, it's not on my left any longer. It seems most odd."

"It's you that's odd! I'll tell you what, though, you can wear my bracelet on your left wrist, and that'll be your left whichever way you're facing."

"And the side which hasn't got the bracelet will be my right," said Erica brightly.

"Aren't we clever!" said Bessie. She went away and came back with the bracelet and put it on Erica's left wrist.

"But that's the one George gave you ... " began Erica, and then broke off.

"I know. That's why I can't a-bear to wear it."

"Oh, Bessie!" Erica blurted out. "I think he must have been a *fool* to like anyone better." Bessie laughed, an odd sort of laugh because her voice was still hoarse, but still the first Erica had heard since Bessie returned. Suddenly Erica flung her arms about Bessie's neck and kissed her, and Bessie hugged her back.

"Let's forget George," said Bessie. "There's plenty more fish in the sea when all's said and done."

"Nicer fish! Oh, Bessie, how lovely to have you back!"

After Bessie had gone, it struck Erica it had been a funny thing to say, since Bessie had been back for months, but it had seemed that she had only just returned that very moment.

The next Saturday Sarah was going into Gloucester to see her sister. As she was fat, and found it a long way to walk to the stop at the *Waggon and Horses*, they hung a red towel over the gate and the driver of the horse-bus pulled up at the vicarage, and Sarah and Erica got on, and the driver whipped up his horses again. Erica got out her bracelet and put it on. She saw Sarah watching and explained how she would always know her left wrist as the one with the bracelet. Sarah looked at her a bit oddly.

"But you've put it on your right wrist, dear."

When that was corrected, she went cheerfully into the class. The bracelet did help a good deal, but she didn't learn to enjoy dancing much. She didn't think she was really becoming very much more graceful, either, which had been the idea. It came to a head one day when she had been caught turning cartwheels on the back lawn; her skirt had fallen round her ears and left her petticoats for all to see.

"It was the back lawn," she pleaded. "There wasn't anyone except Bessie, and she sees my underclothes every day."

"The Misses Brown saw you on their way back from arranging the flowers in church, and were quite shocked."

"They must have crooked telescopes – they couldn't see me from Church Lane. I expect they came spying round the back. Mrs Hunt says they'd creep up inside a drainpipe just so they could say someone's kitchen floor had a smear on it."

Beatrice nearly laughed, but frowned and said something crushing about deportment instead; and Erica said the dancing classes weren't teaching her that, and could she stop them? But it turned out that the dancing classes had been recommended by Mrs Heatherington-Hearnley, and Beatrice wouldn't listen to her. She went slowly upstairs to join the others at tea, and found an indignation meeting in progress about the new decree that they were to have Sarah's rich currant and spice cake only on special occasions, on Sundays and when they had visitors. It turned out that only *some* visitors counted for this purpose, and most of their closer friends were only counted as worth lard-cakes. They tried inviting the sort of friends that Beatrice approved of more, but the cake wasn't worth the strain after all, and they felt worms, too.

Now that there sometimes seemed to be a choice of what you could do, social problems were not quite so straightforward as they had been in the days when you either did what you were told or said "Shan't!" and took the consequences. There were periods when Erica actually felt she ought to try to understand more of the artistic and social good taste of which she considered Beatrice an embodiment. She even ate medlars, when they appeared in their season, because this was a thing people seemed to rave about. Medlars were ugly brown fruit, too sour to eat until they began to rot. Then the sourness was half hidden by a brief syrupy sweetness. Cecily and Chris wouldn't touch them. Clare went quite white because she thought they were a sort of weird slug; Molly spat hers out too vulgarly and was sent away from table. Erica shut her eyes and ate three.

"They have such an *interesting* flavour," she said in her best adult manner.

"I am glad one of you is developing a sophisticated palate," said Beatrice, smiling gracious approval.

It was a kind of reward; but Erica wished she didn't have such a fluttering sensation inside her stomach.

Meanwhile the dancing class tramped on. A new boy of her own age joined it. He was tall and handsome and looked down his nose in a superior way, even if he did wear a brown velvet suit with a lace collar, for goodness sake. They discovered a bond in being both rather bad at dancing, and Colin told her of the custom of "sitting out" at proper balls, when you talked and ate ices instead of dancing. It sounded a wonderful idea, and they managed sometimes to avoid Miss Burnett's eye and sit and talk behind the coats. They hadn't any ices, but Colin would speak at large of the estate and the farms and the deer and the shooting. Erica didn't mind him bragging; it was entertaining and better than Positions and concentrating on your left and right hands. She even thought of inviting him to tea; he seemed just the sort to bring out the spiced currant cake!

She was enlightened by a remark from a rather spiteful girl in the class who resented her monopolizing the newcomer. He was really the *Honourable* Colin and the son or grandson of a peer, and the estate and the deer and the rest of it were real. Erica had enjoyed a lot of the boasting, but she felt decidedly let down when it all turned out to be merely true. Fortunately the long succession of classes came to its natural end soon afterwards, and the acquaintance faded.

There was one other experience that year which was more far-reaching in its effects on Erica, though it wasn't anything much out of the ordinary in itself. There was hardly a time when Erica hadn't known Daisy, who lived at the far end of the village. They hadn't been to the same school and they didn't in fact share many interests or go into one another's homes, but they had kept up a friendly affection without any effort through the years. Daisy's father was an ill-paid clerk in a solicitor's office in Gloucester, though they were very much a village family. Daisy had an amiable golden nature and never pushed herself forward but she was always herself without apology, and her unhurried way of speaking seemed to annoy Beatrice on the few occasions when she saw her. "So *very* Gloucestershire," she would remark in a kind but dismissive tone of voice.

On this particular Sunday, Erica had been down in the village carrying a message from her father, and she was struggling back against a bitter wind. Near the vicarage she met Daisy and her rather clumping younger brother Bill, and invited them in to get some windfall apples from the loft. Each autumn when the good apples were being collected and carefully stored, the windfalls and the others which might not last the season were put into big baskets and put in the loft. These could be taken by the children at any time. Daisy and Billy were pleased and followed Erica into the house. It was Sunday, Erica remembered, and so they must go up by the front stairs. Daisy and Billy clambered up after her, but they had not even reached the landing when Beatrice came out of the sitting-room. She called up angrily to Erica to know what she was doing.

"I'm just taking Daisy and Billy to the loft to get apples."

"Up the *front* stairs?" Beatrice's voice ran up the scale. "Take them round to the servants' stairs. What *are* you thinking of?"

"But, Beatie, it's Sunday – you know, front stairs on Sunday," said Erica cheerfully, reminding Beatrice of the rule she seemed to have forgotten.

"The front stairs for children from the village? Whatever next? Take them to the back stairs at once!"

The sitting-room door closed again, and Erica silently led the way down the stairs and through the hall, Daisy and Billy following her. Neither of them said anything, but Erica could feel their hurt and shame. She could hardly find her way to the foot of the back stairs for the mist of tears which filled her eyes.

Only when they were in the loft did she dare to say anything, so humiliated did she feel.

"I'm so s-sorry!" she stammered. Daisy said nothing. Her face was still very red and her lips pressed close together.

"Oi dunno as oi want any apples," said Billy unhappily.

"Oh, please, Billy, please. Do take them!"

Daisy looked at Erica and then at Billy. She swallowed as though something was stuck in her throat. "O' course Billy wants apples. He was jest a bit put out, like. That's all it were, weren't it, Billy love? But there, you did ought to hear our mam if we goes into the best parlour in our boots. I did ought to have remembered about Billy's boots, and I don't wunner Miss Stock being vexed seeing him walk on her nice carpet in his mucky boots."

"Yes, that was it," said Erica gratefully. "I ought to have remembered too."

But Billy's boots weren't mucky. They were his best boots, put on for Sunday school and no dirtier and not much heavier than Erica's own. It wasn't because of boots that Beatrice had ordered Daisy and Billy to the back stairs.

"Oh, Daisy, I'm so *sorry*," was all Erica could say again. And kind Daisy kissed her and let her pile apples into her apron, and said it didn't matter, but of course it did.

Things went on much as usual afterwards, and Erica's shame and her first anger against Beatrice died down after a while. Her sense of outrage lasted longer; and when even that had gone, something deeper down inside her was settled for ever.

Chapter 14 · The Oxford Junior Local

A few weeks later, Cecily and Erica started school again, not at Appleby Hall but at the Academy of the Misses Atkinson on the far side of Gloucester. They quickly came to think so little of it that they looked back to Miss Pringle's lessons with regret. There was no proper schoolroom. They all sat round a long table in the front parlour, the older girls at the end near Miss Mabel. The younger ones were away at the foot, where they could at least peep out of the window. The rest had a view of brown-painted walls, a globe of the world and an aspidistra in a green-glazed pot.

Miss Mabel taught all but the very youngest. She had no training as a teacher; she was just the undomesticated one of the Atkinson sisters. After the first week Erica more or less gave up, and took to reading under the table and giggling with Rhea Walker next to her. Rhea, full of laughter, was the Academy's chief gift to Erica and later became her best friend. Miss Mabel's leaden lessons could not get her down, and she could even get fun from Mrs Mangnall's *Questions*.

The *Questions* were contained in a thick, ugly book with deep-green covers and a dark red spine, and the tiny print ran through hundreds and hundreds of pages. The only picture was an etching of Mrs Richmal Mangnall wearing a lace cap on frizzy curls and a tight lace collar. Her big dark eyes looked straight out at any child who dared to open her book; but she had a no-nonsense air about her that made Erica say she might have liked her if she'd met her. Her *Questions* were no joke at all: page after page of them had to be learnt off by heart. When short of ideas, which was often, Miss Mabel brought out the *Questions*. There was only one right answer to any question, and that was Mrs Mangnall's. In the second week after Cecily and Erica joined the school they did *Questions on Common Subjects*.

"What is Rhubarb, Erica?" asked Miss Mabel.

"It is the root of a tree growing in Turkey, in Asia and in Arabia Felix, and is used for medicinary purposes," Erica reeled off, and got her mark.

"It also grows in our garden and we eat it in pies," added Cecily. She did not get a mark because that wasn't in the book.

The next week it was the *Ancient History* section.

"Name the Most Ancient Kingdoms, Rhea," said Miss Mabel.

"Chaldea, Babylonia, Assyria in Asia and Egypt in Africa," said Rhea glibly. She paused and then added with a flicker of interest, "What other Egypt is there except the one in Africa?" She had her mark taken off for being pert, but Erica and Rhea thought it was because Miss Mabel didn't know the answer.

Erica's main acquisition from that term's history lessons was a verse from an endless poem which listed everything memorable which had ever happened. She recited it to her father one Sunday afternoon when they were sitting round after dinner.

> Two Thousand Abraham, Fifteen Hundred Moses,
> One Thousand Solomon, the triad closes.
> Now swarm Greek colonies o'er Asia's coast,
> And Homer sings how hapless Troy was lost.

Mr Stock leant back on the sofa in helpless laughter for

several minutes. "At that rate you'll be at the end of the twentieth century next term!" he said. He lifted an eyebrow and added, "What's a triad?" But Erica didn't know.

She took much more to Huxley's Science Primers on Geology and Chemistry and Botany and Physical Geography. They suited her because there wasn't so much detail to be learned by heart, and the broad ideas in them gave her a fine feeling of being knowledgeable and learned.

In the Easter holidays, Erica's father had a letter open in front of him when Erica came into his study one morning.

"Erica, my dear, Miss Mabel says here that you were the only girl who wouldn't kiss her goodbye at the end of term and that she's very hurt."

"Oh, daddy, no! ... I just said ... quite politely, you know ... that I didn't like kissing people. She can't want to kiss us all, and I know some of the other girls really hated it, too." She thought she caught a gleam of sympathy. "I'm sorry, but I don't honestly like Miss Mabel very much. She's fussy and she pretends, and she has favourites, and sometimes she's perfectly hateful to some of the little ones like Parthenope who daren't answer back."

Mr Stock rubbed his white hair ruefully. "Perhaps it all amounts to an adequate reason for not kissing her. But I wonder how I'll answer this letter!"

"How long to the next holidays?" Cecily asked innocently at the last Sunday dinner before the summer term began.

"About twelve weeks," said Beatrice with a suspicious glance. "Why do you ask? You know perfectly well."

"Twelve weeks before the next nice dinner!" said Cecily in mock despair.

"I'm sure the Academy dinners are most genteel," said Beatrice sharply. She was sensitive about the Academy after hearing two terms of comment on it. "I was very impressed by the dining-room – quite different from Appleby Hall's scrubbed tables and coarse china plates."

"I wish there was more food on the genteel plates," said Erica unwisely. "I'm hungrier when I've finished than when I start!"

Beatrice felt she had to go on defending the meals she had

never seen, and Mr Stock started to reflect on the bills he received for them. Cecily fortunately had to be getting herself ready to go and take her Sunday school class – and so had Erica, for she now was to have her own regular class of six small children in the session just beginning.

There were three new children in the Sunday school that term. No one knew much about them, which was very unusual in Woodhuckle where, mostly, everybody knew everybody else. Joe Hutton, their father, was a pigman on one of the farms, a foreigner from over Bristol way, people said. Lizzie, the youngest child, was sturdy, curly-headed and dark-eyed, unlike her fair, frail, timid sisters. Lizzie should have been with the babies, but she had gripped her sister's skirt tightly and put out her tongue and shouted abuse when Mr Edwards tried to lead her away. ("Her were swearing something awful," Alfie reported later with something like respect in his voice.) So she was left in Erica's class with her sister Maisie. She did not listen much, but she sat beside Erica as good as gold, and stroked Erica's velvet cuff and peered up into her face. Erica was flattered in the way someone is when an awkward spitting kitten finally decides to make friends, and she began to feel she must be an Influence for Good. This was a thing people always seemed to have been telling her she could be but wasn't. She began to notice Lizzie's clothes – the hem dragging at one side, the rent, the stains and the old scarf pulled across her chest and pinned behind. She asked Lizzie's sister Maisie about their mother.

"Step-mother," said Maisie briefly.

"Is she kind?"

"She don't hit us like Dad. She don't do much, we 'ave to scrub an' that. She's fretty, like, and coughs something chronic. She's all right."

"I hate my dad," said Lizzie conversationally.

Erica, thinking it over later, decided that the best thing a Good Influence could do now was to make Lizzie a decent dress. She consulted Bessie. Bessie, who remembered more clearly than Erica did the agonies of Erica trying to sew anything at all, looked at her but only said, "That's a new come-out for you."

"Please, please," begged Erica.

"Very well," said Bessie. "I'll help you cut it out. But none of your doing three stitches and leaving the rest to me."

"It wouldn't be *my* present then," said Erica virtuously.

Beatrice was surprisingly easy to get the money from; she even gave her a piece of cloth beautifully stitched with leaves and flowers. She had once worked it herself, and it would make a delightful pocket on the warm, brown woollen material Erica was going to buy. It gave Erica the extra enthusiasm she needed to keep going to the end. Bessie encouraged her, too, but did not help with the sewing – except, perhaps, most tactfully by straightening puckered seams when Erica had gone to bed. After it was done, Erica gave it to Maisie when she saw her in the road.

Maisie brought Lizzie to the class next Sunday in the new dress. She had scrubbed Lizzie's face and brushed her hair, and they both looked excited.

"My, ain't that nice!" exclaimed a child. "An' flowers on the pocket. Where'd you get it, Liz?"

Erica swelled with pride, too, as her moment of triumph approached. Lizzie came and sat beside her and slipped a small cold hand into hers and looked up trustingly.

"My Dad give it me," she said.

"*Your* dad?" said Rose Prudhoe, amazed. "He never."

"He did, too," flashed Lizzie. "He got 'is wages Friday, an' 'e walked into Gloucester after 'is tea an' 'e brought it back. He's good, my dad, ain't 'e, Miss?"

Erica had been staring dumbly. Now she swallowed hard.

"He must be good, Lizzie if ... if he went to all that trouble to make ... to buy you a dress."

A momentary look of doubt crossed Lizzie's face. She opened her mouth to speak, but Rose broke in again.

"'E never did! There's too many other shops on the way. Like the *Waggon and 'Orses*, and the *Royal Oak* ... "

" ... an' the *Victoria*, an' the *Rose an' Crown* an' the *Swan* ... " chanted the rest of the class, catching the joke. They knew the road into Gloucester.

By the time Erica had quietened them, it was high time to get on with the lesson, and Lizzie's dress was not mentioned again. Erica tried to talk to Chris about it when she got back home, but he didn't seem interested enough in the enormity of the affair.

"But Chris, it was a real lie she told, and I'm her Sunday school teacher! I'm responsible and ought to have taught her! If she dies and goes to hell, it'll be my fault!"

"I don't suppose she'll die yet. You've plenty of time to tell her," Chris said patiently. He was trying to read.

Erica decided she would do her duty. Next Sunday's lesson would be on lying. So it was, but Lizzie missed it, because the Huttons didn't come to the class. Perhaps they were avoiding it, but they were an erratic family in any case. Erica met Maisie and Lizzie a few days later in the village street. She was past her first indignation, but she did make a mild remark.

"Oh, Miss," said Maisie, "us didn't want 'em to think our dad couldn't afford a dress."

Erica wasn't able to brood long over this, for her thoughts were soon given a sharp new turn. All the comments on the Atkinsons' Academy must have had an effect and there had evidently been consultations between the vicarage and Rhea Walker's parents. For one day Cecily and Erica and Rhea found themselves in Mr Stock's study discussing with him and Miss Pringle the idea of taking the Oxford Junior examinations. It was a daring thought, for not very many girls did. Admittedly, it meant Miss Pringle again, but Erica and Rhea responded with enthusiasm. They both wanted an aim, and Oxford was a magic word. Cecily was a sober worker and perhaps less romantic about Oxford learning, but she too was beginning to wilt at the Academy and would be as pleased as the others to leave Miss Mabel. After only a few days of term they had said goodbye – without many kisses! – and were excitedly reading the Oxford Junior Local Examination Syllabus and considering choices in English and French and History as well as the duller paragraphs on Arithmetic and Geography.

Mr Stock gave them a friendly lecture on the need to work hard to get it all done in the time. He reminisced about his own university days and the occasion when he'd been sitting in the hall before an examination and seen three other students there looking very anxious. They had been sent up to the university to meet people and enjoy themselves rather than work and were now feeling very hopeless. Mr Stock was moved to make up on the spot his only poem.

> " 'Within the hall, around the wall,
> Three wretched dunces sit.
> They rack their brain, and all in vain,
> To get a bit of wit.' "

One of them said to me, 'The trouble is, Stock, that I've learnt the first dozen of Euclid's Problems off by heart – and I've learnt to draw all the figures, too. What I can never remember is which figure fits with which Problem.' "

They found a side of Miss Pringle they hadn't appreciated earlier. She hadn't the gift of charming younger children into exploring and learning; but, give her a good clear syllabus and an exam at the end, and she could organize work. She still wasn't exactly inspiring, but she kept them moving on as fast as they could manage, reading the annotated play of Shakespeare and trying to grasp the varied Selection of English Poetry. They also did their best with the French story under the Walkers' governess. This wasn't easy, for the governess had been engaged chiefly because her English was poor. The idea had been that Rhea would have to speak French to her or not speak at all. It didn't work out as well as it might have with Erica and Rhea together, because she didn't seem able to talk slowly enough for them to follow. She did correct their written work for them, but when they came to a difficult part of the story, she could only explain it to them in floods of even faster French. They had to plod through most of it on their own with a dictionary. It wasn't a bad story, though a bit weird – all about brigands in Sicily and a man with the evil-eye.

Studying kept them busy and interested, but it was rather an unsettling year at home. Nothing dramatic happened, not like the autumn some years before when a gale brought a chimney down through the roof of the girls' bedroom, smashing the wash-stand, and Bessie had to climb over the debris to them. Erica was almost entirely absorbed in the great examination adventure with Rhea, so that she was only vaguely aware of all the uneasy changes going on in those months. She saw less and less of Cecily even outside study hours. Cecily no longer went around with the giggly Rose Munter, but she was being more and more caught up in the affairs of all the local clubs and societies she was always joining and helping to run. Being conscientious, she worked hard under Miss Pringle, too, but she hadn't the urgent interest of the other two. With the effort of all she was doing she became rather silent at home and paler than usual, though shadows under her eyes did not notice as much as they did sometimes on Erica's darker complexion.

Chris was less at home, too, now that he had to travel to Cheltenham, which meant getting a train on from Gloucester. He was using his opportunity to the full – getting top marks and form prizes. He might have become unbearable, but was saved by his own colossal cheek. For the senior boys came to a quiet understanding, and even thought it their duty, to sit on young Stock, sometimes literally. One whole term he came home with his clothes covered in dust and grime, and passed off the inquiries about it airily. Finally he admitted, in the tone of someone explaining the obvious, that he travelled from Gloucester to Cheltenham and back under the railway-carriage seat. The cricket captain, a boy of few words and hefty muscles, put him there daily, to keep him in his proper place. The cricket captain was very pleased at having thought of that remark and he had a rather repetitive mind, which was why it happened every day.

Erica's father remained his sympathetic self most of the while, but nowadays had periods when he seemed more irritable or forgetful, or when sterner principles showed through his mildness. One day he came across her with a copy of *Jane Eyre* – it had been her mother's, and she had found it at the back of a shelf. She was losing herself in it, but he gently begged her not to read it any more. Overcome by his quiet gravity and the unusualness of the request, she promised him not to open it again. Normally she read anything in the house, and the request was a great surprise, especially as he did not seem to have read it himself. Perhaps (she thought many years later) he had only been thinking of the public outcry and disapproval at the time the book had first come out nearly fifty years earlier, when he was a young man.

But Erica had been quite caught by the story of the unhappy girl, her terrible school, the strange Mr Rochester and his sinister past, and the shrieks in the night. It was a pity then, or perhaps it wasn't, that *Jane Eyre* was in the shelves along the passage which led to the new bathroom and lavatory which had not long been installed upstairs.

"Are you all right?" asked Bessie at the end of one week.

"All right? Of course I am. Why?"

"Well, you're spending a deal of time in the little room, it seems to me." Erica blushed, but could not and did not stop reading *Jane Eyre* until she'd reached the last page and married Jane off to her scarred, blinded, and still adored Mr Rochester.

Sometimes Mr Stock was more actively touchy. When the Double Gloucester cheese was extra strong one day, it made Erica's mouth tingle.

"This cheese stings!" she exclaimed.

"How dare you speak like that?" said her father in a voice of thunder.

"I only said ... "

"Don't repeat it!"

"All I said ... "

"That will do!" he said angrily.

She struggled to say nothing, but then burst out, "I didn't say *anything*, except this cheese stings my tongue!"

"Oh, my dear child!" he said, all kindness again at once. "I thought you said, 'It stinks', and that, you know, is an expression I should not like to hear on my children's lips." They all breathed out with relief, but no one smiled.

His tendency, as he aged, to retreat into theology and his garden annoyed Beatrice sometimes. She had been accustomed to his company at parties or on visits in Gloucester, where his pleasant dignity was a foil for her social sprightliness. She even bickered over small things like his buying azaleas when the money was, she thought, needed elsewhere in the household.

"Fifty shillings! Fifty shillings for azaleas!" she repeated.

"William Long got them from his Gloucester cousin. It was five shillings, my dear, quite a bargain, not fifty," he corrected her amiably. She was even crosser to find she was wrong.

But there were moments of understanding and relief, too, as when he found Clare crying in the garden after an upset with Beatrice. He sympathized, and added, "She *is* an irritating person sometimes, isn't she? Even I find her so." It was a great revelation to Clare to see such a chink in the wall of adults about her. Another time, Erica came rebelliously in to her father in the stove-house where he grew the tender plants. (When she was small, the stove-house with its warm damp smells and dedicated plant rituals had always seemed a place of religious awe and mystery, much more holy than the bright new church.) He looked at her expression but merely said, "There's a job I'd like you to do for me." He led the way into the next shed where there were dozens and dozens of cracked flower-pots which had collected over the years. "I'll need a heap of small pieces for all the seed-trays later on," he said, and put a mallet into her hand. "As small as you can." She broke one or two, and then more, and then spent half an hour until tea-time in a fury of smashing, and felt much better.

One day in the early autumn, Bessie found Erica reading in her room.

"Hello, I thought you were out playing cricket with the boys."

"I never will. I *hate* boys!"

They had been playing a scratch game of cricket and enjoying it, though Hector had been annoyed when she caught him out. It was a hot day, and afterwards they sprawled in the shade: Chris wasn't there that day. She lay in the grass, snuffing its coolness, half-listening to the talk and to Hector starting his sniggering jokes. Suddenly she realized she was alone in a ring of giggling red-faced boys, and that the jokes were directed at her. She jumped up and fled, trembling with rage and shock. Bessie took it in a matter-of-fact way.

"You always get one like Hector in a crowd. Though he's quite right. You are growing a pretty shape, and no call to be ashamed of it that I know."

Put that way, it sounded all right, but it hadn't been down in the meadow among boys she'd always known who had become strangers.

"They *looked* at me," she protested, still half sobbing. "And they said ... they said ... " She broke off, reddening at the memory.

"Oh well," said Bessie tolerantly. "That's boys when they're together. You'll know another time when they get in that mood. You can always say I told you to be back early – so that it don't look particular."

"Yes, I could say that," agreed Erica gratefully; but it was a melancholy moment.

Then work came up again round Erica and Cecily and Rhea, and they settled to the last hard lap of Notes on Shakespeare and Great Poems and those French-speaking brigands in Sicily. Rhea gave a mock-shiver and made a joke about the examiner being the man with the evil-eye, as they whipped themselves on. On the great examination day William Long drove them in the carriage to the school which was being used for all the local candidates. Cecily was tense and holloweyed and gripped a handkerchief, but then she always did take exams in dead earnest.

Erica loved them, and she was blithely sure she had something worthwhile to say about everything, and was annoyed to find that in some questions she could only answer *Either ... or*; she wanted to answer them all. It was delightful to think there was a man who *had* to read what she wrote because he was paid to do it. It was true that when she showed the questions to her father after all the papers were over and told him what she'd said about them, he laughed rather a lot. But it was all done now, and Erica firmly and sensibly put the whole thing out of her mind, at least, for most of the time. She knew it would be weeks or even months before they heard, and it was.

At last there was a long stiff envelope with an official seal lying on Mr Stock's plate at breakfast. He opened it amid a deathly hush. A very odd look crossed his face.

"Congratulations, Erica! You've passed after all!"

There were cries of excitement. Chris threw a bread-roll in the air. Clare and Molly struggled to be first round the table to see the amazing document, with its copper-plate handwriting announcing that Erica Stock had Satisfied the Examiners in a whole heap of subjects and would receive the Certificate of the Oxford Junior Board in due course. Clare gazed and gazed and resolved that one day she too would receive such a document. After a while they noticed that Cecily had slipped quietly from the room, and they understood that Cecily had failed.

Cecily kept out of everybody's way until dinner-time. Erica was going to say nothing, but Cecily surprised her by congratulating her.

"Oh, Cecily, I am so sorry!" Erica blurted out.

"There's nothing to be sorry about," said Cecily quietly. "You got through. I failed."

"They were horrid papers. Everyone said so, coming out. It wasn't your fault." She meant well, but Cecily's calm deserted her, and the blood rushed up into her pale face.

"Shut up! Just shut up, that's all! Don't *you* start pitying me!" She rushed out, choking on a sob.

She cried all day and through the night in a hiccupping kind of way. The doctor was asked to call, and prescribed bromide. When she eventually got up, she remained listless and did little, letting her clubs and societies get on without her. Mr Stock did his best to give her support, but the children were shattered. It wasn't just the failure of Cecily in an exam – for that happens in the best-regulated families – but the completeness of the collapse of the Cecily they knew. She was the oldest of them, and she had so often been the one whose cool sense they had taken for granted in awkward moments, such as a dispute with Beatrice. Going to Cheltenham to school had made Chris more self-contained, but he was no less affected.

Erica spent several unhappy and ill-occupied weeks. There was no longer a class with Cecily and Rhea, and she herself had achieved her aim at the cost of having it turn sour as she reached it. And not a single Oxford Professor had written to say how very impressed he was, not even the examiner. She reflected that her old dream of being Erica Stock, B.A., might be a let-down, too, if she ever got there, and she wondered what else she ought to think of doing with herself.

She didn't wonder long about becoming a nun, but she did feel she might get her ideas straight again about marriage. She didn't particularly want a husband, admittedly, and Jane Eyre had Mr Rochester, anyway. But she did adore small children, and you weren't supposed to have one without the other. She went and pulled out an old book, *The Heir of Redclyffe*, and turned to her favourite picture. There she was, the girl of eighteen, very lovely in her widow's weeds, with her darling baby in her arms, its cheeks flushed with sleep. And Erica knew by heart a paragraph she had once cried over: "It was dim lamplight now that beamed on the portrait of her husband, casting on it the shade of the little wooden cross in front, while she was shaded by the white curtains drawn from her bed round the infant's little cot, so as to shut them both into the quiet twilight."

That was her idea of a perfect marriage. Of course, it meant that your husband had to be dead – and men were *so* unreliable, she thought, as the first bubble of fun in weeks rose inside her and began to make her feel more cheerful and less maudlin.

Things were going on in the background all this time in fact; but, as in many homes, the children didn't get told until they were decided. Then they heard that in a month or so Cecily and Erica were going for a year or more to what was called a finishing school somewhere in the countryside of central France. Cecily cried again and said she was being punished. But the doctor told Mr Stock and Beatrice privately, "For goodness sake, winkle her out whatever she says, or you'll have her moping for the rest of her life."

Chapter 15 · Slow train to Annonay

Erica sat in the corner seat by the window and stared unwinkingly at the turning landscape. Her father smiled at her absorbed face.

"Well, Erica, what do you think of France?"

She pulled her gaze away from the flat fields of Normandy.

"Isn't it odd?" she said. "It's just like England."

The elderly Frenchman in the opposite corner laughed and translated this to his wife, who laughed too. Cecily blushed and tried to look unconcerned. Beatrice tapped her fingers impatiently on the seat-arm.

"What *did* she expect to see in France?" asked her father laughing.

"People walking on their heads and cows with six legs, I expect. She's baby enough," said Beatrice tartly. She had had a lot to do and she was tired.

Erica had gone back to watching the landscape – seeing a countryside with so much that was familiar yet different: farmhouses painted another pink, fields much bigger and more open, and whiter and dustier roads. Some things were quite new, however – men in dark blue smocks and wooden shoes, women all in black with black shawls over their heads, and ploughs and carts drawn by oxen instead of horses. Soon she was laughing and chatting away to the old man in a medley of English and French – accuracy was never the first thing with her. Cecily was embarrassed at the attention her sister was drawing to herself and did not notice that her own pretty fairness and slender height were attracting as much: Erica with her sallower complexion might have passed for French.

They spent the night in the first hotel the girls had ever stayed in; and on the next day they boarded a slow train. By the time it reached the town of Annonay the sun was low, and the town looked attractive in the golden light; but they were tired and rather apprehensive about the new school. The hired carriage took them through narrow streets with queer strong smells, then climbed a hill which brought them out above the town. They stopped by a high brick wall at a wrought-iron gate. They glimpsed a big untidy garden and a low house with blue shutters and a creeper-hung veranda. Night-scented stock filled the air as they walked up the gravel path. They were received, and there were refreshments; but Mr Stock and Beatrice had to leave almost at once for a train, and the girls were alone among strangers.

To their relief the first stranger was the English teacher. She said she was Miss Moore, but they might as well get used to calling her "Mademoiselle-Miss" like everyone else. She led them into a parlour to a supper of soup and white bread broken off a yard-long loaf. The supper was good, but the parlour was so quiet they were afraid to speak above a whisper. Then they were taken to the Head Teacher in her salon.

Madame Blanchard was fat and short, but her plump face fell quite naturally into amiable smiling curves. Cecily thought, "Just like fat Mrs Barnes at the shop" and then was ashamed of being such a snob. Madame Blanchard turned up the small gas-jet, beckoned Cecily over and inspected her.

"I like to see my new pupils," she said. "Yes ... Mademoiselle Cécile is a good, reliable girl and we shall be delighted with her."

Erica skipped into the small circle of light, half laughing and half defiant.

"She also will do. A kind heart, but slightly impetuous and *entêtée*."

A little later Erica asked Mademoiselle-Miss what *entêtée* meant, as she and Cecily were being taken to their room along a corridor smelling of pine and lavender. "Stubborn," said Mademoiselle-Miss without inquiring further, and Erica stayed silent.

The room was very small. The iron-framed double bed had sheets, a thin blanket and an enormous feather-filled quilt. They sat down on the bed, subdued and very tired, and began to undress.

"I'm sorry she thought me stubborn," said Erica.

"It was unforgivable, making me stand in the light to be stared at," said Cecily resentfully. "I don't like this place."

They got into bed, threw the unbearably hot quilt on the floor, blew out the candle and slept at once despite their gloom.

The small white room was full of sunlight when they woke. Crowded round the bed, they now saw, were a white-painted chest of drawers, a minute table and one basket-chair. A red and green square of carpet was an island on the white-painted floorboards. They giggled at the ewer and wash-basin: they were more like a large milk jug and sugar-basin.

They discovered the room's real glory when they got up to dress. It looked right across the roofs of Annonay below them to woods and a tumble of hills, backed by mountains which were clear and sharp against the bluest of skies. A girl of about Cecily's age, with smooth hair and a competent manner and an attractive smile, came in and said,

"Please, soon it is *le petit déjeuner*, the breakfast. Is there anything you need?"

"Some hot water?" asked Cecily tentatively.

"Not hot water in the morning!" said Madeleine, very shocked. "That is difficult for the stove, they need for the cooking," she explained. "You know the rule about speaking, do you, yes? Everyone speaks their own language the first day. Then we speak only the French always. Of course," she added laughing, "I do not suppose they will listen at the bedroom keyhole!"

They had their breakfast at one of the wooden tables on the veranda. There were heaped baskets of fresh croissants on a stiff white tablecloth, and steaming bowls of coffee, and the sun twinkled through the leaves of the great vine. Madeleine settled them down and left them to look at all the other girls chattering away in French and German and English. There were bright, quick girls from Paris, girls from the south with glossy black hair and olive complexions, fair Germans, two sisters with black eyes and curled hair from French Equatorial Africa and brown-headed English. Erica took a hot croissant from a basket and tried to decide between honey and apricot conserve. She heard a complaining voice with a strange accent on the other side of her.

"Ach, this is breakfast, is it? No porridge, no eggs, no baps, no marmalade!" She saw a tall girl with high cheekbones and a reddish tinge to her fair hair. Erica smiled uncertainly.

"Are you English, too?"

"I am not. I am from Scotland." She didn't sound very friendly.

"I don't know any Scotch people."

"Scottish, not Scotch," said the girl with disdain. "I suppose we'll have to see each other a lot as my room's opposite. My name's Helen McKenzie and I'm from Edinburgh."

Erica introduced herself and Cecily, and added straightly, "You don't have to be friends with us: there are lots of other girls."

"Foreigners!" said Helen scornfully. "We are on a different level. Our parents pay more, and we do not sleep in dormitories and we have tea in the dining-room."

"But I want to learn French," said Cecily mildly.

"Oh, that!" Helen shrugged. "If you're going to be governesses or something, I suppose. I shan't be earning my living and English is good enough for me."

"Scottish, surely?" said Cecily, stung out of her mildness.

Two weeks later Erica finished her letter home and began one to Rhea Walker.

Dear Rhea,

So here I am at Pension Blanchard! Madame Blanchard is very fat and wears straw hats with bright colours pushed to the back of her head, which looks awful. I like her now, and Cecily says she has a kind heart, and two girls don't have to pay any fees at all. Madeleine's mother left her when she was small, and ran away, and Madame's adopted her. She's sixteen and she's learning to be a teacher, to take over the school when Madame retires. Lucie's mother was the cook here, but she died and there wasn't anyone to look after Lucie. She adores Madame and will kick or scratch anyone who's rude about Madame. Some girls say rude things just to set her off! Old Marie the housekeeper is very funny. She's smaller than me and wears a big white cap which makes her face look like a doll's, only wrinkled. She locks up the Pension at night and goes round with a tiny stone lamp like that Roman one your father showed us. Honestly. It's got a hole in the top and the wick just floats in oil. I don't know why she doesn't take a candle, it would be brighter.

Two English girls have been here nearly all their lives and all the English they can say is, "You leetle peeg!" They're sisters. The only girl I don't like is Scotch, she calls it Scottish.

Erica paused, remembering yesterday at dinner. Helen asked Erica – well, ordered her, more like – to pour her a glass of water, and Erica did. Helen raised her eyebrows and said,

"My dear girl! So vulgar to fill a glass to the brim. Where were you brought up? In a Board school?"

Despite herself, Erica was stung by the Board school, as she was meant to be. But not filling a glass was a new piece of gentility to her. She went on with her letter.

You can always get at Helen by calling her English. We had to go and register at the Town Hall, *la Mairie* – I think that's right. The big clerk got up and bowed and said, "You are all English, I see" – only in French, of course. Helen said she was *Écossaise*, and he put his hands out like the French do and said, "*Anglaise, Écossaise*. It's

all the same thing. You will be entered as English."
Helen was *furious*. I expect Scotch people are all right really.

We're starting to understand the lessons all in French. We have to talk it all the time, so grammar doesn't matter so long as you're understood, and we get on swimmingly. The girls play singing games in break. Cecily and me tried to start rounders, but Madame said it was tiring and some girls had been sent to her for the mountain air because they are delicate. But we play croquet, only there's a ridge in the lawn and the ball rolls anywhere, you can laugh or cry!

Our room's lovely. You look right across the town – it's like a pretty doll-town, but not so nice when you're there. The factories cure pigskin for leather gloves and smell *most* peculiar! The people who make the gloves look thin and ill. Mostly I look over at the mountains.

Erica paused again. Each morning she woke in the first grey dawn and went to the window as bird after bird started up and all the thick mist was filled with chirping and trilling. The mist grew lighter and lighter, and at last the sun rose and coloured the houses and trees. The mist faded back, and there – far up in the sky – was Mount Miandon, the highest peak of all, glowing in the morning. When there was only the common sunshine of a summer's day everywhere, Erica crept back into bed again until the school bell rang. She wanted to say the mountain tops made her feel God was near her soul, but Rhea might laugh. She picked up her pen and dashed off her last sentences.

There aren't any baths in the school. On Friday someone goes round shouting, "Who wants a bath?". And we walk in a line through the town to the public wash-house. Some girls don't ever go. One of them says her mother has never allowed water to touch her hair because it would spoil its lustre. It does shine, but I had to put her ribbon on for her the other day, and her hair was sort of soapy slippery. Horrid!!

With much love, ERICA

She and Cecily continued to find Pension Blanchard endearing and odd. They enjoyed it largely because of its oddities and because it was so delightfully different from all they knew. Only two months ago Beatrice's moods and the affairs of Woodhuckle were the centre of their world, and now they were right on the edge of it. All that mattered was keeping eyes and ears open so as to miss nothing. Helen McKenzie was just the opposite. Faced with the strange French world, Helen was partly hostile and partly frightened, and tried to let in as little as possible that was new. Perhaps that was why she and Erica continued to dislike each other and tried to score off one another when a chance arose. Helen often won, for she spent more time thinking alone in her room, while Erica was downstairs cheerfully gabbling her awful French.

In the French dictation class they all had to exchange exercise books to correct each other's work. The teacher was strict; every grammatical slip and every spelling mistake counted as a fault and meant a mark off. To her annoyance one day, Erica saw her exercise book go to Helen. After a while Helen raised her hand and asked in wide-eyed innocence,

"How many words did you dictate, Mademoiselle?"

"I am sure I do not know, Hélène. Why do you ask?"

"I was just wondering, Mademoiselle, if Erica could really have more faults than words!"

Erica had a revenge that evening without planning it. She was doing homework when she heard a scream from Helen's room opposite. She found Helen standing on her bed, clutching her skirt round her.

"There's a rat under the bed!" she shouted. "Catch it this moment, Erica!"

Erica was inclined to jump on the bed, too, but she controlled herself and said with a smile, "I'm not a terrier."

"Get my umbrella and chase it quick, you idiot!"

So Erica got the umbrella and rattled it on the springs under the bed, and a rather small rat emerged, ran to a far corner and sat on its haunches. After her first start, Erica saw it was more frightened than she was. Helen was in another panic.

"Why did you drive it that way? Couldn't you think of the door? I don't want to stand here all night!"

"It would just about serve you right," retorted Erica. "Chase it yourself. I'm busy."

The rat made a dash through the open door at this point, and Erica saw it disappear under the door of the big attic at the end of the corridor.

"No, no, don't go," begged Helen. "It might come back. Or there might be another. Do stay, there's a dear."

"You aren't usually so polite," said Erica. "It's just because you want something. I don't know how you can be so barefaced."

Very satisfied with this high-sounding and crushing phrase, she strode back to her room to finish her work. It is true she now sat on the bed with her feet well tucked up, but Helen never knew because she had fled downstairs to be with the French girls whose company she generally spurned.

Helen was often sarcastic about one girl called Klara, who came from Alsace – so Helen could make the English girls smile by calling her "a little Alsatian". Klara wasn't particularly clever or pretty, but very good-natured. Being from Alsace, between France and Germany, she spoke both languages badly: the Germans laughed at her German, and the French girls at her French; she could never distinguish between p and b, for example. Erica was led by Helen's sneers to offer to teach Klara some English.

"I'll say each new word carefully," she told Cecily. "Then she'll never have heard English said wrongly, and she'll get it right. I won't have Helen laughing at her so."

Klara was a grateful pupil, and Erica decided to teach her a little poem to say at one of Madame's Saturday social parties. Klara's accent was almost perfect when she practised with Erica:

> "I remember, I remember
> the house where I was born,
> the little window where the sun
> came peeping in at morn ... "

The day before the party, Erica wrote it all down for her, so that she could go through it by herself. It was a fatal move. For Klara, seeing the words on the page for the first time, started getting her *b*s and *p*s mixed up again. When the time came, she stood up and began with,

>"I rememper, I rememper
>De house where I wass pawned ... "

Only the English girls and Mademoiselle-Miss saw the full joke, perhaps; but Helen was quite convulsed, because she was laughing at Erica, too.

The next day was a Sunday, when nearly the whole school went to church in a crocodile line. There were very few Protestants in Annonay, but there were two churches fighting for their custom, as church and chapel sometimes fought at Woodhuckle. Madame, spendidly impartial, went with her school to *Le Temple* and *L'Église Libre* – The Free Church – in turn. The Temple was like a rather dull church at home, complete with stained glass and incomprehensible sermon. Erica preferred The Free Church, held in a hall over stables. In the silences they heard the horses below them snorting and pawing the cobbles. There was a plain oak table for an altar, and no pulpit. Pastor Leblanc stood facing them and talked in French simple enough for most of them to grasp.

He also visited the Pension with his wife once a year to take "goûter", an annual tea. The pastor's wife supplied the *patisserie* – delicate twists of pastry with cream and sugar and fruits. Helen was trying to say how much better Scottish cakes were, but she was already on her third pastry. At the end, they found, all the girls were to drop a curtsy and say, "*Merci, madame, merci, monsieur,*" as they left. Cecily was taken aback, but did so gravely; Erica grinned as she bobbed, thinking how furious Beatrice would be to see her curtsying like the village children. Helen stalked out without a word. "I was put in a false position by not being told beforehand," she said stiffly and without apology afterwards.

When the summer term ended, their father and Beatrice, who had been in Italy, collected them and took them to a hotel in the Alps. They saw higher mountains and snow on them in August. They also saw two American women cycling through in trousers: they were fat and hot and they stuck out behind. Erica looked critically at them and said, if those were bloomers she was sorry she'd ever said she wanted to wear them.

"Erica – that word!" said Beatrice sharply. Suddenly the old angry resentment welled up in Erica and blotted out the holiday feeling. It passed again in the amusement of watching a steam tram chugging and clanking along the street. But there were other moments of irritation, and it was with very mixed feelings that they said goodbye to Father and Beatrice at the end of the three weeks and went back to the Pension.

There was still a month before term, and the big house was nearly empty. Madeleine was there, of course, for it was her home, and she was happy to see Cecily; they were two sensible girls with similar outlooks and they found it easy to get on. Lucie was enjoying having Madame almost to herself. Unfortunately, Helen McKenzie was there, too, and in a bad mood. Her father had decided that it was too expensive to have her travel to Edinburgh and back, and she was deeply mortified in her bitter way.

The weather stayed fine and hot, and they almost lived in the garden; even Marie peeled potatoes and prepared vegetables outside. They ate at a wooden table under a linden tree. Then Helen would taker her book and occupy the ivy-shaded arbour built by a former owner. She kept everyone else out of it by her ill-temper; so the others improvised arbours under clematises and honeysuckle. They were shaky and full of insects and caused squabbles.

One very hot day Erica had finished helping with the washing-up – a fairly novel chore to her – and went with a book to the arbour she called hers. But Helen was there. They argued, but Helen remained stubborn and rude, and Erica left. No, Helen should not get away with it this time, she thought. She crept round the back of the arbour and called to one of the others:

"Catherine! Come and see! An *enormous* spider spinning such a long thread. Quick, it's just going to fall on Helen!"

Helen was out in a moment, screaming, and Erica was inside. Helen screamed again with rage when she found out, and the others laughed loudly. Madame threw up a window and heard from Helen that Erica had dropped a spider down her back. Madame looked from one to the other, but it was impossible to guess what she believed.

"I am sorry whatever has happened, but I cannot have the summer peace disturbed. The arbours must come down." She was met with a babble of pleas and explanations.

"Oh, very well. But you must all go inside now, and learn the 133rd psalm. I will hear it tomorrow morning."

They rushed to the classroom to get Bibles, to be finished as soon as possible. They hoped it wasn't that terrible psalm with about a hundred and seventy verses. They were relieved to see how short it was, and giggled at the opening: "Behold, how good and how pleasant it is for brethren to dwell together in unity."

In the cool of the evening after the sun had set they sat in the hall to sew and talk. Sometimes Madame told them stories of her early days, when she had nursed soldiers during the siege of Paris in 1870, while her young husband served as a soldier on the defences. If a girl was finicky about her food, Madame might smile and say, "You should have been in Paris during the siege. You'd have been glad enough to catch a mouse to eat!" Erica was moved to furious private rages at the tales of the pain the wounded went through, with all medicines and pain-killers in very short supply, and at stories of children in the streets crying with hunger.

"Why, why, why?" she broke out once at such a story.

Madame tried to explain. God knows all and loves all. If he permits pain, it must be because he has some higher purpose beyond our understanding. We must just be patient and trust. Erica, listening to her serene voice in the hushed twilight, was almost convinced.

Chapter 16 · Always laughing

Soon the rest of the school had returned, and the new term was leading them on into the winter, when the cold from the mountains froze the water in the little bedroom ewer and it took courage to throw off the thick quilt in the mornings. The dining-room seemed wonderfully cosy by comparison, though its only heat came through the kitchen hatch. A maid once spilt a pail of water in the passage from the dining-room to the garden and by the time she got back with a cloth it had frozen, and the girls were sliding up and down the passage.

The hall was the only really warm place apart from the kitchen. Its enormous stove could feed all the pipes to the classrooms; but Marie was convinced that all Madame's profits were going on coal, and she kept the stove burning as low as possible. In the end a teacher would appeal to Madame, who would throw up her hands and exclaim, "Ah, Marie is determined I must make my fortune from this school. Run and tell her I don't want to make my fortune and she must unlock the coal-store at once."

But Marie worked all hours to see there was enough good food for the Christmas Eve supper which Madame gave to some poor Protestant women of the town. The next day, Madame took Lucie and Erica when she went to take presents to a family. They walked through narrow lanes to the river – where the tenements rose sheer from the water – climbed rickety, smelly stairs and came to a dark back room where the woman lived and ate and slept with her thin little children.

"And Françoise?" asked Madame, after they had talked a little.

"She is asleep. She has had the toothache and could not bear the noise of the others. Will you see her? It might cheer her up." She indicated the chair behind a screen.

Françoise had been a cripple all her life, with a big head and small, useless legs; and now that she was fourteen her mother found her too heavy to carry up and down. The dentist would deal with the tooth free if she could be brought to his surgery. Erica looked at Françoise sleeping in the only armchair, her heavy head on her arm. She was so pale that the blue veins stood out on her forehead above her pinched face. A half-stitched glove lay on the floor.

"She is a good girl," said her mother. "She tried not to stop working for the pain. She does not want to be a drag on us. But what will happen when I am gone?"

Erica had not met anything like this in Woodhuckle, and she found herself resenting the injustice of Françoise's deformed life and wondering what would become of her when she grew up, if she did. Madame, talking to her mother, said she thought the pastor would be able to find a suitable strong man to carry Françoise down and get her to the dentist. That would cure the toothache, thought Erica fiercely, but what then? The picture of Françoise sleeping in the chair remained vivid with her for a very long time.

Cecily and Erica were very much at home in the school by now, and both enjoyed it – each in her own way. Erica bounced round making and unmaking new best friends at frequent intervals, almost as often as she changed her dress. This was in fact a fashion of the class, but Erica was a good deal more light-hearted about it than others were. Some girls made earnest vows of friendship, agreed always to call each other *tu* instead of *vous*, met in quiet corners and swore to love one another for ever. Two or three weeks later they would part, with or without a scene, and the class would take sides for a day or two.

Cecily had no need to seek friends. As at home, she attracted something like devotion without trying. Her friends jostled to walk beside her and were happy to iron her clothes, go to keep her a seat at a function, or even clean her shoes. It puzzled Erica, who eternally ran errands, found things lost and kept the young ones amused without earning that sort of privilege. As Cecily's sister she did gain a certain amount of prestige as a sort of liaison officer to royalty.

The new term brought some new pupils; one or two of them were, they knew, problems accepted by Madame out of the amiability of her nature. The girls argued about this – that Madame ought to charge more, that it was hard on the teachers, that the difficult ones didn't improve anyway.

"Oh, come now!" said Klara. "Look at Helma. I don't believe anyone has had to throw water on her for ages."

That was true. Helma, a small, quiet, pale girl, had been no trouble at all – until someone hurt her feelings. But that was very easy to do, and then Helma ran and shouted and screamed, and no one could get near her even to find out what had happened. The doctor prescribed cold water, in a jug, if she could be caught. Once Erica saw Mademoiselle-Miss chase her all round the garden before cornering her among the blackcurrant bushes and dousing her. It looked cruel, but it stopped the screams. Helma became mouse-like again, changed her dress and sat in Madame's room for a while to make sure she didn't catch cold. Over a period she had become happier and less mouse-like.

Madame had asked them all beforehand to be particularly kind to the first of her pet lambs this term. Victorine had been brought up very closely with her cousin Léonie since they were babies, and now at fourteen Léonie had been sent to America to join her father, who had asked for her. Victorine had sobbed for weeks, and in the end it had been decided that fresh air and other young people were what were likely to do her most good. She arrived crying, but many homesick girls did that. She was still crying the next morning, though, sobbing between mouthfuls of bread and butter and through prayers and through lessons, till she had to be sent to sob in the garden so that everyone else could get on with their work. On the third day, Victorine, still sobbing, shocked them by praying aloud in their morning meeting. She begged forgiveness for her sins and asked for the return of Léonie: on and on her unoriginal petitions went, until Madame touched her and said quietly that such personal prayers were better spoken privately to God. Victorine rushed out still crying. Two days later her parents fetched her. Madeleine, returning from shopping, saw her leave and reported that she stopped crying the moment she found herself outside the door of the school.

The next trouble built up more slowly. Keys kept disappearing till there were times when the whole life of the school would be held up, as classrooms could not be unlocked and lessons could not start. One evening the passage to the dormitories was found locked, and most of the girls could not get to bed. Madame was out visiting friends, and Marie, who was in charge, took the lost key as an outrage and a personal affront. The girls laughed and joked at first, but the young ones got cold and began to cry. Some older girls suggested that the door should be broken down, but this was too much for Marie – *What*, and Madame would have to pay good money to mend it?

She fetched her oil lamp and a candle and led the way upstairs. The girls trooped up after her along the corridor where the separate rooms were. More girls came out of some of them and joined the procession. Marie opened and went through the attic door where Helen's rat had disappeared. The girls were more nervous now; the place was strange and gloomy. Someone declared she was sure she saw a man lurking in the shadows. Marie went through to the trap-door at the end, pulled it up and disclosed a ladder leading down to her own room.

"It is in case of fire," she explained. "Now, you can get to your bedrooms from there. Down you go."

No one moved. The ladder looked weak and shaky in the

dim light. Marie's room had its curtains drawn and the girls standing round the trap-door opening were peering down into darkness. In the end, Marie sent Cecily and Erica (who had joined in for the fun of it) down the ladder to help the young ones. Then the older ones felt encouraged and came down too, chattering excitedly. But a small group of them still stayed at the top, crying that they were too frightened. Suzanne in particular stood there dramatically clutching her heart and declaring she would die of fright if she set foot on the ladder. Eventually Marie, half her size, threatened to carry her down, and she might have done so if Madame had not come back just then. Her presence brought Suzanne and the rest to the bottom at once.

None of the girls got to know how the culprit was discovered; but next day Erica and some friends were looking out of a passage window and saw Marie and a girl called Elsie among the fruit trees in the garden of the convent across the street. Marie and Elsie were searching from tree to tree, and they could hear Elsie saying, just like a small child, "No it wasn't there, it must have been here." It turned out that Elsie – whose father, curiously enough, was a prison official – wasn't a simple thief but had just been quite unable to stop herself taking and hiding things in that way. But for years Erica thought that a kleptomaniac was someone who stole keys.

There were half a dozen girls who were spending the Easter holiday at the Pension. Madame Blanchard announced to them that she and they would all go on a long trip down the valley of the Rhône, visit the towns of Arles and Orange and the Roman aqueduct at the Pont du Gard, and go right on down to Marseilles and the Mediterranean. They went and they had what Erica in a letter called a splendiferous time, travelling back just before term began. For the last few miles they had to change from the express to the slow local train, full of peasant women with piled market baskets. It was nice to see the familiar wooden carriages and their wooden seats, and they found a carriage which was empty but for a bearded old farmer. They piled in, full of high spirits which Madame sensibly did not damp.

The farmer took some snuff and eyed them. He turned and offered his snuffbox to Mademoiselle-Miss sitting opposite. Helen, next to her, thought it was being offered to her and turned away petulantly, saying in English, "Disgusting old monster! Tell him girls in Scotland do not take snuff!" Lucie very promptly translated this, and to everyone's joy he said he had never heard of Scotland. They explained that it was north of England.

"Ah! I have heard of the English! So young Mademoiselle is English?"

Helen's savage glare was too much for them, and they all laughed loudly. Erica laughed loudest and longest, and the farmer shook his finger at her. *"Hé, hé, une vraie petite diable!"* This set Erica off again; everything seemed hilarious that day, even being called a proper little devil. The farmer asked Mademoiselle-Miss if she was Erica's mother.

"No, no," she said hastily. "But Madame Blanchard over there is her head teacher." The farmer rose, went over and addressed Madame very solemnly.

"Madame, allow me to give you a warning. That child is too free. It is bad for young people, especially girls. Now, I have four of them at home. Always, at the first sign of giddiness, I shut them up in their bedroom on bread and water until they show a proper submission. I tell you, madame – you will have trouble with that child!"

Madame Blanchard was not at all offended at the old man's harangue. She thanked him with great courtesy and went on to ask him more about his farm and his daughters. Erica watched her in smiling appreciation: how Beatrice would have put this rough old man in his place! Or condescended graciously.

The farmer got out at the next station. As he did so he looked once more at Erica. "Remember the words of a father!" he said impressively to Madame Blanchard. "Bread and water before it is too late!"

As they started off again, Erica, half laughing and half apologetic, looked towards Madame. She only laughed back.

"There, Erica. Wouldn't you like to be one of his daughters! Now I know where to send you when I can't manage you."

"He'd make me more stubborn than ever," said Erica. "I'd starve rather than give in to that sort of father! But if it will please you, I will try to laugh less."

"No, no," said Madame. "Laugh while you can. There will be plenty to cry about before you're done with this world."

The summer term began the day after they returned; it was the last term that Cecily and Erica would be spending at the Pension Blanchard. Cecily, who was now seventeen, became even more thoughtful than usual and had long serious talks with her friends about her plans and their plans for the future. Erica declined to think about it at all.

"By the time I get back I shall be just sixteen. Almost grown-up, perhaps, but I'll not give it a thought till I have to!"

She plunged into the life of the school and refused to be serious or remember that her skirts were now longer and her hair was turned up. There was plenty to amuse her, and sometimes she thought there was no end to the delightfully funny things that happened at the Pension. She was always laughing – or had just finished laughing or was about to laugh. There seemed nothing left of the passionate, cross-grained girl who could make life a misery for herself and others during previous years at Woodhuckle. There was little to be cross-grained about in the cheerful orderliness which surrounded Madame.

Erica sometimes wondered what Beatrice had heard before she decided on this school as somewhere for them to go to be "finished", and what she thought would be done to them. When Hermione Bantock had been sent to France to be finished, it had been to Paris. She had gone there to learn how to dress well, how to move and dance elegantly and know what to say at parties and on social occasions, and how to say it with poise. At the Pension Blanchard girls learnt quite different skills. Classroom lessons were long and were strict, but the girls also took a part in the running of the house. Each morning, two girls from one class or another went with Marie to the market to help carry the baskets. It was certainly an alternative education to watch Marie trotting from stall to stall turning over the fruit and vegetables with suspicion, and shrilly refusing to pay a *sou* more than she thought things were worth.

The fruit season brought girls into the kitchen to help in the preparation and to stir the great vats of boiling conserves. Marie hovered like a hawk, and a girl – well, girl after girl sometimes – might be sent back to her class for surreptitiously popping a sly strawberry into her mouth instead of into the vat. Marie relaxed at quince time; though Klara was called the universal dustbin, not even she could eat quinces. The vine which wreathed the veranda provided dessert for a long time. Each day a girl was sent to find the ripe bunches. Each bunch had to have one grape pulled from it and stuck over the end of the stalk to prevent the bunch drying out; but if more than one grape had gone when the bunch reached Marie ...

Rhea heard about an even more agricultural side of school life.

Dear Rhea (wrote Erica),

We have killed our pig! It has been fed on kitchen scraps for a whole year. Marie fed it devotedly, for she knew how much money it would keep from the butcher. Yesterday was the great day. The man came out from Annonay, and we were all sent off for a walk so that we shouldn't hear the squeals when he Did the Deed. You know what pigs are like.

We thought that was the end of it, but when we got back the ironing room had been emptied, and there on the scrubbed ironing table was the Body (*and* the innards) waiting for the top class. Cecily went a bit pale, but she made herself turn the enormous mincer, and Anne-Marie, who says she's so delicate the smell of roses makes her faint, ladled revolting meat into the mincer to help her *chère Cécilie*.

I had to help make black puddings. Do you know how? You pour blood – actual *blood* – into horrible skin bags full of salt and lumps of fat and goodness knows what else. I might have been sick on the spot, but Helen squeaked and said it was no job for a well-brought up girl, so I *had* to say I didn't mind. I poured bowls and bowls of blood through a filter thing and waited for it to drip into the beastly puddings. Mostly I kept my eyes shut – I wish I could have kept my nose shut, too, ugh, ugh!

I was glad afterwards I'd managed, it's good to try anything once – but *not* the black pudding when it was served today. The other girls who'd been with me couldn't face it either. Madame laughed and said, how delicate! I don't suppose you *ever* make black puddings at Cheltenham Ladies College, for all you say it's such a good school. This Pension is still full of surprises!

Much love from ERICA

In fact, Madame herself had a love of surprises. She kept the girls hard at work most of the time; but then, if the weather was set fair, she would announce that it was a shame to waste such lovely days and that they would make a little expedition tomorrow. They would set off carrying loaves of bread – baked into rings which hung conveniently on the arm – and cheese and spicy sausage and packets of chocolate. They took the local train to the Rhône, or walked in the woods or far up the mountain country. Once, a party of them got up very early indeed and climbed Mount Miandon itself to see the dawn, and eat breakfast over the great view.

On another occasion Madame arranged with a farmer near the Rhône that they could pick as many cherries in his orchard as they could eat. Erica was suddenly very popular, for she didn't mind climbing to the top of the trees to get the difficult cherries. They usually took their own food and called at farms to buy milk. Once they had to drink it out of soup plates, and Madame laughed and laughed watching – but she had the only cup. She would get them to sing songs to show they were grateful for the milk and the picnic place; and, though their voices sounded thin and small in the open air, the farm people seemed to like it.

Back at the Pension itself, life was not without incident, as on the night when four senior girls were missing from supper; they had been seen whispering together earlier. Lucie, sent to fetch them, came back pale and breathless.

"Madame! Chère Madame! I think Suzanne has gone mad! She's on the table and says she's Napoléon!" Madame got up at once, looking stern.

"Do take care, Maman!" begged Lucie. (She must have been frightened for she was only to call her adopted mother "Maman" in private.) "Suzanne threw the carafe at me and it smashed on the wall! She said she'd throw the basin, too, if I didn't go. The others are on their beds groaning."

Madame said she could deal with any number of Suzannes, and left. She returned after supper and told some of the seniors what had been happening. The four girls had received food parcels from home and had hidden them in their dormitory instead of giving them to Marie to look after as usual. They had finished everything, including about four pounds of strawberry jam, which they'd eaten with spoons. They felt sick, and Suzanne opened the bottle of champagne her mother had sent for medicinal use, a spoonful a day. But Suzanne had drunk the whole bottle; the others felt too ill already.

It was not funny to Madame, and she added at the end of her account, "Kindly do not turn them into heroines. I do not want you to talk to them about this stupid affair." So, when the four had recovered from their stomach-aches and their headaches and tried to brag, the conversation was firmly turned to other subjects. Erica said to Cecily in their room one night, "It was fairly typical of Suzanne, I suppose, and perhaps we're as jealous as we are pi! All the same, I don't want to be horribly sick so as to feel like Napoleon!"

Erica herself was nearly in serious difficulties of another kind once. She had found the school cat up in Madeleine's room trying to eat Madeleine's canary. She was so angry that on an impulse she threw the cat straight out of the window, which was open. It landed right on the straw hat of Madame, who was coming down the path. Madame quite shouted at her to come down at once and explain, she was so startled. When she understood and had had a moment to recover herself, she laughed and said, would Erica remember another time that cats might have nine lives but headmistresses hadn't.

Rhea received one more letter from Pension Blanchard in that final term.

Dear Rhea,

Believe it or not, we've all been in danger of starving to death these last few days! Madame went off to Paris for a reunion of people who had been nurses in the Siege of Paris, and Marie at once started to economize to save Madame's pocket: she can't help it. We didn't realize at first because there were three huge bubbling golden-brown pies. Then Lucie said they were turnip pies, which didn't sound very good, though some of the French girls said there was nothing nicer, and so we all set to! But we just *couldn't* eat them. Even that strict new teacher Mlle Poiret – the one who told me she'd never heard anyone speak French so fast or so badly – she couldn't go on after the first spoonful, though she said we were making a fuss about nothing. Mademoiselle-Miss sent Lucie for Marie and politely said that the fat must have been rancid or something, and could we have bread and jam. Marie was offended and said we'd already had our allowance of jam; and Mademoiselle-Miss said to us, "Oh well, it's dry bread tonight, then, and there'll be something nice tomorrow." But Marie just looked and said she couldn't allow good food to be wasted, and the pies would be served until they were eaten.

So out they came next night – cold this time, and flabby and repulsive! And Madame away a *week*! But yesterday at supper-time there was a delicious smell of baking potatoes – and there they were, mounds of them with lots of butter and cheese and everything. Mademoiselle-Miss had telegraphed Madame in Paris, and Madame had telegraphed straight back. We saw the telegram: THROW TURNIPS TO PIGS. TONIGHT ROAST POTATOES WITH BUTTER. DON'T WANT TO MAKE FORTUNE.

How we ate!!

With much love, ERICA

PS. We're arriving home on July 28th. I wonder what it'll be like, and what Chris and the others have been doing. I don't seem to have thought about Woodhuckle all this year, and now I can't think of anything else.

Chapter 17 · Not for ages

When she woke on her first morning at Woodhuckle, Erica's bedroom seemed stranger than the small white room at Pension Blanchard had done on her arrival at Annonay. She lay gazing round in sleepy vacancy until a faint scent of bacon being fried for a very English breakfast curled round her nose and brought awareness flooding back. She was awake, she was at home and she was at last past her sixteenth birthday. It was the end of an old way of life and the beginning of a new one, whatever it was going to be. She leapt out of bed and started to dress.

She did not have time at first to think about herself much. There were too many changes in the house and in the village to see and be told about and exclaim over, and too much news to hear. She listened to the full story of the smallpox scare at Gloucester, for example. It had been so serious, the Woodhuckle and Woodhall Flower Show had been cancelled! The Parish Council had met and decided to turn an empty cottage into an emergency isolation hospital, and arranged vaccination of the children at school. Some of the mothers said it wasn't right because if God meant you to catch it, you shouldn't thwart him by being vaccinated, but the vicar had exerted himself quite forcefully for a mild man. He also had to go and keep half the village out of the bedroom of the only man who did catch smallpox. They hadn't seen smallpox before and were curious. The patient was elderly and the most cantankerous man in the three counties, and he wouldn't be moved from his filthy cottage to their new isolation hospital. Smallpox wasn't going to kill *him*, he said obstinately; and it didn't.

In the vicarage there was a new carpet in the dining-room, and in the sitting-room there was a remarkable addition to the family – a pink and white cockatoo, which had been presented by one of the parishioners when he was clearing out his house before going off to settle in America. It really seemed to talk like a human being, though it hadn't many ideas. The changes in Molly and Clare seemed considerable, too. She had left them as decidedly junior children in short frocks. Now their hems were lower and their hair was held by proper school-girl bows.

Even Chris had seemed a little strange at first; it was hard to recognize in this elegant youth the boy who had travelled dustily under the railway-carriage seat. But behind the elegance he was the same inquisitive Chris with exuberant ideas that he had always been, and not above welcoming his sister warmly. There had been awkward moments to begin with. She tried to tell him about Annonay and Madame and the other girls and their travels; but his quick questions made her wonder if she'd been to France at all. He asked her how high Mount Miandon was, and she didn't know. He wanted to know which emperor had built the Roman Arch at Orange, and she had forgotten. It was easier when he was talking enthusiastically about his College and his hopes for a scholarship. It reminded her once more of her own dream of a degree, and how little she had done towards it. She should, she thought, have paid more attention to planning for the future, as Cecily had been doing. But the matter came to a head quite soon.

One evening, Cecily and Erica went to their father's study

to discuss the arrangements which he and Beatrice had been trying to make. Rhea Walker was to be allowed to stay on at Cheltenham Ladies' College to study for an Oxford degree at the University Class there, as there wasn't a women's college she could go to at Oxford. Now, did Cecily and Erica want to join her? If so, he had worked out, the fees could be found. Erica accepted at once; Cecily refused altogether.

"I'm nearly eighteen and too old for more school," she said. "It's time I started earning my own living."

Her father struggled to bridge the gap of sixty years between them. He tried to make it clear that he sympathized but that she was not compelled to earn; he could always support her, and perhaps by the time he died she would have married. But Cecily was firm.

"I don't want to marry, and I couldn't think of staying at home doing nothing. I think I shall begin by teaching."

Mr Stock accepted this, but not all their friends did. Some reminded her of all the clubs she ran and all the other work she might be doing before the time came for her to marry. Others, with Beatrice, urged the advantages of training before teaching. Erica was on Beatrice's side that night, and she carried on the argument as she and Cecily prepared for bed.

"Why not join Rhea and me? I dare say I'll be a teacher, too, but I mean to get my degree first. I'm not going to be a governess like Miss Pringle."

"What's wrong with Miss Pringle? She taught us all right without training. Teaching can't be all that hard."

"You don't sound very interested in teaching." Erica paused half out of her dress. "What do you mean to do, really?"

"I don't know," said Cecily slowly. "But I don't want to stay in Woodhuckle. I'm going to start with teaching because it's the only way I can earn a living. Then I'll find something I can do better than anyone else, even if finding it takes me twenty years. I'm not eighteen yet; I can wait." She lay back in bed, her grey eyes reflectively staring at the ceiling as if she saw some vision of her future there. Erica looked at her: was this what Cecily would be like in twenty years – calm and firm and sure of herself? It was only a moment's glimpse;

Cecily's eyes came back to reality.

"Erica," she said reproachfully, "you've left your best dress lying on the floor *again*."

Erica meekly picked it up. She was always finding herself doing what Cecily wanted, without meaning to; as when Cecily's red flannel petticoat had fallen round her ankles in the village street. Cecily had calmly stepped out of it and walked serenely on. Erica had to pick it up and run behind her with the petticoat over her arm.

Next day, swinging herself on the old swing on one of the apple trees, Erica pondered on the enigma of Cecily – why she had broken with Rose Munter, why her exam failure had been so terrible, what she really thought of the boys who now ran after her. She drifted on to her own affairs. Did she want to do something grand? What *could* she do anyway?

"Nothing," she told herself in depression. "Anything," she corrected herself as she swung higher and higher. "*Elle avait seize ans. Âge sublime!*" she chanted at the summer sky. "No coward soul is mine!" she added enthusiastically.

She slowed down as she saw Tom Upthorpe coming into the garden with a rose. He called her name. She did not answer at first; he'd only want to talk about himself. Then she pulled a green apple and threw it with unwomanly accuracy. He saw her, came across and offered his rose with a bow.

> "Rosy is the west,
> Rosy is the south,
> Roses are her cheeks,
> And a rose is her mouth."

Oh well, he was going to be an actor, and actors had to practise. She cocked her head.

"That's not your rose. It's from our front garden. Was it for Cecily?"

"Certainly not. She said I'll make a very bad actor."

"Ah, so you did offer it!"

"I did *not*. I'll not be bossed about by a girl a year younger!"

"She doesn't boss. She says what she thinks, and she's often right. If she said you'll be a bad actor, you probably will be."

At that he tipped her out of the swing and chased her round

the garden. She took refuge in the hayloft, threatened to kick the ladder away and jumped from the loading doors. So did Tom. Then Clare and Molly joined in; and by the time a tea-bell rang they were all hot and panting as they went in, and Erica was feeling that her heroic attitudes were slipping a bit.

Eddie Mayton was there, and she sighed. It was naughty of Tom and the rest to laugh, really. Eddie was all a young man should be – handsome, hard-working, kind to his widowed mother and the mainstay of his young sisters. But he was so anxious to please Cecily that he never stopped offering her things and breaking into other people's conversations. In the middle of one of Beatrice's best stories, it was, "Oh, Miss Cecily, you have no jam! May I pass it to you?"

As Beatrice frowned, he looked wildly round for the jam. Cecily deftly removed it from under his nose and pushed it out of his reach.

"*No*, thank you, Mr Mayton, nor anything else! And please apologize to my sister for interrupting her."

Eddie went red to the eyes and apologized so abjectly that Beatrice was touched and set herself to soothe him; but he sat through the rest of tea like a whipped puppy.

"Oh dear, why do such *extraordinary* people fall for Cecily?" asked Erica as she and Chris walked back to The Limes with Tom.

"Lack of backbone," said Chris. "They see her coming and think, 'Ah, someone I can flop against.' Never mind Eddie. Wait till you see Archibald."

"He can't be worse than Eddie," said Tom. "*I* wouldn't stand being ticked off in public by a girl, I can tell you! Anyway, I'm after other game. I'd want a different sort of wife – a little dark rosebud with a pretty smile." They had reached The Limes, and Tom vaulted the gate, waved and went in.

"Is Tom making sheep's eyes at you?" Chris demanded as they turned back.

"Not sheep's eyes. Actor's eyes," said Erica. "And he'll find his rosebud has thorns if he tries to be masterly."

Chris laughed. "It's a good thing you're going to Cheltenham. It'll give you something better to think about than young actors."

"All right, grandpa. I promise I won't marry till someone can say, 'I offer you my hand and heart and *all* my worldly goods, Miss Erica Stock, B.A.'!"

Cecily was to leave them at the end of the year on the first stage of her search for a career of her own. Erica's new life began in the autumn, and she settled happily to it. She was no longer as single-minded as she had been at twelve; there were too many things to be interested in. All the same, term-time living fell into a pattern which centred very much round her work. She would set her alarm for six o'clock and wrap it in layers of clothes so that it shouldn't wake Cecily. When it went off, she lit a candle, reached for the top book on the pile by her bed, then snuggled back and studied until nearly seven. After a quick breakfast by the new-lit fire she and Chris flung out of the house at half-past to cycle the three miles to Gloucester. They cut through the horse-trams and the carts in the middle of the city, threw their bicycles into the station yard and rushed up the slope. Even when they were not late, they sometimes ran for the joke.

"Quick! We'll miss the Cheltenham train!" Chris would say urgently and loudly enough to be overheard, as he pulled out his watch.

"Run! Run!" Erica would cry with equal urgency and just a little louder. Occasionally they succeeded in starting a mild stampede, and plump businessmen in top hats wallowed, panting heavily, up the incline.

She and Chris had to part on the platform, and didn't even speak. Cheltenham College boys and Ladies' College girls never talked or travelled together; but once Erica asked a small boy to give a note to his sister for her. Chris reported cheerfully that the boy had announced the shocking incident to the whole carriageful of his friends.

"Stock of the Lower Sixth has a very fast sister. She *spoke* to me!" Erica was indignant at the impertinence of a boy younger than Molly.

"Ah," said Chris, "he has a sister, you see. It makes a man feel his responsibilities. I asked him what he'd feel like if he had four sisters like me. He looked very bowed down at the idea."

Erica's class finished at one o'clock. She caught the 1.20 train, cycled back alone from Gloucester and arrived well after two o'clock to a kept-warm meal, before settling to the work she had brought back. It was a strenuous life but healthy; her eyes sparkled and her cheeks glowed. One Saturday morning as she bounded downstairs Alice, who was passing, exclaimed cheerfully that she was almost pretty.

"Almost, indeed!" said Erica good-humouredly. She paused to glance approvingly in the mirror, caught a movement behind her and spun round in slight embarrassment at being caught. An old woman with a tired face was sitting at the back of the hall with an envelope in her hand. Her mouth was working and her cheeks were wet.

"Why, whatever is it, Mrs Pudsey?"

"It's the letter," said Mrs Pudsey. "The postman brought it." She seemed to think this explained everything.

"But what does it say?" asked Erica in bewilderment. "You've not even opened it."

"Oh, I wouldn't do that. The Reverend will, if that's what has to be done." She spoke as if it were a highly skilled and strange task, as it was to her. The vicar appeared, and they went into his study. When she reappeared, she was garrulously relieved, though her eyes were still red.

"And I only axed him to read it," she repeated as Erica showed her out. "I didn't ask anything. You tell him, I'll never be in debt again. Never!"

"It was only thirty shillings," said Mr Stock defensively at breakfast. "The baker let her run it up and was threatening her. She thought the letter was a debt-summons. It was an advertisement from a Gloucester money-lender who must have overheard something."

"Half the tradesmen in the town will be after you," said Beatrice, "if you're so soft-hearted. She's improvident. If she'd set aside a little bit weekly, she'd soon be clear."

"Out of her nine shillings a week?" asked her father quietly.

Once upon a time Erica would have flared up at Beatrice's remark. But since she had returned from France she was seeing her step-sister more as a fussy and sometimes snobbish or waywardly impetuous middle-aged woman than as someone formidable and able to upset her completely at any time.

From the effort of having to make her own choices about the future Erica was beginning to think more about the lives people led – about the wages of the farm-workers, for instance, or about the state of some of the houses in the village, or about wives having to obey their husbands. Plenty of wives were independent enough in practice, but there seemed to be little hope for those who were not. Mrs Agnew, in one of the new villas along the Gloucester road, was one who let her husband bully and shout at her. He gave her too little money, then complained at her dowdy dresses and stayed out in the evenings because she was fretful and the food wasn't good enough. Beatrice, who didn't approve of women being downtrodden, supported her. One day she had dropped an invitation to tea through the Agnews' letter-box; but Mrs Agnew neither came nor excused herself. This was odd, and Beatrice asked about it when she next saw her.

"What *do* you think she told me?" she exclaimed to another friend next day. "Mr Agnew *locks the letter-box* when he goes to work and takes the key with him!" Mr Agnew, who had a handsome high colour and a fleshy figure and tended to fulsome compliments, was not much liked; and each new instance of his masculine tyranny was reported with many expressions of sympathy for Mrs Agnew.

Some months later Beatrice's friend hurried into the sitting-room unannounced. "Such a terrible thing has happened! It is too shocking ... so sudden! Poor Mr Agnew, ... and nobody has told the children yet!" Beatrice signed to Erica who left the room believing Mrs Agnew was dead. Later she learned the truth from Sarah and the others in the kitchen. Mrs Agnew was not dead. She had run away.

At once public sympathy veered, and those who had been so sorry for Mrs Agnew now hadn't a good word to say for her. They said she had acted unforgivably. Their hearts bled for the deserted children. Some of them even bled for Mr Agnew. The sequel concerned the vicarage closely. For after Mr

Agnew, unable to bear more of the village gossip, had moved with the rest of the children to a sister's in London, Joseph, the eldest boy, came to the vicarage to stay until he could go out to join an uncle in Canada.

They had hardly known him before because he had been away at a boarding school. Erica remembered him from the days before she went to France as a thin boy with dirty knees. She was unprepared for the beautiful, melancholy young man who appeared at table. She took covert glances at him as he sat with his eyes cast down on his plate, and admired the dark eyelashes that shadowed his cheeks. She wondered if he was shy or depressed, that he said nothing and ate little.

Afterwards he and Chris were to go out on their bicycles and try coasting down Birdlip Hill. Erica went upstairs and tried to read. She had recently decided to broaden her outlook by wider reading, and had resolved to read every book in the spare bookshelf, starting from the bottom left-hand corner. Some of the books were very solid indeed, even with the help of a rule about omitting Collected Sermons. The last one, *Sir John Mandeville's Travels*, had been actually entertaining, but now she had come to something entitled *Kirk White: Remains*. After three pages she realized she had taken in nothing and was thinking about Birdlip Hill and melancholy eyes. She went downstairs to look for something better and was surprised to see Joseph sitting there with a book he was obviously not reading. Apparently a fault on his bicycle had prevented him going out. She explained herself and tentatively asked what he was reading. He solemnly handed her the green-leather volume. She read the gold letters, *Maine: Ancient Laws*, and laughed.

"Chris wanted me to read that. But I *couldn't*! Do you find it interesting?"

"Oh, no, I'm not a brainy chap. Just as well, I suppose, if I'm to go cattle-rearing on my uncle's farm." He sighed, and Erica looked at him sympathetically, wanting to say something helpful.

"Do you mind terribly, I mean, about your mother?" she said jerkily at last. "No, no," she went on hurriedly, "I mustn't ask."

"But do ask," said Joseph. "Everybody else is afraid to." He broke off. Molly's voice calling to someone could be heard outside, and nearer at hand there was the sound of crockery being clattered on a tray.

Over the next few days they went for many walks, and Joseph unburdened himself of a great deal. He talked of his home and of his family, of his love for his mother and anger at his father, of his resentment at her betrayal and his pride in his father's position. He veered between agonized shame and furious defiance, and sometimes pretended indifference. He did not ask Erica about herself, but she felt pulled into his world. She was stirred beyond herself, and she thought she was in love. One day her father asked for her, and she found him at his desk fiddling with the pens.

"Erica my dear," he said, "it has been suggested ... I'm told that during the game of Hide and Seek at Molly's party yesterday you and Joseph spent a very long time in the cellar. Why did you not come up?"

"Because no one found us," said Erica after a fractional pause. "We were happy talking."

"What were you talking about?"

"Mostly about Joseph having to leave school early, and what the Canadian winters are like, and what he'll do after his uncle's farm."

"Run away, dear," he said a little awkwardly. "I wish people would not read so much into ordinary friendships."

Up in her room she found she was breathing rather quickly. "You are a bare-faced liar," she told herself severely; but she had spoken only the truth. The party for Molly's little friends had been tedious, and talking was more interesting: it was by chance they had not been traced sooner. Joseph was to leave for Liverpool and his ship in a day or two, and he had been more restless and self-occupied than usual, and she had listened harder.

The day of his departure came, and he was packed with his box into a cab; and they watched and listened as it clattered off down the dusty road and disappeared. That night she cried in bed out of pity for him, and felt flat for a day or two. Then she began to recover her spirits and resumed her active round: somehow Joseph's memory didn't last very long. Perhaps it had all been a bit too one-sidedly intense.

She was helped by the relaxed atmosphere at the vicarage at this time. Spring wasn't quite with them but it was not far ahead, and Cecily was expected for a substantial break at Easter. Mr Stock himself once contributed to the lighter spirit. He had taken to going about the house with the cockatoo on his shoulder. He was quite proud of this trick, and the pink and white feathers against his silver hair made an attractive picture. One day he came with it into a tea-party Beatrice was holding, and he was letting the cockatoo gently nibble his finger.

"Oh, Mr Stock," fluttered one of the visitors, "aren't you afraid it will bite?"

"Oh, no, he would never do a thing like that."

Unfortunately, he shook his head to emphasize his words; the cockatoo, not liking the sudden movement, gave his ear a sharp nip, and Mr Stock was startled into an exclamation he did not often use. Some of the tea-party were startled too, but Erica laughed aloud.

The pious Children's Magazine which Clare and Molly had decided to produce for the parish contributed its moment of hilarity, too. The first two numbers were fine efforts and really very clever. By the third number they were finding it hard to think of new ideas. But Clare was very chagrined when she found Chris and Erica laughing heartily over the fourth number as they read the hymn she had dashed off at high speed, in the best journalistic tradition, to fill the final paragraph. It worked up to a splendid last verse:

> Jesus our Captain is,
> 'Twas he who died for us.
> 'Twas he who did the Will of God
> And never made a fuss.

The day before Cecily was due, Molly's feet were heard running along the passage, and she bounced in obviously full with news.

"Guess who's coming to stay for Easter!"

"The baroness," said Erica, not bothering to lift her eyes

from her book. "There was a letter from Germany for Beatrice on the hall table."

"Ah, but I know more! Guess who's coming with her – her son!"

"Of course," said Erica, sitting up so suddenly she dropped her book. "He's coming to propose to Cecily now he's twenty-one. I quite forgot. She won't have him, of course. Unless perhaps he offered her vast sums to build a Girls' Club in that London slum of hers."

"She probably wouldn't then," said Chris. "Look at all Cecily's Undesirables who've asked her to marry them. And they were English, not like Harry von Düring."

"You horrible jingoist!" said Erica. "Me, I like foreigners. Just imagine being a Baroness and living in a Medieval Castle in the Mountains. I expect there's an oubliette, if it's what I think it is, and dungeons, and wolves howling in the winter. Lovely! I used to try to get her to invite me there, but she never did."

"You did have one holiday with her," said Clare.

"The Isle of Wight is *not* the same thing," said Erica. "We sat on the hotel veranda most of the time. The Herr Baron was going through the Bible to find when the Jews first believed in Hell, but his eyes were weak. So while everyone else was swimming or playing tennis, I was reading him the Bible."

Cecily arrived for her holiday, and two days later the Baroness came with her son. She was as pink-cheeked and scented and selfishly charming as ever. Harry von Düring was not like her, but so much like everybody's idea of a young German that he almost seemed a caricature. He was stiff, blue-eyed, kindly and was already beginning to spread in the middle: he even clicked his heels and bowed. On the morning after his arrival, they all said "Good morning, and how are you?" when he came in to breakfast. He clicked his heels, put his hand on his middle bulge and said very seriously, "Thank you, I have an pain in mine sto-mack."

But he could sing romantic songs in a beautiful bass voice in the evening; and Clare and Molly watched him like hopeful hawks whenever he was in the room with Cecily; but they never caught him out in a single sigh or longing look. If he was a suitor, he was not pressing. Cecily was having much more trouble with her latest local admirer, a superior young clerk called Arthur Legard. Arthur worked in Gloucester but spent most of his spare time lingering at Woodhuckle, to the vehement disapproval of Cecily's sisters.

"I believe he thinks we *like* having him here all Sunday and every Sunday! Hasn't he got a church of his own?"

"I spoke to him about that," said Cecily seriously, "and said it was wrong not to support one's own parish church. He said I was very right; so I think he won't be coming this Sunday."

But no sooner were they settled in their pew than they saw Arthur mincing his way down the aisle. Cecily kept her eyes on her prayer-book or on the officiating clergyman. Her father had a rather feverish cold and was not there. During the sermon Erica had a note passed to her from Beatrice: "Tell Arthur we can't invite him to lunch. Might catch flu. *Don't* let him come in."

Beatrice and Cecily had to stay behind after the service. The others found Arthur in the church porch and Erica delivered her message. Arthur said he wasn't afraid of infection. He walked back with Erica and Harry, and simply followed them in: Harry went to his room and Erica had to entertain Arthur. When she heard Beatrice and Cecily at the front door, she rushed out to intercept them.

"He's here!" she hissed. "It's not my fault. He just won't go!" Beatrice's face warned her and she turned. Arthur had followed her into the hall.

"Well, I'm sorry," she said to Cecily, as they went upstairs to change. "Listeners never hear good of themselves. At least I've saved you. He simply can't come again."

A snort of laughter made her look up. Harry had been leaning over the banister enjoying the scene. Erica grinned back at him cheerfully. Harry hadn't got a bad smile – when you could make him smile, which wasn't often.

After the meal Arthur sang Irish airs and accompanied himself, as Cecily refused to bring out her violin. Harry, whose ear was good, looked pained. Erica thankfully escaped to the Sunday school class she was taking.

She still enjoyed this contact with the young ones, though she no longer had her early simple hope that she would inspire one or two of the stolid Woodhuckle children with a truly elevated faith. She took more notice now of which child needed new shoes, or looked pale from hunger or had no winter clothes. This was partly the result of her being influenced by the patriotic socialism and the ideas for public reform she had picked up from Robert Blatchford's *Merrie England*, which she had bought in a cheap edition "produced by Trade Union labour on English-made paper".

But that Sunday she observed the rapt attention of one child as she talked to them about the African mission work, and the smile of almost unearthly bliss on her face as she listened: it was Lizzie Hutton, of all children. At the end the others went out, but Lizzie sat on, heedless. Erica drew up a chair and asked reverently which of the missionary stories had touched her so much. Lizzie turned her dark eyes and put her small hand on her heart or thereabouts.

"Oh, Miss!" she said in a quiet rapture. "My little belly is quite full!"

Erica had recovered and was giggling to herself as she reached home. She told the story with great liveliness over tea.

"And there was me thinking I'd inspired another Mary Kingsley!" she concluded.

"A child without a soul," said Harry heavily. "I am sorry she has disappointed you."

"It's not her fault," said Erica quickly. "Those children never get enough to eat as a rule. But the farmer's son is getting married, and he's given all his men a round of beef. I expect they ate till they nearly burst."

"Very funny," said Harry with a solemn nod. "You tell the story so well, you make me laugh."

The next day when Erica went in to see her father, he told her that Harry had formally asked for her hand in marriage.

"But his mother wants him to marry Cecily!" she said in blank astonishment.

"So he told me," said her father with a smile. "However, he prefers you, and has persuaded his mother. What am I to say to him?"

"Do you mean he asked *you*, without even a word to me?" said Erica, still trying to take in this extraordinary business.

"I was a little taken aback, too. It was the way it was done in my young days, but not always even then, and I thought things had quite changed. I suppose Germany manages differently. *Do* you want to marry?"

"Not yet at all," said Erica. "Not for ages. I feel much too young."

After she had left him she wondered just why she had been so sure she didn't want to marry. It wasn't from cold feet or panic, and a lot of what was being offered was attractive. Living abroad in the romantic castle, with a position, and money and a chance of some adventure. Harry was nice in his funny stiff way, too; clever, kind and knowledgable, apart from being the catch his mother thought him. The alternative might be long years as a teacher with poor pay and little or nothing at the end. But she needn't dramatize it – she simply knew she couldn't say yes.

Relations were just a little embarrassed after that. But the Baroness's visit was nearly over, and a few days later, after the usual long, slow fuss of preparation, she gathered herself together, kissed the sympathetic Beatrice a warm goodbye and departed with Harry, who was a little subdued.

On the Sunday afternoon after they had gone, Cecily and Erica were happily having tea by themselves in the dining-room, suitors all forgotten, when a well-known voice was heard in the hall. Cecily stood up in alarm. They heard the visitor being invited to step into the sitting-room.

"Thank you, I should prefer to come into this room," said Arthur's precise voice. "I think the young ladies must be in here."

Cecily looked round frantically. There was only one possible way of escape. As Arthur entered, he saw only the legs of his beloved disappearing through the serving-hatch into the kitchen.

He did finally take the hint from that, and they saw him no more at the vicarage. Not many weeks later he wrote to say that he was engaged to a most delightful and accomplished young lady. Her Mama had consented, but as her daughter was still very young she had stipulated a year at a finishing school before their marriage. Cecily (the letter implied) could now realize and regret the great chance she had missed.

"The baby-snatcher!" exclaimed Erica. "I hope that school has some serving-hatches!"

Cecily, who had been home on a second short visit and was darning her stockings before packing, smiled at her work.

"Do you really not mind? Not a tiny bit?" said Erica curiously.

Cecily raised her grey eyes from her stocking and smiled again. She positively twinkled, in fact; and suddenly Erica thought she understood Cecily and was enormously glad that she herself had refused Harry. There was really a great deal in life besides proposals. She startled them by jumping to her feet and flinging her arms wide in a gesture of freedom as she declaimed her favourite tag:

"*Elle avait seize ans. Âge sublime!* Sixteen! Sixteen! A wonderful age!"

"You're jolly nearly seventeen," said Clare, who had heard it before.

"So I am," said Erica, smiling sweetly at her. "Well, sixteen was pretty good. I should think seventeen would be even better."

There had been a difficult moment some while before at the Ladies' College, when Erica stood before the headmistress for breaking a rule. Miss Beale had said in her high, awful and austerely regal way – not directly to her but to the teacher standing by –

"That child will come to a bad end!"

But Erica wasn't remembering that now. She saw her life opening out in front of her, with no ties and everything to expect, and her heart was dancing.

"Do stop fidgeting and sit down, Erica," said Beatrice.

Afterword by the author

The original Erica was born in 1880. Her name wasn't Erica, but like the Erica in the story she lived with her brother and three sisters in a small village near Gloucester. She grew up, went away and worked, married and had children of her own. By the time they too had grown up and gone out into the world, she was quite old. She went to live in another small village, and came to know the children there. She helped and taught some of them who were having trouble keeping up at school, because working with children had always been what she best liked to do.

It was then that she found herself thinking about the village where she had lived as a child, and she began writing down things she remembered. She put them down as they came into her head, even some of the conversation; and if she didn't remember names, she made them up. Sometimes she changed them anyway, and perhaps this helped her to be more frank about other people and about herself. Some of the things she remembered about herself weren't at all flattering, but they didn't seem to matter so much now she was old.

After she died it seemed a pity that these memories should be lost and that no one should know about a girl who had been very much alive. Although she was no longer there, people she had talked to during her long life could fill in some of the gaps. Her sister (Clare in the book) added her own special recollections and explained a great deal.

Erica's home village could still help over some things. At the baker's shop you can buy even now the sort of lard-cakes that the cook Sarah (her real name) made for the children when they were told they couldn't have richer cake. Their house and the church and the brook and the village street are still there, despite changes; and Cheltenham Ladies' College is still in Cheltenham. Then there were old maps and journals and directories which could be looked at in a library, and they helped too. The present story grew from all these things.

No one can now tell the story of the original girl exactly as she was, but this is an attempt to tell about a girl who might have been her – who did the things she did, and, above all, a girl who thought and felt the way she did.

Sometimes guesses (within the limits of known facts) had to be made about just how things had happened. But there was little need to invent the details of their everyday life – there were so many: down to the colour of the muslin curtains, the clothes she was dressed in on Sunday when she was small, and even the man on the horse-tram who wanted to know how much a herring cost.

Many names, but not all, have been changed for practical reasons; but as for why Erica hasn't been given her own name – well, it *was* a queer one, and she didn't think much of it herself. When she was writing down her memories, she even called herself by a much more romantic name; so perhaps she wouldn't mind being Erica here.